SOUTHWEST BY SOUTHWEST

ESME FRANCIS

for

CAP'N JOHN

CAPE BOOKS

Published by Cape Books
St. Just, Cornwall

Printed by
Headland Printers
Penzance, Cornwall

ISBN 978-0-9533022-3-9

SOUTHWEST BY SOUTHWEST

The echoing call rang out across the granite cliffs and shore, "Tammy!" and the solitary figure on the headland came running along the cliff pathway to meet the caller. They laughed and chatted in the sunshine, swinging their lunch, as they climbed down into the cove below.

"What's yer sister doing?" queried the old skipper, leaning on the harbour wall, sucking at his pipe. The boy, with his bag slung over his shoulder, shaded his eyes against the sun.

"She's with Kathy. They're sitting on the sand eating sandwiches."

"Haw ... " a deep grunt.

"What're you looking at, Grandfer?"

Zach Trewin squinted through his telescope at the bright sunlit waters across Porthgwyna bay, his lips puckered up in a tuneless whistle. A thick silvery lock of hair swept the lines of his weathered brow.

"I'm watchin' the far horizon, lad, at that bulky cargo coaster. An' look, there's the sails of a tall ship behind that an' a number of mackerel boats and old toshers in the bay. There's also a couple of fishing trawlers making their way across, an' a-ha – there's the bow of the revenue boat speedin' by, casting up that white wash." The gnarled fingers tamped his pipe.

"Are you going out on Father's boat later?" asked Matt. "Can I come?" He anxiously eyed his grandfather, knowing he might let him have his way more than his father.

"Haw! Put some warm clothes on – don't let yer Mother know!"

Matt bounded away down the slipway with a yell, flung off his shirt and leapt into the sea to join his friends in the rushing surf. Later, he quietly let himself into the cottage, hurriedly picking up jumpers, thick socks and waterproofs, hiding them behind the cupboard, ready to go out fishing.

When he heard Seth, his father, collecting his tools together, he slipped out of the back door, ran down to Zach's cottage and followed him down to the quay and onto their crab boat, the Clarissa Rose.

Seth Trewin wasn't long coming. He started up the engine and set the bows to the open sea. He glared at young Matthew when he saw him in the cabin.

"Now who let you on board?"

Zach laughed, "I did."

"Mother's goin' to give the pair of you a bit of her tongue when you get back," grumbled Seth.

The wind was a fresh westerly, tipping the waves with white flecks. They pulled in their lines of crab pots, emptying them of lobsters and crabs, and then baiting them for the next trip. The evening was quickly drawing in as they finished and Zach turned the boat to round the headland.

"Where're you going, Grandfer?" asked Matt.

"Aah – one more pull 'ere, m'lad," Zach searched the surface of the water for marker buoys.

"There," shouted Seth, and he pushed out his grappling hook to haul in the rope. Up came barrels, one after another, which he rolled and set them on end to the side of the deck.

The night was quickly falling as Zach turned the boat towards the shore, and they slipped into the harbour. A full moon came out from the cloud, bright as daylight as they pulled in to the quay.

Clarissa was there on lookout and threw them a rope.

"Hurry!" she hissed, "There's customs men 'ere – everywhere."

But the revenue boat saw them there and came roaring behind in pursuit, so they hurried away from the harbour to hide in the darkening night.

They kept the boat close to the cliffs and in the shadows of Pedmendhu, but their followers swept in and flushed them out. They sped on, running the race of the wicked tide of the reef, and out round again, slipping into Nanjizel bay, and idled there against the blackness of the cliff.

The revenue men searched all along the coast, and along to the light of the Tater Du lighthouse. So the Clarissa Rose hid in the darkness of the night, Seth letting her drift upon the tide like a soft whisper on the wind, and they left those on the other boat far behind.

Just before the dawn came rising, they slipped into Porthgwyna alongside the mackerel and crab boats, and tied silently up to the quay.

Clarissa was there to meet them, and Matt helped to roll the barrels along the deck while Zach and Seth hefted them onto their backs, stumbling up the steep steps of the quay. They took them through the back lane and door of Zach's cottage and rolled them down to the cellar floor. Then Clarissa hustled them away, hiding them in the attic before daylight came.

Seth was thinking of the scolding his wife Hannah would give them, but Zach chuckled to himself, as they drank from hot mugs of cocoa laced with brandy. His eyes lit up with a smile and the craggy lines of his face creased as he looked at a tired Matt.

"Ah – she's a grand lass, is yer Grandma. A grand lass is Clarrie, m'lad."

It rose in a twisting spiral to the azure heavens. Grey smoke tendrils rising from the parched earth of tall yellowing grasses.

The brittle heather and gorse fronds, still in tight bud, waiting for the rain to bring them bursting into bloom, covered the cracked soil in wide swathes over hill and cairn, sweeping down to the sea.

On the cliff farm, Davy Pender was herding his sheep into fresh pastures, when he looked up towards the windswept heath. To one side where the craggy cairn of Chapel Carn Brea reared up, the smoke now funnelled into a black plume, clouding up from bursts of yellow and red flame, forking out between the gnarled furze stogs and heather. He quickly closed the gate and ran across the fields into the barn, shouting for his two lads.

"Ben – Jan – get up the moor – there's a fire starting – take the beaters with you!" His sons came out of the door, looked upwards, then ran, snatching up the beaters that were kept against the wall.

Their father watched them taking off like colts across the heather, climbing higher and higher up the steep slopes.

"They'll soon sort that out," said his workman, sluicing out the dairy.

Flaring tongues spread alongwards and upwards, sucked and blown by the fresh wind, glowing blue and copper-green at the ground base, then radiating scarlet showers of bright sparks which triggered off a myriad of separate flames.

The smoke swirled around the lads, as coughing and spluttering, they beat the peaty ground, working their way through the brakes of furze, and disappearing into the smeech.

Their father burst into the kitchen to call the firemen, "My lads are up there, but we need more hands," he shouted into the telephone. Then he ran out, calling for Archie to help round up the cattle and sheep, and move them down to the cliff fields, away from the fire.

The bitter taint of the acrid cloud swirled down the valley and around the hamlet of cottages and isolated farms and dwellings, stinging throats and eyes.

Work came to a standstill, as Zach Trewin looked upwards to seek the direction of its source. He ran along the lane to Seth's cottage and burst through the door.

"The moor's on fire!" he shouted. Seth pulled open the shed door and wheeled out his old motorbike, and they leapt into the saddle and roared up the hill.

Ben and Jan moved across the moor, leaving smouldering ash behind them, but the fire was rapidly gaining new ground sideways, away from them. They were blackened from head to foot, their eyes glinting in grimed faces.

They heard shouting and saw the blacksmith striding up, having left the horse he was shoeing in the stable. With him was a crowd of neighbours carrying beaters and spades.

Pengelly had closed the inn and brought his customers with him, collecting Dan, who was laying the stone wall, and Jacca the Postie.

Some joined the boys beating the flames, while Pengelly and the others dug trenches and brakes to cut off the direction of the fire. But the heat had set the heather peat glowing and the flare was travelling quickly underground and breaking out around them in jets of flame.

Seth, who'd just come back from fishing, saw a great swathe of the moor and downs alight as he and Zach came to the rise of the hill. They leapt off the motorbike and joined up with the grocer, who'd left his lass in charge of the shop, to snatch up beaters and spades to stop the spread of the fire.

The carpenters and builders, working on the new row of houses appeared and behind them were farm workers and hands, all running across the fields. The vicar, having donned a black cape and boots, joined the fire engine and tender that came roaring along the winding coast road. In fact, firemen from Penzance, St. Just, and as far as Hayle and Camborne, arrived, as there was no supply of water for the hoses on the vast expanse of moorland, and they had to depend on as much manpower as they could get.

The ground was also dangerous, because of the many adits, holes and shafts left from many of the old mines dotted about the landscape.

Jessie smelt the smoke as it blew in through the house, bringing with it black flecks and smuts. She rushed around closing doors and windows, calling out to the children to run down to the long barn, as she could see the line of beaters and the fire coming closer, enough to threaten her roof.

Lucy, her youngest set up a wail, darting back into the house, to hurriedly reappear, clutching her hamster in its cage.

Word went round to those who felt it safer to evacuate their dwellings, to make to Jessie's field barn. There the women brought kettles and flasks and made tea and stacks of sandwiches to keep the beaters going. They also brought blankets and clothing for those who'd have to stay through the night.

Zach and Seth fought their way through the gorse and bracken to join Ben and Jan and they worked their way along the higher ridge, beating down the flames that threatened to go over the top. They were surrounded by wreathes of blue-grey smoke, coughing as they swung the beaters, their eyes watering so much that they worked almost blindly.

Suddenly, before them came two more equally grim figures,

Eddy and James from one of the lower farms. They shouted, only to swallow the smoke, spluttering at each other.

Eddy pointed to the right and they saw old Gundry's cottage, sparks beginning to smoulder where the wind had blown them onto the wooden part of the roof. They struggled through the gorse and hammered on the door, shouting for him.

A face peered out of the window, half-asleep, then a moment later the door opened.

"Come out, yer daft begger," yelled Zach.

Gundry gasped with the sudden intake of smeech, "M'pigs," he rasped.

The thatch on the sty had started to burn as they rounded up the pigs, with the piglets running all ways, into a ploughed field. Old Gundry, meanwhile, had disappeared into the murk, then came out with a piece of wire netting, shunting his hens along to join the pigs.

When they turned, they could see large areas of flames gaining on them, so they began to dig a trench, breaking up the dried brittle grass. Gundry drew buckets from his water barrels and dampened the ground, though they were soon emptied.

The stringent vapour was overpowering and when they could see past the clouds of smoke, the whole moors were a luminous blaze, the sparks like flaming jewels, flowers of the fire blooming in the dusk.

Gundry sat down, breathing heavily, finding it hard to get his breath in the thick air.

Seth and Zach lifted him up by his elbows, "Come on – you can't stay 'ere."

They took turns helping him along, making for the ploughed fields.

"Get up to the cairn," panted Ben. "It'll screen us from the smoke, at least."

They struggled over the tussocks of coarse grass and heather, and came upon the towering slabs of granite looming above them. Here they crept between the giant stones and huddled against the farthest side, while the smoke billowed up and over the top. The air was clearer here, whistling between the gaps in the stones, and they leant back for a rest.

They could hear the ominous roar and crackling of the fire growing nearer, bringing with it suffocating clouds of dense smoke and haze. Shouts from the firemen rang out above the noise of the blaze.

Night began to close in and each time they crept out to check on the fire, they could see it was beginning to move away and die down. Wreathes of grey tendrils rose up everywhere, and the ground was hot to walk on.

A voice suddenly called out from below and Ben recognized Davy's hoarse bellow. They crawled out into the bright glare of torchlight.

"Here ..." shouted Jan.

"I thought you'd got barbecued," his father came up to them. "Who's that with you?"

"Ah ..." grunted Gundry, stretching his stiff joints, "I 'ope m' hens 'aven't got roasted."

"I feel as if I 'ave," groaned Zach, looking out from a blackened face.

They followed those with the torches, picking their way across the burnt tracks down to Jessie's barn, and quenched their rasping smoke-filled throats.

Wearily Zach and Seth set out to find the motorbike which they'd hurriedly flung against a field wall, and they roared off as black with smoke as the dark night.

When they burst through Clarrie's door, she shrieked at the state of them, while Hannah scurried off to fill a bath of hot water.

The firemen worked in relays all through the night and when

morning came, the moors were a sorry sight of blackened slopes and crags. They worked on for the next few days, beating out any outbreaks that threatened to flare up again.

Eventually, the rains came at last, washing the black ash into the ground, and nature began to slowly recover herself, throwing up new shoots to clothe the area again with green bracken and sprouting bushes of purple heather and yellow gorse.

3

"Tammy!" – Matt heard Kathy's call as he'd heard it many a time ringing out from the cliff path. He watched as his sister ran downwards to the cove to meet her friend and they walked, chattering nineteen to the dozen onto the beach in the bright sunlight.

Jem, one of the fisherlads, was stacking crab pots into a small boat.

"Want to come for a trip?"

"No, thanks," Tamsin tossed her hair.

"Go on," Kathy nudged her.

"You come with me."

"I get seasick."

"I'm staying here, then," Tamsin turned away.

"You'll see the seals on the Brisons isle today," Jem grinned at her.

"Well …"

"I'm only going to pull some pots and put these out."

"Go on," Kathy lay on her towel, closing her eyes.

Tamsin hesitated, then she climbed into the boat and Jem winked at her as he pushed it out into the water and jumped in.

He turned the engine, and after several splutters it roared into life and they were put-putting away from the slipway. The water was so clear that they could see the shadowy shapes of the rocks and seaweed on the seabed.

They stopped to throw over the pots stacked in the boat, then they went around the rocky islands, where Jem picked up a marker float and hauled in the rope, pulling up six crab pots from the depths below.

In the first two were a few crabs and in the next, a blue lobster. Tamsin squeaked with delight and Jem was pleased, for a 'blue' brought in good money on the fish market.

He baited the pots, skewering strips of mackerel around the inside of the neck, and threw them back overboard to fish again the next day.

They went in closer to the islands and there on the rocks lay a dozen seals or more, basking in the sun. Jem threw a mackerel at a grey head bobbing in the water. It rose up and caught it, swallowing it quickly and watching for another, its long whiskers twitching. Jem handed a fish to Tamsin to throw and they spent the next half hour tossing mackerel to others that came around the boat.

Tamsin laughed as the fish were caught and Jem laughed too and snatched a quick kiss from her in between.

" 'Ere, Jem Morgan, you behave," she drew back from him, but she smiled at him, just the same.

He turned the boat and they went further out to try for some pollack. He stopped the engine and they put out handlines and drifted.

Tamsin was the first to catch one and was highly delighted at her success, for which Jem snatched another kiss to encourage her. Then he also caught one and a few mackerel.

"A proper little fishergirl, you be," he slid his arm around her.

"Jem – you are a one," she gave him a small push, "Jo'll see us from the lookout." He overbalanced against the boat's side and it rocked suddenly.

"Here!" he grasped at the gunnel, knocking one of the oars into the water.

"Now, look!" he pulled out the other oar and tried to hook the paddle towards them, but it slowly floated away.

"Oh, I'm sorry," cried Tamsin.

He started the engine, but it spluttered just as it had done in the bay.

"What's the matter with it?"

"The darn thing's bin playin' up all week. I'll 'ave a look at it," he reached into his toolbox for a spanner.

"Will you be able to do it?"

"Surely, I thought I'd cured it yesterday."

"I don't want to be out here all day," she said.

"It'll be alright in a minute," he had parts of the engine out in pieces.

There was a slight haze drawing nearer from the horizon with wisps of cloud passing over, and the heat of the sun cooled behind it. Tamsin pulled on a jumper she'd brought with her.

Jem put the engine together and tried it again, but there was no sound from it.

"What're we going to do?" she asked.

"I'll 'ave to scull us in with this oar. It's a good job the sea's calm."

Tamsin groaned, "How long will that take?"

"Can't say – 'ave you got anything light coloured? We can tie it to the oar. If one of the other boats see us, they'll give us a tow."

"No – I haven't."

"Not a hanky?" Jem searched his pockets.

"No – nothing."

He looked at her, "Ha – your costume's yellow. That'll show up nice."

"No!"

"You won't get back till tonight!"

"Oh, my Gar! Father'll kill me!"

"Come on, then. You've got a jumper on – I won't look."

Tamsin tightened her lips undecidedly, turning her head away from him, then she slipped off the top of her costume under the jumper, while Jem studied his engine, a slight grin on his lips.

She held it out to him.

"That'll do – handsome," he tied it onto the oar and stood it up like a mast. The small piece of yellow material fluttered in the slight breeze like a seagull.

"We should be alright now. They'll home in on us like little pigeons," he laughed.

"Oh, Jem ..." she giggled.

Neither of them had noticed that the haze now swirled about them.

"Fog!" she shrieked.

Jem turned to try the engine again and suddenly through the mist, a grey shape loomed up beside them, a tosher from the next cove.

"You want any help?" a voice shouted at them.

"A tow," yelled back Jem.

"Who is it?" a dark figure pushed forward to the side of the fishing boat, "Ha! Jem Morgan is it? It'll cost you. I'll 'ave one o' they lobsters you got under that sack."

"I want no favours from you!" Jem waved his fist angrily, "You bin at my pots again. I see you in the fog last week." The antagonism between the rival coves was as always.

"You ain't got no proof. Do you want a tow or not?"

"You'll 'ave no lobster from me!" shouted Jem.

"Row back then! Ha – what's that emblem you got there – the sign o' the two titties? Haw-haw-haw"

"Give it 'ere, Jem," Tamsin was tearful.

"What about the maid. She coming home with us?"

"You can – if you want," muttered Jem.

"No," she said.

"Her father'll give 'er hell," came the raucous voice.

Jem said, "I won't mind if you go ..."

"No. Not with them – I couldn't."

"She don't fancy your company," Jem yelled up to them. "So, piss off!"

15

"Pray for a good wind then. Haw-haw."

They could hear the laughter and shouts as the larger boat slid away from them into the fog.

"Why didn't you go?" Jem undid the wisp of material from the oar and gave it to her.

"An' 'ave it broadcast all round the village? Besides, I don't like that lot."

"Let's 'ave another go at this engine then," Jem tried the starter again and again. Once or twice it gave a cough and their hopes were rising, when they heard voices once more through the fog.

A small boat appeared, its occupants rowing. It was the Pollard brothers who had gone fishing earlier that morning.

"Well – well. What 'ave we 'ere. Rob?"

"Two little doves. Run out 'o fuel, boy? Haw-haw ..."

"It's broken down," Jem muttered.

"Haw-haw. Pull the other leg, boy. Anyhow, we got trouble with ours, so you can give us a tow in."

"I can't! I can't get it going."

"You 'ear that, Rob? I do b'lieve he's tellin' the truth."

"Of course he is," Tamsin snapped at them. "We ain't hanging around out 'ere for fun."

"I got a couple o' sparks out of 'er just now," Jem turned to the engine again.

"Go on, Pete. Get over an' help him an' I'll 'ave another go with our'n. Whoever gets going first, tows the other in." Rob pulled the two craft together and Pete climbed over into Jem's boat.

"I've given it a wipe over," Jem made room for him. They could hear Rob turning his engine two or three times and Pete did the same with theirs, and suddenly it roared into life.

"There y'are, boy. Got a rope?"

Jem pulled out a length from under the seat.

"Right. Tie it here an' I'll get back to Rob with my end." Pete clambered over the gunnel and fastened the rope to his own bow.

"Away you go!" yelled Rob.

They steamed on for a while, then Pete called out, "We should be getting near the shore."

"Yes." Jem shouted back at them, "Shorten your rope a bit."

"What?"

"Shorten the rope. It's making the boat yaw."

"Right."

"I can hear breakers!" Tamsin leaned over the side. The cliff loomed out at them as the fog lifted slightly.

"Breakers!" yelled Rob.

"Steer to the right!" Pete waved urgently.

"Shorten the rope," shouted back Jem, as he moved the tiller round.

A surging wave rose up beneath them, foaming on top. Jem's boat swooped up upon it and they hung in the air as the roller swept by. Tamsin screamed as the boat fell with a smack into the trough.

"Hang on!" cried Jem.

He looked back and saw the Pollards on top of the wave, the two figures sprawled in the bows, and he could hear their shouts as their boat swooped down. He felt the pull of their weight on his stern, but he opened up the throttle and headed into the cove and onto the slipway.

"I thought we were going in on the rocks," Tamsin gasped. Jem grinned as he heard the voices behind.

"Hey, Jem lad, can't you steer better'n that?"

"Tammy!" Kathy came running across the beach with Matt.

"Where've you been?" he shouted to her. He'd wandered down to the shore, peering into the haze trying to see if their boat was coming in.

"Fishing," Tamsin laughed and flickered a look at Jem.

"Come on, it's time we got home," called Kathy.

"Coming," Tamsin turned to Jem.

"I s'spose you won't be coming out again, after the engine an' all," he strung a couple of pollack together for her.

"Oh, go on. It was fun really – coming up for tea?" she looked at him under her dark curling lashes.

"We-ll …"

"Mother made scones this morning."

"We-ll," he started to undo a bolt on the engine.

"An' a batch of strawberry jam last week – an' I'm picking up some cream on the way," a smile quirked at the side of her mouth.

"What about your Dad?"

"He won't mind – 'specially if you bring him some fish."

"We-ll," he glanced quickly round at the other men, "I'll catch you up."

She giggled, " 'Bye," and ran after Kathy. She caught Matt by the arm and made him swear not to say a word to father, or else!

Jem sauntered across to Rob, "About time you got a new engine," he called cheekily.

"Aye. I don't b'lieve we'd survive another trip with you, lad!" Pete gave him a playful elbow in the ribs.

4

Zach and Matt waited at the top of the steep hill for Eli Rowe with his wife Mary Anne and their son Harry, to come by. They'd climb up into his cart pulled by his faithful white stallion Nathan, and all go to Penzance market.

Matt and Harry went to school together and had many of the same interests. They held their own conversation with each other, while the adults loudly voiced their opinions on their relatives and neighbours around them.

On market day Eli rose at dawn, and while mother and Mary Anne did the milking, he harnessed up Nathan and loaded the cart with the week's produce. Baskets of butter and new laid eggs, sacks of potatoes, carrots, turnips and broccoli. In the summer, there would be strawberries and clotted cream, raspberries and gooseberries.

Then he rounded up the stock of animals going to market and off they went, the cart leading the way with Mary Anne atop, her hat tied under her chin with braid, and Eli, Zach and the boys driving the cattle.

The market up at the Causewayhead was hectic and noisy as always. Eli put a nosebag on the horse and he and Zach stood and watched the auction. Then while Mary Anne and the boys were on the stall selling their goods, the two men would nip in the inn for a midday noggin.

Old Nathan was as quiet and patient as a dove, blowing and snuffling in Matt's hand when he gave him an apple or a lump of sugared pastry.

He'd pulled the cart day in, day out, along the stony highways and rutted tracks. That old stallion, he'd drawn the plough in the stone walled fields, harrowing, raking, turning and sowing, plodding up and down the furrows and back.

One evening during the winter, when Eli went to bring the herd in for milking, he found one missing, and on walking round the field, discovered a cliff fall. Part of the cliff had fallen away, and the rab between the granite had been washed loose by the heavy rain. Stone and turf had rolled down the steep cliff into the sea and the ledge and fence was left dangling in mid air. One of the young flighty heifers had missed her footing and had gone tumbling down the cliffside, to lodge in a cleft some way down, with the stunned heifer lying on the ledge. He ran back to the farm and his shouts brought Mary Anne and Harry, and Matt who was also with him, running out to help.

Matt ran down to the village to fetch Zach and Seth and they found what ropes they could and Eli harnessed up Nathan.

When they reached the cliff, Eli tied one end of a rope around himself and attached the other end to Nathan, as Zach and Seth held the horse steady and watched him lower himself down to the heifer.

On reaching her, he carefully tied ropes around her, and then gave the signal to those above him to pull. The two boys held onto Nathan and urged him forward while Mary Anne watched Eli to see he didn't get hitched up on spars of rock. Zach and Seth hauled on the rope and with Nathan, pulled both Eli and the heifer up the face of the cliff.

Nathan was like one of the family, in all the many ways he and the family helped each other. When he was put out at the end of the day, he kicked up his heels and galloped across the field and rolled on his back for sheer joy.

That winter Eli began to feel that time and age had begun to creep up on him, and when he laid down his tools, he sat back more and more in his chair to take his ease.

He and Zach were sitting each side of the log fire that was

banked up, giving out a heat that flushed their weathered faces, while the warmth of the glass of whisky in their hands warmed their stomachs.

"I'm thinking that perhaps it's time I let cousin Penwithers take over," Eli said.

"You're probably right," agreed Zach.

"Henry's too young, an' m'daughters are now married with families an' lives of their own," Eli sighed.

"Time you took it easier," nodded Mary Anne.

"I'll put most of the land up for sale, but we still want to go on living here in our old home, our family farmhouse," Eli decided.

So the milking herd and some of the pigs were auctioned. Mary Anne kept the chickens for their eggs, and the time had come too for Nathan to be put out to grass as he deserved. To wander the sweet-scented heather moor and rough cliff land behind the house.

The place fell quiet and empty for a while. Eli, Zach and Seth took to racing pigeons with the pigeon club, Mary Anne joined the art group and wandered about with paint brushes and easel, and Matt and Harry continued going to and from school, and exploring the moors and the beach.

They often watched Nathan galloping across the bracken and gorse headland, with the white crests of the waves flinging up the misty spray against the rocky shore below. They'd see his silhouette against the sky, looking down onto the sands and Progo arch, which was cut out of the cliff by the ever restless motion of the sea.

Cousin Penwithers bought up the land and also two other small farms adjoining. He began to dismantle the granite walls to enlarge the fields, and soon the place began to look like a vast plain, to Eli's regret.

The roar of machines and tractors took over the harrowing,

raking and sowing, racing across the terrain at high speed, throwing up stones and earth in a dusty cloud behind them.

Morning and evening, the boys would go out onto the moor with half a bucket of grain for Nathan, and he would come galloping up to them, drooling over Harry's shoulder with affection, or he would often be by the gate waiting for them.

One morning as he was feeding, with the noise of the tractors filling the air, the boys heard another sound, an ominous sound. The old familiar grating of the dilapidated knacker's van, rattling down the hill. Nathan too heard and recognised the van. He lifted his head from the bucket, whirled round on his haunches and took off across the headland.

Unknown to Eli, Penwithers had determined to round up the old horse, and he and the knackerman set off in the van, with his workmen spread out behind him in pursuit.

The boys shouted at them, "No – no …!" waving their arms and satchels frantically, the books tumbling out into the mud, but to no avail.

Nathan galloped across the slopes of Gribba point, his mane streaming out, racing the wind, heels thudding and the turf flying, with the lurching van, the noisy shouts of the men and the pounding feet following hard behind.

Harry ran to the farmhouse to find Eli and Matt raced off down to Zach's cottage. Seth had gone out fishing, so Matt and Zach hurried back up the hill to see Eli and Harry running across the cliff fields. They could see the men chasing after the stallion, with Nathan galloping away in the distance.

Eli roared at Penwithers, with Zach and the boys all shouting to attract his attention.

Zach ran with rasping breath, over the steep rise of Polpry cliff, and saw Nathan skirting the crumbling mineshafts, going hard down the narrow dip and up Boscregan Cairn, then up higher to the craggy slabs of Ship's Cairn.

There he paused to look back at the figures struggling up the rise, then off he went like an arrow down the mossy slopes of St.George's stream. He splashed through the little brook and up the other side to Ding Dong workings, and up again to Cairn Clougy and round the ruined powder house.

Eli's heart was gasping in hoarse gulps as he ran round the bottom of the cairn to the rushing falls of Tay river. Nathan had to scramble down the stony track that had fallen away into scree and rab, but down he went, skittering over the stepping stones across the river, and plunging through the swirl of water.

Then up and up the steep winding track set into the cliff edge. Up he climbed, leaping from one ledge to the other until he reached the narrow cliff path running from the foot of Cairn Mellyn, and sweeping above the Gazick slipway where the fishermen had their small boats tied up.

A group of them came out of the low fishing huts on hearing the shouting voices, and stared up at the white horse racing across the cliff above them as Matt and Harry reached the rough track and started to wearily climb up after him.

When Zach reached the top path, he looked back and saw that Penwithers had forsaken the van, and he and his men were running up the other side of the cairn and across the fields to cut the stallion off.

Nathan thudded his hooves into the turf, galloping like the wind, up the twisting track of Cairn Creagle, the crying cairn, its granite crags rising above the sea which foamed at its foot.

As Penwithers moved forward to head him off, to Matt's horror, the stallion sprang high into a soaring leap, slowly turning and plunging downwards through the salt-laden spray, to vanish beneath the white tumbling surf.

He rushed to the granite ledge, calling and crying out his name, looking down the dizzy height of the cliff, with anguish and grief in his heart, remembering all the joy and friendship they'd shared together.

"The devil take you, Penwithers!" roared Eli, as they searched the cliff and shore for his horse. "That old horse was living out his last days easy, with us. I told you, you backguard!"

"He was roaming all over m'land," argued Penwithers, red faced.

"You're a rotten …!" yelled Harry, heartbroken.

Matt clutched sorrowfully at his friend's arm as they spread out, hunting along the cliffs until dusk fell without any sight of Nathan, who'd disappeared beneath the waves.

It was about three days later, that Walt Nicholls was walking back from the inn late at night, when he was startled by a thundering of hooves behind him. On turning round he suddenly jumped back as the shape of a white horse sped by, and swiftly disappeared into the night.

He was somewhat shaken when he reached his own door and had to sit down with a stiff toddy to calm his nerves.

When he told Zach the following morning Zach laughed, saying he'd better curtail his evening ale.

During the following weeks, the white stallion was seen in the lanes and on the moors and cliffs by a great number of people, appearing as a pale image in the dark of the night or a silvery shimmer in the moonlight.

Matt and Harry took their dogs out on the sands in the early mornings, and one day Matt looked down and saw that the dogs were following prints made in the newly washed sand. They were the prints of horse shoes.

"Look!" he cried, catching hold of Harry's arm.

"Horse prints!" shouted Harry, "Nathan's …"

They followed the prints across the beach and down to the

edge of the sea, where the surf surged and washed the sands.

The horse shoe prints led into the sea and disappeared. They looked all over the beach and cliffs but could see no sign of the horse, so they made their way to Zach's cottage.

Zach went down to the shore with them and they showed him the hoof prints and they followed them until they disappeared into the waves.

"Ah," Zach shook his head sadly, "Nathan's gone to his own world with his fellow mates, the sea horses, Harry."

And on many mornings the boys would come across Nathan's hoof prints, as if he had just enjoyed a gallop over the sands in the previous night.

Penwithers doesn't go up to the headland any more, especially at night. For some time later, he was working the top field and had jumped out of the tractor to set the plough, when he heard the thudding of hooves. He looked up and saw the white stallion galloping towards him. It reared up onto its haunches, wildly pawing the air, and lunged forward.

Penwithers fell, rolling aside, but one hoof caught his arm and bruised it so badly, that it stayed purpled and withered until the end of his days.

He scrambled to his feet, leaping and stumbling over walls and stones, with the hooves thundering behind him, until he reached the safety of the barn in the valley below. Each time Penwithers sets foot on the headland he is followed by the sound of hooves, and he beats a hurried retreat.

The ghost of the white stallion is still seen, his mane streaming out in the wind, galloping across the bay in the moonlight.

And Matt and Harry often find the prints of horse shoes going across the fresh firm sands just washed by the tide, in the early mornings.

5

In the whistle of the wind the bell's lone toll echoed and moaned around the grey tower of the granite church, and Seth, standing at the side of the small grave, heard the low tolling of the fateful hour.

His whole being was frozen in time as he looked down at the tiny box that he held in his arms. He didn't feel the sharp angles of the wood that dug into his flesh and his blurred gaze bore almost into the inert shroud where his dark-haired daughter now silently slept.

Then as in a nightmarish dream, he gently lowered his burden into the dank earth. His sorrowing wife, Hannah Jane, quietly wept at his side, her head bowed in grief against the wind.

Their youngest child was now returned to the earth from whence she came, slipping away from where neither Hannah Jane nor himself could reach her. He clasped her hand cruelly, crushing her slim fingers in his cold grasp, while the world seemed encased in a bitter mantle.

The tears streamed down the face of their son Matt, with the loss of his little sister, as he stared down into the tiny grave. He stood next to Zach and clutched his grandfather's hand. Clarissa Rose sobbed into her handkerchief, grieving for her happy grand-daughter, with her other arm round the shoulders of Tamsin, holding her in her comforting embrace.

Zach gazed down into the grave, his eyes misty with a sorrow that struck painfully at his heart. He silently cried out for the gay spirit of life that was his treasured grand-daughter.

Seth, a fisherman from a long line of fishermen, lived in the middle of the bay with his wife, daughters Tamsin and Zara and his son Matt, and the whole of their cottage was filled with light by the elfish quintessence of Zara, weaving her laughter and song around them.

She would go with Zach along the beach, tossing her beach ball into the air to him, running and laughing in play. He and Matt would take her with her fishing net, to the pools in the rocks looking for small crabs and blennies, and together they would go with their fishing rods to the end of the beach, fishing for bass. Matt and Tamsin with their own rods and Zara holding on to Zach's larger one with him.

When Seth was away at sea, Hannah Jane would walk across the white sands and Zara would skip and leap over the pools and run shrieking into the blustery wind, calling shrilly to the seagulls wheeling above.

And it was on such a day, when a wild westerly was blowing and a high surf was pounding on the beach, that the long arm of the surge swept far up onto the sands, enfolding Zara in its embrace and taking her far out into the deep.

Hannah Jane screamed into the wind, running up and down the wet sands, crying her name, and all through the night the villagers searched, seeking and calling.

As the tide turned, Seth found his daughter washed by the waves between the grey rocks, and he took her up into his arms and looked down at her still form in stunned bewilderment.

Now they stood on the bleak hillside, hidden by the chilling mists as the dark clouds gathered in a swirling veil, and the wind rose whining in the swaying trees, scattering harsh flurries of rain.

Beyond the cliffs the wild sea raged, smothering the reef in a pulsing roar – and far out on the horizon the outline of white sails appeared.

As the huddled group of mourners lingered by the grave, Seth lifted his eyes slowly to the sullen sky and out to the turbulent waves, and watched the white sails and masts rise and fall against the angry tide.

The coursing waves curved in sporadic rolls and the masts disappeared - then rose - then vanished again, and a shower of hail swept down and blotted out the shoreline.

Then as the clouds lifted, there again the white sails that bent before the wind – flailing and floundering in the tremulous swell – white sails reeling towards the rocky shore.

A brittle crack split the heavens as a flared star shattered the lowering clouds, lighting the shore, the cliffs and the sea. Another – a signal calling him, urging his leaden feet to move. His bitter heart shouted silently, "Why – why – when my own has gone, why?" his whole being raging with his sorrow.

He heard Zach and the others moving away, their footsteps hurrying over the stony track going down to the quay.

Hannah Jane pressed his arm and raised her eyes to look hard into his, "Go, Seth, go …" she whispered.

His eyes dropped away from her gaze and he stumbled away from where his daughter lay, and ran with his grief down to the shore. Hannah Jane sighed, letting the single white rose that she held in her limp fingers, fall fluttering down into her daughter's tiny grave and slowly made her way back to the silent cottage.

Then away went the lifeboat through the stormy wave, flinging the salt spray high into the air, with the wind tearing through cordage and spar.

Zach creased his eyes and clenched his jaw against the lash of icy flurries as he peered through the spume for sight of the stricken vessel.

Then the shadow of masts rose up, veering towards the reef, with shredded sail and plunging bows, only to vanish amongst the tumbling surf where the sharp-edged teeth of granite rock showed.

They raced up the hunch-backed seas, searching through the troughs and the creaming surge, but only the turmoil of the storm met them.

Then a tangled mass reared up in a torrent of water and they surged towards it, searching for any sign of life in the flotsam of timber. But nowhere upon the listing wreck was a soul to be seen, as it reeled away from them in the rip of the current.

They turned away into the wave and then the sound of a cry in the howl of the wind wailed above the snarl of the tide. Again it came as they swept in and neared the reef where the broken craft lay upon its side. But as they searched, only the water-logged stays rose up upon the black rocks trembling in the seething race, and only the buoy with its swaying light pierced through the gloom and rang its warning into the coming night.

Then again rose the cry, a childish keening that was shrill and high. And to Seth it was like his own child, calling out in the wind with the mournful clang of the buoy's lone sigh.

He cried hoarsely out to the storm, his hands clutching the rails of the lurching boat, his eyes stinging with the icy shards of rain.

Then as the buoy's rusty frame straddled the wave, they saw the tattered scarecrow of a man clinging to its side. His eyes were rimmed white with encrusted salt and his ravaged lips drawn taut and wide as he screamed into the night. The buoy swept down into the trough out of sight as serried ranks of waves coursed over the reef.

They turned the boat again to start a run closer to the tossing bell and as they neared, it reared up before them with the sea-wracked figure still clutching its frame. Then they saw close by his feet a bedraggled bundle of rags, that wailed in terror with the roar of the turbulent sway.

As the crew watched, a climbing wave smothered the buoy,

and when it emerged on the following ridge, the welling seas had taken their toll and had swept the gaunt figure away in the swirl. Every way they searched, around and over the rushing waves, but he was gone into the maelstrom, then as the buoy rose up again they could see that the ragged bundle was still there.

Then again the cry pierced through the darkening night – calling, calling to Seth. He reached for the life-line and with a despairing shout, plunged into the racing swell.

Zach cried out to him, grabbing hold of the line to pull him back, but was swept into the heaving waters by a breaking wave. The icy grip of the ocean froze the marrow in his bones and closed over his head. He struggled and thrust out towards the surface and a fierce surge of current threw him up and he saw the black shape of the lifeboat and felt the bitter scourge of the gale on his face.

The crew's shouts blew away with the wind as he flung his strength at the grey rolling hills, and the smoking crests spun him high in their frenzied rills, as he struggled to reach the buoy.

As Seth topped an oncoming wave he caught a glimpse of its dark frame rising up before him, then it was hidden in the shadows of engulfing water. He was washed away in the white trails of the spume with the grey cloud of the night whirling about him.

Then he rose up on the back of a sloping wave and the black swaying buoy towered above him, ready to crush him as it was thrown down by the force of the sea.

As it sped towards him he clawed at it, seizing a hold as the wave rushed by. His fingers were almost wrenched from their grasp as the buoy spun aside and slid down into the following trough. It was then that he saw Zach being swept towards him. As he rose up on the next wave Seth pulled at the life-line, throwing his father against the buoy. Zach clutched at the metal framework, gasping and coughing out sea water.

The sodden bundle was still clinging there and as Seth snatched at it, the face turned to cower from the lash of the spray and he saw a child – his child – that shivered and trembled in the stormy night. A child who'd been hastily roped to the bell by the wild-eyed man in his desperate plight, before the sea had taken him.

Zach locked his frozen fingers into the bedraggled clothing as the buoy lurched and reeled in a wild switchback ride. Seth tore at the rope binding the child to the frame and as it parted he clasped the child in his arms. He threw back his head and shouted his triumph to the wind's shrill whine, then with Zach keeping the line taut, together they leapt into the raging seas.

The watching crew hauled at the coiling life-line as the clamorous waters arched and foamed, breaking around them in speckled plumes.

Seth held the child tightly, turning it as he might against the onslaught of the waves, and he cried out his child's name as Zach gasped and spluttered beside him with renewed strength to reach the boat.

The crew shouted to them against the howling of the wind, pulling hard on the line, drawing them nearer and nearer, and as they were tossed and tumbled in the fray, frantic hands scooped them up from the frenzied spume.

Then the reeling craft turned for the land, and the hearts of each of the crew were full, as the two men and child shivered together in the blankets that had been wrapped around them.

Seth held the small child as they sped through the stormy waves for the cove, his salt-blurred vision seeing the long dark strands of hair and the small pointed face, so like his own daughter. His bemused mind, battered by the spite of the seas, hovered in a vague world of consciousness and his soul cried out for joy that he now held his lost child again.

The cliffs glowed yellow with the lights from the windows of the cottages in the cove and straddling up the hill. Lights were also moving and bobbing along the paths, held by the villagers coming down to the shore. For they could see the swaying mast of the lifeboat lifting and falling in the rolling combers.

As it rounded the inner edge of the reef it wallowed and disappeared into the well of grey seas, seemingly for ever, but then the flicker of lights appeared again, pushing onward around the black crags. It surged forward in the tidal race, then hung in almost suspended motion as the engine battled against the undertow. Then onward it flew again, and those on the shore stood with held breath and clenched hands, their wild hopes running with the boat.

As it neared the shore the waiting villagers were silhouetted against the night, wading into the foaming surf swirling around their thighs, and flinging the stinging salt spray into their faces.

With outstretched hands they dragged the ropes, wires and pulleys ready for the craft as she came in, to pull her up swiftly from the greedy grasp of the sea.

Zach stepped shakily down upon the land. Clarissa Rose ran to him, her arms embracing his trembling frame, helping him up the beach.

Seth held the child against him, ignoring the reaching hands ready to help him. He walked across the shore and there was Hannah Jane with Tamsin and Matt running towards him, their eyes filled with tears at his safe return.

Hannah Jane flung herself upon him, crying his name, over and over, then she felt the child stir in his arms and looked down at the small face uplifted to her.

Seth looked at the child as he stood there upon the shore, and he saw his child in the dark sea waif, his lost child returned to him once more.

He held his arms out to Hannah and she took the child, enfolding it against her breast, and her smile lit the joy in her face as her tears mingled with the falling rain.

6

Zach went down to meet the Queen. The King and his wife were visiting Falmouth, and Zach had put out his best jacket and shirt the day before in readiness.

"We're all going," said Hannah Jane. Tamsin and Matt were to be there with their schools and their little sister, the sea maid Jessica, as they called her, for no-one had come forward to claim her, was going with Clarissa Rose and Zach.

Seth and his crew would see the procession from the docks where they would berth their boat.

During the week they'd sailed on the Clarissa Rose, accompanied with many of their neighbours in their boats, making quite a flotilla rounding the point to Falmouth.

The morning showers were passing over and the spring sun began to shine from a sky beginning to turn blue over the coastline and sea.

Zach and Hannah, with Clarissa and Jessica, made their way along the harbour, where a new jetty was being built and still needed the finishing touches to complete it.

They walked through the narrow streets into the town, stopping by the flower seller for Zach to purchase an early white rose for his buttonhole and a posy of flowers for Jessica.

Though they were early, there were already crowds of people gathering, choosing which was the best place to see everything happening and to catch a glimpse of the King and Queen.

Jessica and Hannah Jane were pressed up against the park railings with Zach standing behind them.

A colourful array of flags and banners were waved by the gathering crowds as they heard the gun salute, fired by one of the frigates in the bay signalling the arrival of the Royal couple at the Falmouth Docks railway station. Here the band was playing, with hundreds more people waiting to greet them as they stepped down from the train and out into the sunshine.

Matt stood with his school friends along the way where the King and Queen would arrive. They pushed and jostled each other impatiently, turning their heads this way and that to watch the movements of an occasional official or policeman and to see any sign of the procession.

Zach Trewin's feet were starting to ache and he was getting thirsty in the warm sunshine. Hannah Jane was gossiping with a group of friends beside her, while Jessica had sat down on the ground with her head pushed through the gap of the railings, watching the excited crowd around her.

Standing on a step of the pavement, Matt saw his grandfather and waved his arms at him to attract his attention. His mother lifted Jessica up to see him with his school group and Tamsin amongst her school friends, and she happily waved her flag and flowers at them.

Soon there were hundreds in the excited crowd growing noisier, gossiping, laughing and shouting to each other. Matt squeezed through those around him and pushed his way until he found Zach.

"Isn't it exciting, Grandfer?" he shouted. Zach laughed to see him and ruffled his hair.

Clarissa Rose exclaimed, "Matt! Get back with your school group. You won't see as much here."

"There's nothing coming yet," he said, "are you alright, Grandfer?"

"It's getting hot 'ere with all this crowd, I could do with something cold," came the reply.

Matt was looking towards the corner of the road where the ice-cream man often stood, and sure enough he was there now.

"I'll get you an ice-cream," he shouted. Hannah started, "Don't you go running off my lad."

"Tha's alright, I'll go with him," Zach put his hand on Matt's shoulder, "we'll stick together."

Matt went ahead of his grandfather, and they made their way weaving in and out of the mass of people. There was quite a queue at the corner, but with an ice each, Zach also had a welcome orange drink to quench his thirst.

"Tha's revived me, lad," he said, "now we'd best be getting back."

As they made their way through the crowd they could hear the sound of hand clapping and cheering from the other end of the road.

"Come on Grandfer – they're coming!" shouted Matt, dragging him by the hand towards his school friends. The two ice-tubs that Zach was holding for Hannah and Jessica were lost in the forward surge of the crowd.

"He's with us – this's my school here," declared Matt to one of the officials standing nearby, who saw his school tie and blazer and nodded them through to merge with the rest of the school group. So Zach stood with the schoolboys beside Matt's friends, his tongue licking the last of his ice. The cheering grew to a crescendo with loud clapping and a sea of waving flags.

"The King's coming!" shrieked Matt.

"The Queen's here !" shouted all those around.

Zach leant over the heads of the others and there came his King and Queen. He was in stately uniform and she was in a colourful rose-coloured coat and hat. Behind followed the Ladies-in-waiting and other familiar Cornish dignitaries.

The King was smiling, happy to see them all there in great spirits to greet him, and everybody cheered and clapped, celebrating their appreciation of his steady reign.

Many of the children were leaning over, with posies of bright flowers clutched in their hands, and the Queen came over to them, walking and talking and accepting their gifts.

Soon she had a large armful of colourful flowers as she smiled and thanked each one. She took Jessica's small nosegay, smiling at her and the little seamaid's eyes sparkled with delight, and the Royal couple walked from side to side happily greeting everyone.

Matt's school waved their flags and Tamsin's group had their own sprays of flowers held out towards the Queen, and she passed the bouquets on to those with her to hold them, as she accepted more.

Zach carefully took out his white rose from his buttonhole and with outstretched arm, offered it to his Queen.

"Ma-am," he said. "Well done, m'handsome," and she took his rose, holding it up and breathing in its delicate perfume and smiled her thanks.

The Royal couple then moved on, with many more flowers offered on their way, amongst the applause of well-wishers.

Matt tugged at Zach's hand, "Come on, Grandfer, the King and Queen are going on the new liner. We're going round to see if we can see them on it."

Zach was pulled along through the moving crowd by Matt's friends, until they were surrounded by so many people that they could go no further. The boys climbed up onto a narrow ledge and Zach could just see over their heads.

There were all kinds of boats in the harbour packed with people on board. They could see the Royal couple being introduced to dignitaries and to the skippers and crews of many of the boats, Seth on the Clarissa Rose being one of them.

The King and Queen went on board the revenue craft, putting out to sea to tour the harbour, inspecting the tall ship, Sir Galahad, which was dressed overall with sailors manning the yards, and they could hear them giving a salutary three cheers, ringing out loudly across the water.

Zach was humming to himself the old song, 'I love the white

rose in its splendour, I love the white rose in its bloom …' and stood there watching the distant figure of the Queen in her rose-coloured coat on board the liner.

Matt thought, "When Grandfer met the Queen – he'll never stop talking about it!"

Zach looked around him at the happy smiling faces. What a day! What a grand day!

7

Seth's brother Ezra, hadn't followed him or their father into fishing for a living.

Instead he'd become one of the numerous miners working in the nearby Wheal Venton tin mine, and his two sons, Jake and Simeon had joined him, walking the mile or so there and back before and after their shifts.

Zach was in his small garden, hoeing his carrots, when there was a sudden tremendous roar that shook the ground and startled all those in the small terraced cottages, and he knew something had happened at the mine.

He called to Clarrie and they ran along the lane where they found Seth and Hannah Jane hurrying out of their door, and on to Ezra's cottage, where his wife Ella came running out to them.

They were joined by the rest of the villagers, all hurrying towards the headgear silhouetted against the sky, and to the mine's count house.

Beneath the ground a violent blast of air swept through the 8th level, and the miners working away at the tin lode dropped their tools and began to run as the ground overhead creaked and cracked, with dust and stones falling, a 'God send' warning.

The sweeping air current swirled the men along, tearing jackets off their backs, flinging stones in their eyes, and throwing them against the granite rock.

Ezra screamed to his two sons to get out. He shouted their names over and over till the dust filled his lungs.

Then came the collapse of the deads and waste rock overhead crashing down, the whole mass breaking through to the old flooded workings. The rushing wave of water swept him along, overturning a wagon from the rails, and building up piles of stones and props.

He was flung against the wagon and clung to pieces of wood as the torrent raced by, to pour down a winze in a descending waterfall.

Jake and Simeon working further along the level, were caught up and whirled along in the flood of water, sucking them under with the flotsam of debris.

As Simeon was tossed upon the current he saw a timber stull wedged above the water, and lunged forward, flinging his arm over it, and shouting for his brother.

Jake grasped hold of Simeon's boot to haul himself upward, and Simeon pulled himself along the timber, bringing Jake up with him. But his brother was tiring, his hands slipping on Simeon's ankle as the boot was wrenched off, and he fell back into the water and was swept away.

Simeon screamed his name into the black level, as he clung miserably to the timber.

Many hours passed during which rescue parties made great efforts to release anyone who may be trapped. The water level began dropping so they were able to drive tunnels through the rubble, but most of the miners had been instantly buried by the collapse.

Ezra found himself lying under several broken timbers, unable to move. Again and again he made efforts to shift the wood, calling and tapping on the granite stone.

Hours later, he began to hear faint voices and sounds of digging. He shouted, his voice hoarse with dust, but could not make himself heard.

Gradually, the sounds came closer of pick and shovel echoing in the darkness.

" 'Ere – 'ere – I'm 'ere!" he shouted repeatedly.

To his relief came a faint answer –

"Where are 'ee?"

" 'Ere – I'm 'ere!" his voice croaked with the dust.

A hole appeared through the debris and he could see a flickering light.

"I see 'ee …" he screeched, as a pick began to widen the hole and one of the men crawled through.

" 'Tis Ezra!" he shouted back to the others, as they pulled away at the rock and began lifting the debris to help him out. He was bruised and cut, but with their help he crawled along the levels to safety.

When he came out into the chill of the grey dawn, he fell into the arms of Ella, who cried tears of relief. But when he asked for their sons, she sobbed against his shoulder and he sank to his knees in despair.

Zach and Seth comforted the couple as much as they could, while Clarrie and Hannah wept with Ella, as they waited anxiously for the rescue group to find his sons.

A small slight figure touched Ella's arm and she turned and saw Zelda, who slipped her hand in Ella's, thankful that Ezra was alive. But her heart full of Simeon, with his ring on a chain beneath her bodice, cried out for him.

For most of the day they waited, silent watchers standing in the mist, the rescue group bringing up a man here, a boy there, most who had succumbed to the flooding waters.

"Ezra!" came a shout, "Over 'ere…."

He stumbled over the rough ground helped by his father and brother. On a makeshift stretcher lay a bedraggled form.

"Simeon!" whispered Ezra, and Ella and Zelda wept, their tears streaking the red slime on his cheek.

His shoulder hung out of shape, dislocated from hanging onto the wet timber against the force of the flood.

Pengegon, who came to doctor those rescued, wrenched it back in place as Simeon screamed out in agony.

"Jake?" queried Ezra. But Simeon howled the more, "He's gone, Da – he's gone!"

The men carried him home and laid him on his bed. Ella tended to the wounds of both her husband and son, but nothing could help to heal the wound in their hearts of the loss of Jake.

Many weeks passed, the work continued in the other levels of the mine. Simeon, quieter now without his brother, worked again but his heart wasn't in it.

His parents, being older, were more resigned to the sad knocks of life. Zelda though, was distraught, for Simeon neither spoke nor looked at her with their past love in his eyes.

Ella was woken early one morning by a sound. She quietly pulled a shawl over her shoulders and crept down the stairs, to come upon Simeon fastening the straps to a pack.

"Ah, no! Simeon, no …" whispered his mother.

"I must," he turned, his eyes dull with sadness, "I let 'im go – don't you see? I let Jake go and he drowned."

"No, no," pleaded Ella, "it's not your fault – God doesn't always let us hold on to the things we want."

"I let 'im go," cried Simeon, "I couldn't hold 'im - I see 'im in every adit and rock. I must go where he's never been – I'll find work an' send you money towards the rent."

"He's right," Ezra came up to them, "bid 'im luck, Ella."

Simeon held them both, then picked up his bag and set off over the moor.

Ezra put his arm around Ella, and they both watched until he disappeared over the rise of the hill.

Simeon found a ship at Falmouth, one of the collecting stations for the hundreds of mining emigrants, sailing to join the larger ships at Bristol for California. The long voyage, with salt beef to eat and the terrible seas were a real hardship.

His first sight of San Francisco was a sprawling settlement of log huts, where he joined others crowded on bullock-carts to the gold diggings.

He registered a claim and set to work to sinking a narrow shaft, with just room for a ladder and to swing a bucket. He sank small winzes, and worked away with pick and gad.

The months passed as he worked all hours of the day and night, talking to Jake, talking to himself, often finding nothing, but hoarding any small pieces of gold he did find and burying them in a secret place.

Now and again he would go down to the rapidly spreading settlement, and exchange a small amount of gold for money for food, and the rest he sent off to Cornwall to Ezra.

The streets were filling up with hostels and liquor bars, where many miners spent most of their findings. But Simeon would go back to his hut and brood, eat a little, then climb down the shaft and start work again.

One day he was working at a new vein he'd found, when the perspiration on his brow grew heated with a dizziness in his head, and he fell onto the pick.

After a moment's blankness, he began to shiver with intense cold, then heat, and knew that he'd caught a fever.

He lay there for some hours, knowing that no-one would miss him for maybe days. He could no longer picture Jake in his mind, and he realised that he hadn't thought of him for some time. He now longed for him, but he wouldn't find Jake nor Zelda in this place, and he grasped the pick and struck out in anguish at the rock around him.

It fell away in a large run of debris and stone, partly burying his feet and tools. He scrabbled around for the shovel and began to fill the bucket for a last haul, if he could manage in his weakness, to climb up to the surface.

As he dug into the pile, he could see a change of colour in the sample. He picked out another and another, and as he searched the vein he saw a golden gleam in the ore.

His excitement grew as he worked all day and into the next morning, proving the richness of his lucky strike. Then with his find in a body-belt under his shirt, he set out for home.

Quite a few miners returned, embarking on the long voyage of many weeks, some with wealth but many with almost nothing to show for their hardships. Ezra and Ella would listen to their tales of adventure, but there was no news of their son.

Then one morning, Zelda, walking to the top of the moors where she went every day to watch the path, saw the familiar figure coming over the heather.

They heard her crying out his name, and Ezra and Ella with joyful hearts came out to meet their son, in his broad-brimmed hat, with his shirt open at the neck and in high rolled boots, striding towards them.

8

The last days of summer were warm, throwing out the glorious colours of the late roses and dahlias. But the trees stood colourless – no fullness of red apple or golden pear. What few plums on the branches were shrivelled and unformed. The once thriving orchards had failed for the second year, and the widow-woman leant on the gate with a heavy heart, gazing with despair at the trees.

She must now think of selling up, before a third year sent her into the poorhouse leaving nothing for her sons.

Her workman, Walt, grumbled about being without work, then he grunted, "What you want is bees!"

"Bees!" she stared at him.

" 'Es – go an' see Zach and Eli at Pencherrow farm, down the valley," he wheezed, as he shuffled away.

Over the winter she pondered on her problem, and when early spring arrived, she decided to cycle down the steep valley lane.

There was no-one around the white-washed farmhouse, so she walked over to the paddock, and saw puffs of smoke rising up from the bushes.

Zach, a figure in overalls, hat and veil, was bending over an open hive. He saw her and came over, taking off his gloves and veil. She told him about the poor fruit harvest as they walked towards the kitchen, and he said that he and Eli would come over and look. The kitchen shelves and table were stacked with jars of last summer's golden honey, containers of yellow-white honeycomb, lids and labels.

She picked up a full jar, gazing through the glowing colour, reading the label – 'Cornish Honey, Zach Trewin & Eli Rowe,

Pencherrow Farm, Nanquidno Valley.'

The next day Eli and Zach walked the fields and hedgerows of her land, and they pointed out where they could position hives for the most benefit.

"Will bees make all that difference?" Lizzie Whitta was dubious.

"If the weather is kind, you'll 'ave hundreds of bees working on the blossom, collecting nectar an' pollinating each flower," said Eli.

Walt offered his help to move the hives in the late evenings when the bees went in for the night. A strip of wood was wedged across the hive entrances to keep the bees inside as they moved them.

Walt backed Eli's van up to the group of hives and he and Zach lifted them into the back. There was a muted humming from the bees inside as he drove out into the potholed lane, Eli saying, "Steady – they don't like being jolted!"

They reached the orchard gate, and placed the hives where Walt had cut back the grass. Zach took out the wedge from each entrance and a few bees began to crawl out, "They won't go far," he said.

They took more hives to the orchard, and then were on their way with another three hives to put on the moor to take advantage of the wild flowers and the autumn heather harvest.

Walt was driving across the track when suddenly the front wheel hit a tussock and tilted sideways. The hives in the back slid to the corner of the vehicle, with a rising hum from the bees. Lizzie looked fearfully over her shoulder, but they were still sealed up. Walt's door leant drunkenly in the mire, and he shouted, "We're in the bog!"

There was no-one around to help, but Eli saw a gate in the distance and the men hurried towards it, and worked it off its rusty hinges. They levered it as far as possible under the front wheel, then pushed the back of the van while Walt started the engine. The vehicle slithered on the sinking wood, but suddenly gripped onto firmer ground, and they set off again to site the hives.

March month began mildly, the willow catkins, aconites and dandelions were out in the valley, and the hedgerows buzzed with a low humming as bees and insects flew from flower to flower.

Then came days of gales with salt-blown winds from the sea. Zach went about putting heavy granite blocks on the hive roofs to prevent them from being blown off. He also went round feeding a mixture of sugar and water syrup to those that had eaten their stored supply of food and needed more.

When April began, the sun shone through again and the orchards burst out in picturesque white and pink blossom of plum, pear and apple, the snow-white flowers of the blackthorn and the yellow gorse. Thousands of bees winged their way from tree to tree and when eventually the petals fell, Lizzie could see the tiny fruit sets on the branches.

The summer days grew hot and the bees were at their busiest on the white clover and the fiery rose-bay willowherb, the crops of strawberry and raspberry flowers, and the vast host of wild flowers and orchids on the cliffs and moors. When the blackberry blossomed and then later the heather bloomed, the whole valley was serenaded with the humming song of the golden throng of bees.

Eli and Zach added extra super boxes of combs, which the bees rapidly filled with honey until some hives stood shoulder high.

One afternoon a swarm clustered in a dark mass on a branch of the tree near the house. Lizzie shouted for Walt and went

47

round closing the windows in case any of the bees came inside. He and Zach found a box and held it beneath the branch and shook the cluster carefully into it. They placed it in front of an empty hive and tipped the bees onto a white sheet on a sloping board, leading to the narrow entrance at the bottom of the hive. The bees began in great numbers to walk up the slope into their new home.

Zach beckoned to Lizzie to come over, "It's alright – they're too busy goin' into their new quarters to bother about us. I'm lookin' for the Queen, you can spot her against the white cloth."

Lizzie looked down, searching the swarm of insects. "There she is," he pointed, "she's important as she lays the eggs, the swarm'll die without 'er." Lizzie could see that the Queen bee was double the size of the worker bee, a royal Queen.

The strawberries and raspberries fruited in abundance with large sweet fruit. The pickers came and the fields were filled with the voices of those sorting and packing.

Then in August, Zach and Eli began taking the honey off, first smoking the bees to calm them, then lifting off the boxes of honeycomb, which the bees had filled and capped with wax to stop the honey from running out.

They left enough combs of honey behind as food to feed the bees over winter, for the bees were so industrious that most of the honey was surplus to their needs. The boxes were taken to Eli's white-washed dairy, which was full of containers, extractors, ripeners, jars and pieces of muslin hanging from racks.

Zach took out the frames of honeycomb, uncapping the cells containing the honey, by slicing through the caps with a sharp knife. Eli collected the pieces of wax in a container to be melted down for candles and wax bars.

Zach placed the combs in the honey extractor, the handle of

which Eli rotated at great speed, the combs spinning round with such force as to spin the honey out of the cells into the bottom of the extractor. It ran out through the lower tap and through a strainer into the ripener container. They left it for a few days for the air bubbles to rise, then Mary Anne and Lizzie helped to fill the jars with the honey from a tap at the base.

When the combs were taken off later from the ling heather, the honey was darker, thicker and had a tangy flavour which stung pleasurably on the tongue.

The whole farmhouse was filled with the sweet aroma of honey. As Zach filled the jars, Mary Anne and Lizzie stuck on the labels and packed them into boxes ready to deliver to the local shops, and for when callers came knocking on the door to buy.

Zach emptied the wax cappings into the solar wax extractor, a box with a glass top, and set it at an angle in the sunlight. The heat of the sun melted the wax, which ran down into a rectangular mould, and set into a solid wax bar. He showed Lizzie how to melt the wax again and pour it into candle moulds of all shapes and sizes. Eli also mixed some of the wax with turpentine to make a beeswax polish.

One evening Zach rinsed two five gallon glass carboys, and filled them with a mixture of honey and water with added yeast. He set them aside by the sunny window to ferment into mead, and Eli found a bottle from the previous year for Lizzie to taste, filling the glasses with a light sauterne-like liquid, which was smooth and refreshing.

Then came the day when Lizzie and Walt were leaning over the gate, gazing down on the valley. The month had been warm and the sun had ripened the fruit to fullness. The trees were heavy and the branches laden and hung low with apples, rosy-bloomed and golden, round blue plums and yellow pears, the conference pears still richly green.

"There y'are – bees…!" grunted Walt knowingly.

They watched the pickers coming with ladders and bags over their shoulders, calling and laughing as they moved through the trees, gathering in the abundant fruit harvest.

9

'If you see her with a rose in her mouth, do not look or listen – or you'll hear her call up the storms, and you'll hear the ghosts of the drowned crying out – and you'll perish!'

Penberthy was superstitious. A hard man, a man of the sea, of the wind and the weather. He drove his crew with rarely a let up in their work. Getting up all hours of the morning and out to sea in mostly all weathers, rain and hail, sun and mist. The only time they lay up was when the sea became ugly and the breakers rolled in with a great swell, enough to turn a craft over on its side.

But like all men and women who live and work with nature, Penberthy was superstitious, and took great heed of the old sayings.

"Nature goes its own way an' can't be trashed by wishful thinkin' of man's ways," he would say.

He lived alone in a small granite cottage in the cove, left to him by his father. Since his mother died he fended for himself, having neither brother nor sister. He rose in the early hours, took his boat out to sea, and when he came home later, cooked for himself a plain simple meal. This was mainly of fish that he or one of the other fishermen had caught, with a loaf of bread and a mug of strong tea.

He collected fuel of wreckwood from the beach and furze-stogs for his fire, settling down to a toddy of rum spirit, and fell asleep under the harsh glare of the lamp.

His dark canvas trousers, smock and thick jumper, were worn until they frayed badly enough to be thrown away and replaced by exactly the same.

His hands were scarred and ingrained with tar from repairing the boat and crab pots, line and nets.

He would go into Newlyn to land his catch, collect the money and pay it into the bank, keeping back enough for repairs to the boat, his crew's wages and to buy bait, provisions and pipe tobacco for himself. Most items he bought at the local village store in the cove.

He had two crew that spring, Nicky, an old hand, scrawny, with an everlasting drip at the end of his nose. He lodged with his equally scrawny sister in one of the cove cottages along the lane.

There was also Tom, a young lively lad who hadn't long started with the skipper and was saving up to get a boat of his own.

They made an uneven crew, but jogged along with each other as well as they could. There weren't that many jobs about, and it was difficult to earn a good wage.

Penberthy walked down to Zach's cottage and pounded on the door one evening.

When Zach called out for the caller to step in, he was surprised to see him, for Penberthy wasn't often in a social mood.

"Nicky's broke his hand," stated the skipper, "he caught it in the winch. Can you crew for me for a few days?"

Since Zach had passed the Clarissa Rose over to Seth, he was often asked now and again to fill in on one of the local boats if they were a man short. He gave Penberthy a look, for he wasn't known as a patient man on board a boat.

"I'm stuck for a hand," the skipper growled, "I got pots out all baited, an' I'll 'ave to lay up if I can't find anyone else."

Zach hesitated.

"An' young Tom'll 'ave to lay up too with no wages."

"Ah – tha's grim," said Zach, "I'll see you in the morning

then. Only for a few days mind."

Penberthy turned to go, but welcomed a drop of whisky and the two began talking about fishing.

The following morning the crew headed out to sea, taking marks from the land, setting their line of crab and lobster pots, Penberthy on the tiller with Zach and Tom throwing the pots over in turn, to fish in the depths of the sea.

Then they hauled in the dan and ropes of other sets, pulling each dripping pot on board and taking out the crabs and lobsters that had been caught. Zach put the lobsters under the wet sacking, apart from the crabs who were pushed into a partition of the boat, winding bands around their claws to prevent them fighting each other. Tom baited the pots and threw them overboard to catch again for the next day.

The cliffs reared above the waves all round the Land's End coast, with the Pen Wlas crags towering to the sky. They threw up dark and shadowy shapes and figures about which there were numerous tales and rumours told.

Zach saw the reef of rocks stretching away from Sennen, known as the Cowloes, Bo Cowloe and Little Bo. When the weather lowered, a strange whistling could be heard around the rocks, which was said to whistle up a thick seafog. When Penberthy ever heard that he immediately halted the fishing and turned the boat for home.

Further out he could see the sharp triangular rock jutting out of the sea, marked by white foam, known as the Shark's Fin. As the tide rose and it couldn't easily be seen, Penberthy gave it a wide berth, keeping well away. For the saying went that the shark was lurking below the surface, ready to pounce on any craft that came near.

But one of the most awesome rocks of peculiar form, rearing above the waves was known as the Irish Lady.

An Irish boat was wrecked there at the foot of Pednmendhu and all on board were swept into the sea. Those watching from the cliff edge saw only one figure left alive, that of a lady clinging to the rocks, crying out before she was swept away.

The rising shape of the rock resembles the likeness of the lady, in a long black cloak and hood, about to walk into the sea, supposedly calling out for her lover. The ghosts of the drowned of these shores haunt the coast, and the superstition is that a drowned person's voice is heard evermore afterwards, calling his own name on the breeze.

The ghost of the Irish Lady with a rose in her mouth is often seen, and those who dare to walk on the cliffs at night would not care to look or stay to listen. For the legend goes that she'll call up the storms, and those who hear the voices of the drowned crying out will perish.

Penberthy was very aware of the old tales, and kept a wide area of sea between himself and certain locations.

That morning the boat was rounding the cliff headland of Pednmendhu, setting and hauling the crab pots.

" 'Ere, Tom lad – don't just stand there," a shout from the skipper, "give a 'and with this rope."

They pulled hard, but it had snagged way down beneath the waves, on the rocks of the seabed. Penberthy revved the engine and took the boat out in a wide sweep, to pull the rope in the opposite direction, but it wouldn't come.

"Darn - pernickety…" there came a stream of cursing. "We'll 'ave to go to the other end an' try to lift'n there," and he sent the boat surging through the swell.

Zach was leaning out, looking for the dan and floats marking the place where the string of pots lay beneath the water. The sea was becoming restless with small white flecks capping the waves, the sky gloomy with the hazy hint of fog creeping in.

"There!" he pointed to the small speck showing in the distance on the top of the wave, and they raced towards it.

Penberthy coasted up to the dan, shutting the engine down, and Tom leant over, grabbing it, and he and Zach pulled on the wet rope as hard as they could.

" 'Ere she is," Penberthy counted the pots as they came up, When they came to the fifth, the rope snagged again.

He opened up the engine and thrust the bows to port, then starboard, then suddenly the rope freed itself and up came the rest of the set.

They had come around the other side of the headland meanwhile, and there rose the dark, craggy shaped rock of the Irish Lady. Her black hood set above the long, black voluminous cloak ballooning around her.

Tom looked up warily at the towering figure, almost life-like, rising from the waves in the shifting mists.

Penberthy turned round and saw him, "Don't look! – tend to yer gear, lad," he shouted, "don't look – or we'll all perish!"

"Na – tha's old wives tale," Tom scoffed, "you b'lieve that?" he said to Zach.

"Aw, well…" Zach looked sheepish, "they d'say if anyone sees her standing there with a rose in 'er mouth, she'll call up the storms and they'll drown. An' their voice'll be heard evermore callin' their name in the wind." He kept his head down as he coiled the rope.

"You're as bad as the skipper," laughed Tom, " 'tes nothing but an old rock." But Zach saw that he kept his head turned away as he baited the pots.

"There was an Irish boat wrecked 'ere, an' a lady was the only one left seen alive, clinging to the rocks before she was swept away," Zach muttered, "an' now she watches for ever, lookin' for 'er lover."

"G'arn," snorted Tom.

"Well, nobody walks the cliffs there at night, tha's fer sure."

"Dear life…" roared Penberthy, "let's get these pots baited an' get home."

Tom ducked away from him, and he and Zach baited the rest of the pots and threw them overboard again to fish for the next day, paying out the rope as the boat moved forward leaving a trail of frothy wake.

The fog came sweeping over them in thicker swirls, and Penberthy opened the throttle wide to its fullest speed.

"If we hadn't wasted time on unhitching that last set of pots, we'd be well on the way back by now," he growled.

Suddenly, a rogue wave reared up before them and rolled the craft almost onto her side. The sea was everywhere, washing everything away in the surge, buckets, gloves, floats, oars –

Penberthy shouted to the others. They were hanging on to the gunwales as she righted herself, with the engine spluttering, but still roaring away.

Then it was that Penberthy looked over his shoulder, and there looming over them was the towering, black hooded figure of the Lady.

His heart leapt, and he swung away from the sight, but not before he saw the seaweed curled like rose petals, draped across her face.

He cried out – and another wave reared up, its foam cap breaking upon them, with the wind shrieking wildly around their ears.

The bows shuddered upon the jagged teeth of the reef, cracking asunder, and the men were swept under the frenzied surf and taken away on the racing swell.

Zach was tossed and tumbled, sliding downwards towards the darkness of the deep. Then a rippling whorl flung him up onto the rocky ledges at the foot of the cliff.

He clung desperately, his fingers trying to grip the slippery granite as the wash dragged and sucked at his body. Each time the waves receded he pulled himself up a little higher, until he was out of their reach. He lay there exhausted and choking from the salt water.

When he looked back, he could see nothing of the boat, of Tom, or the skipper.

The fog swirled around him on the stormy wind. Then as it fitfully lifted he saw above him the haunting rock shape of the Irish Lady, and standing beside her was the shadowy figure of Penberthy, who raised his arm to him, calling "Penberth – y … Penberth – y …"

Zach cried out, covering his head with his arms to stop himself from looking, or hearing that ghostly voice, crouching as low as he could with dread filling his very being.

He shivered and shook all night, crawling higher up the cliff as the tide roared in and drenched him in fountains of icy spray.

When the morning dawned, there they found him, still clinging to the rocks, as stiff and salt-bleached as a drowned corpse.

Seth and the cove men had come out searching for Penberthy's boat when it was known that he hadn't returned.

Seth jumped onto the flat granite rocks at the foot of the cliff, and they hauled Zach off with ropes.

On the way back they took it in turns to rub and slap some warmth into his cold limbs, and he gradually came back to life.

They found pieces of the boat, an oar, some rope – but there was no sign of Tom or Penberthy.

Months later, he and Seth ventured one early evening, up the steep zig-zag path over the boulders and yellow gorse, to the top of Pednmendhu.

There, they looked down upon the dark rock figure of the Irish Lady. Her long, black cloak spread advancing into the sea, she gazed outwards over the waves.

"After all," he told Seth, "she is just a shape, a formation of granite rock, part of the cliff."

Then, as they turned to go, the setting sun's shadow moved across her hooded face, throwing golden rose petal rays against her cheek – and faintly on the breeze came – "Penberth – y … – give me a 'and with this rope … Penberth – y …"

And they ran for dear life, stumbling and tripping over the stones and boulders and down the cliff, until they reached the safety of the cove.

10

Clarissa Rose opened the letter that had come that morning and read through it again.

"The poor little souls," she said, "all alone in that foreign land."

News had come of their cousin who had passed away, leaving his two daughters with no-one to turn to.

"You 'ave to write to them," she added.

"Me?" Zach gulped a mouthful of tea, startled.

"You'm head of this family," stated his wife.

"Aw Clarrie – you c'n do it," he said.

"I'll tell you what to write, but you 'ave to do it." Clarissa opened a drawer and took out paper and pen.

"You'm to say they're more than welcome to come 'ere with us, or with Seth and Hannah Jane. An' they've still got their grandfer's cottage 'ere, an' we'll get it all dusted an' aired ready for them," Clarissa pushed the paper in front of him.

" 'Old on – wait a minute can't you?" Zach began to laboriously write, carefully forming his letters.

"O' course they're welcome," he grunted, "but all this 'ere writing …" he paused.

"Keep writing!" insisted Clarissa.

"Look to the far horizon when you are low," said the old man, "when life is a grind, climb to the highest rise and look to the far horizon where earth meets the sky. There you'll see between land and heaven a slim ray of light, a ray of hope."

He took Karen's hand in his, "Look hard and long and it's there, the thin streak of light shining between earth, sea and sky. So press on towards the ray, press on to that glimmer of hope on the far horizon."

Tears gathered in her eyes as he said goodbye and wished her well. She picked up her bag, took her younger sister's arm and they walked out into the warm Californian morning to the train.

On the step they turned and waved to him, then entered the door to a new world.

The old man had meant well but her horizon looked very far indeed, thought Karen taking her seat, while Ellen sniffed into her handkerchief.

Their father had passed quietly away with a bad case of influenza, their mother long gone with Ellen's birth, and the elderly man, their solicitor, had informed them of their dwindling finances. The house was rented and being sold over their heads, but one good item was the old Cornish homestead that their grandparents had left to come out to the new land of America and this was still theirs.

Their father's cousins Zach and Clarissa Rose had written to welcome them, so they had unwillingly parted from all their friends and were setting out to a new life.

The journey was long and tedious. When they arrived in England they had to change trains several times on the way to Penzance. The last one was slow and the carriage became colder and colder. Karen pulled pullovers and socks from their bags, and they wrapped themselves up in miscellaneous items of clothing. Coming from the warm Californian sun, neither had brought scarves or gloves.

They reached Penzance in the early hours of morning, both frozen to the bone. It was sleeting and an icy wind whipped around their legs as they stepped out onto the platform.

They looked for their cousins but no-one was about. Karen peered round the corner and met the full blast of the wind, taking her breath away.

There was a lone vehicle waiting for the last train, with a figure sitting hunched up inside. She waved her arm desperately, but to no avail, so she ran out into the driving sleet and drummed loudly on the window.

"Can you take us to Porthgwyna, Cairn Cottage, where Captain Tremain used to live?" she shouted.

"Tha's a long way out o' town," he grumbled, but slowly climbed out and opened the boot for their luggage, as they struggled with the rear door in the wind and thankfully entered the warmth of the car.

The engine was not new and the gears grated, but at least they were on their way.

The town lights disappeared and they soon seemed to be climbing into darkness, where rock and stunted trees swung close.

"Cap'n Tremain – ah, I remember 'im. 'E 'ad a sail ship, brought cargo an' such to Penzance, I b'lieve," their driver said, his gnarled hands gripping the wheel.

"You know his house then?" asked Ellen.

" 'Aven't bin there fer some while, but I d'knaw the likely direction of it." He suddenly pulled the car into a sharp turn and the road climbed steeply. " 'Ere's the turnin'," he grunted.

Karen clutched the back of the front seat as the back wheels spun and slid to a stop.

"Now what!" He pushed at the door and went out to look.

"We're in the mud! You'll 'ave to get out an' help."

"Oh, no!" both girls cried out despairingly. But they bent their heads into the rain and pushed as hard as they could.

"Now…" he shouted and the car buried its nose into the gorse bank.

"Stop!" he shouted again and got out to look at the bonnet. "No 'arm done. Get back in."

They scrambled in, their hands numb with cold.

He rolled the car back and then surged forward onto the harder surface. The lane became steeper and narrower, until at last they swung around a craggy outcrop of boulders and came to a low dark building set back against the gorse bank.

" 'Ere y'are – Cap'n Tremain's cottage," he got out and lifted their luggage from the boot, looking closely at the fare Karen gave him. Then he struggled back into his seat with a "Gettin' too old fer this, y' knaw," and disappeared into the black night.

The wind and sleet stung their faces, and Ellen could hear the sea pounding below them somewhere. It was pitch dark. There were no lights showing from the windows, as they picked up their bags and stumbled along the uneven path to the door that showed pale against the granite walls.

Karen knocked loudly on the wood then tried the latch. It opened and they were blown into a narrow passageway. They hurriedly slammed the door, thankful to be out of the gale.

There was no-one there. It was very cold and chill and they couldn't find any means of lighting. They hadn't anything with them, but Ellen had picked up a used box of matches left on the train. She pulled it out of her pocket and struck one.

They were standing in a room with just one chair, a ladder and brushes and containers of paint. The match died away but she had seen a candlestick on the shelf.

She lit another match, and shading it with her hand walked over to light the candle, which threw dark shadows around the room. The granite stone of the walls had been re-pointed and left bare and a single rug lay on the wooden floor.

They took the candle into the next room which seemed to be the kitchen, with cold stone flags, an ancient stove, a large iron bath and dark wooden cupboards. Another room had some old furniture with an oil lamp. Karen shook it and found it still had some oil, so lifting the shade she put a match to the wick. A flame shot up with a column of smeeching smoke.

"Turn it down," shrieked Ellen, coughing.

When they had it at an even glow they found it made quite a good light, and took it with them as they climbed a draughty staircase, which led to two small bedrooms with iron bedsteads without mattresses.

"We should've gone to a hotel at home, at least it would've been warm," groaned Ellen.

"But this is ours. It won't cost us anything – I'll get a job and we'll manage," said Karen.

They went down to the kitchen and wrenched open the stiff back door. Here they found an outside toilet in a small shed, and in the yard was a heap of discarded wood from the renovation of the first room.

"We'll see if we can get that stove going," suggested Karen shivering, "maybe we can get some heat from it."

They tipped out the cold ashes in the stove, opened the grill and pushed in the scraps of paper and wood that lay around and set a match to it.

The strong wind sucked up the flames, burning out any nests that might have lodged in the chimney, and the stove began to give out some warmth.

Thankfully they spread out clothes from their luggage, and with the rug from the next room, made warm bedding and gradually thawed out their frozen hands and feet. They turned out the lamp to save fuel and during the night threw on more wood to keep the fire going.

They were woken from their sleep at daybreak, by a loud knocking on the door and voices coming along the passageway. Two women accompanied by a tall man stood looking at them in amazement.

Karen leapt to her feet, "I'm sorry! We were told by the driver who brought us here that this was Captain Tremain's cottage. We're his granddaughters."

"Dear life!" exclaimed Clarissa Rose, "You were meant to come home with us. We thought you were comin' tomorrow!"

She and Hannah Jane went forward and embraced them, "We saw the smoke comin' from the chimney."

Zach patted their hands, saying, "That's old Josiah! Silly old codger – this was where Cap'n Tremain used to live at one time, but 'e built another cottage with ours, further up the lane."

"Seth is in the middle of doin' this up," said Hannah, "it hasn't any furniture or anythin' in it yet."

"We found that out!" laughed Karen.

"Come 'ome now to a good breakfast," said Zach, gathering up their luggage, and they went out onto a grassy plateau and found a bright sunlit morning, with the cliff falling away down to a blue sea.

Karen looked at the beautiful vista of the bay with the wild flowers on the granite cliffs, and there between the sea and sky, she saw a silver-green ray of light, the glimmer of hope shining on the far horizon.

11

It was born of the wind of the summer heat. Of the sun's white glare in the wide blue heaven that seared the green fields to desert brown, scorching the cliffs, the heather, gorse and bracken. Sheep and cattle were thirsted and wilted, as they lay prone beneath the rock cairns throwing meagre shade, and leaf and wild flower shrivelled and withered on the banks of the dry stream beds on the moorland.

It was born of the hot wave of the summer sea. Of the sleeping pulse of the languid tide, where the fishing boats drifted on the lazy swell, and the raucous seagulls swooped and soared above the mast.

There it stirred the Atlantic in a deepening low, with the air pressure tightening - then swiftly dropping - and a troubled wind gathered in keen searching gusts - a wild wind, with cold fingers of icy splay increasing during the night – and when dawn broke the ocean waters rose and heaved, great hills of green grey rollers, rearing and falling in giant mountains and troughs, racing swiftly towards the shores.

Then the storm force hit with a thunderous roar, the brute strength of whirlwind soaring and whooping with the rain in torrents, flailing gutter and roof and lashing the windows in a frenzied spite.

Black clouds clashed in long tremulous rolls, and white lightning forked and ripped the sky apart. Fire swept the earth with loud thunderbolts and the cyclonic wind howled in screaming cry.

The grey light faltered in the leaden-washed sky with the trees bending and swaying, their tops touching their trembling bark. Great trunks rocking, uprooting, and crashing down to the earth, with branches hurtling by in the dark morning.

Zach peered out through the bedroom curtains and saw the sycamore thrashing against his greenhouse, shattering the glass into sharp swirling fragments.

He shook Clarissa Rose, shouting into her ear above the noise of the wind. She was already awake, having flung the bedclothes over her head to shut out the roar of the driving rain.

They hurried down the stairs and into their clothes and waterproofs. Clarissa struggled with the door as the wind tore it almost from her hold, and Zach pushed through carrying his saw.

He threw a rope over the limb of the tree and Clarrie clung fearfully to it, pulling it away from the greenhouse, as he climbed up the swaying trunk and sawed at the branch.

"Stand away!" he cried, shouting above the gale.

With a crack it fell to the ground, strafed them both with glass, twigs, leaves and garden litter, and was then blown away across the cliffs.

In a noisy clatter, the roof slates went flying, spinning and whirling like a flock of black crows.

Zach fought his way against the wind, holding onto the ledges of the granite walls, to Seth's cottage.

There, in a swooping eddy the summerhouse rose, plucked two feet high on the spiralling air. Its store of demijohns of summer wine were sucked out across the lane and rolled down the path towards the henhouse.

"My wine – my wine!" shrieked Hannah Jane into the screaming wind, and they bent double into the gale, running after the jars and carrying them into the cottage.

Seth rolled a large boulder against the hatch of the henhouse, for fear the birds would be blown over the cliff and out to sea.

Then he flung heavy hawsers up and over the summerhouse roof, and anchored it down with boulders and granite stones to the walls and fences. Clarissa and Zach clawed and clung to ropes and chains, as the wind's shrieking howl snatched away their calls.

Matt and Tamsin ran excitedly from the gate and the door, to hanging on to the ropes, while Jessica watched round-eyed from the window, until Hannah shrieked at them, "Get inside you crazy loonies!"

The two men then struggled up the lane to Eli's farmhouse, where he still had a small flock of sheep. They found him with Mary Anne staggering across the home field to the big barn. So together they fought the fierceness of the hurricane that blew them against the hedges, and almost over the top of the wall, so that Eli just saved himself by seizing a branch of the elder tree that sheltered the corner. They then stumbled from bush to bush, holding on to them to help themselves along, until they came to the gate.

Some of their flock of Dorset ewes were huddled by the wall near the entrance, their ears flattened back by the blast of the down-draught that whistled through the barn. They stared at the men uneasily, showing the whites of their eyes as they stamped their feet nervously. The young lambs, now fast growing, were inside, sitting close up to their mothers, burying themselves in the thick wool.

Eli and Seth closed up all the shutters and stable-doors, to prevent the lambs from being blown over the hedges. So they were left in a dim gloom, with the noisy slam of the skylight rattling against its frame.

The salt-laden wind shredded and tattered every shrub and flower in Mary Anne's garden, and tore away gate and rail, and toppled the long garden seat end over end, to plunge into the pond in a trail of splintered matchwood.

The tall great pine lurched and heeled and the cement-washed rooftiles of the farmhouse curled up on the wind, ripping away from the seams.

Down in the village harsh daylight funnelled through the schoolhouse rafters, and the stark pale beams of the baker's roof shuddered in a maelstrom of spinning slate.

The inn was a patchwork of bleak gaping holes, and Fore Street was closed down against the swirling spate of debris whirling along the pavements. In the courtyard, the tables and benches flew across the hedge and field.

Any vehicles that ventured out were rocked on the moorland road, as they caught the up-lift of wind-whipped whorls.

Cottages, houses, farms, mills and barns, all were riffled and blasted by the wind-scourged rain.

The villagers lit their oil lamps in the darkness of the day, and candles flickered in the windows of the village to give light. Meals were cooked early on the old oven ranges and log fires blazed up the chimneys.

All during the long night the seas sent up a continuous roar, as the raging waters rose higher on successive tides. A mountainous mass of wild tumbling surf, tore long kelp and wrack from the deep to fling onto the paths and high up onto the grassy turf of the cliffs.

On the next flood, the creaming surge of the waves hurled the salt spray higher and higher, sucking out the sea-walls of harbour and quay. White flurries of spume were flung in fountains to the sky, soaring over roof and spire in neighbouring villages around.

Each breaker that broke and buried the slipway, tore out huge craters in the surface. The small boats were scattered aside and holed and were awash with debris, even though they had been pulled up to higher ground.

Boathouse doors and walls were wrenched out, washing away the contents of boots and waterproofs, smocks and coats. Waves roared through the cove in a seething race, sweeping away crab pots, lines, ropes and oars.

Seth and Zach ran down to the cove and joined the group of fishermen standing in the lee of the thick granite wall. They watched the boiling waters sucking and tearing at the very cliffs and crags of the bay. They watched as their items and equipment were whirled by on the riptide.

Every now and then as a momentary lull came in the waves, they would rush down to the waterline to rescue what was left on the slipway. Then, as a cry went up from one of the watchers, they'd run for dear life for the safety of the wall, before a thunderous sea rose above them, threatening to sweep them away into the deep.

All shipping headed for shelter in harbours and creeks. The crews of the trawlers groaned and cursed as their nets out at sea were spoiled and tangled along the stormy shores.

Then as the next day dawned, the whirlwind slowly abated its savage breath, and there washed up on the wind-driven sands of the bay, lay a whale – alone – a huge magnificent cetacean.

A grey Emperor of the deep – of the oceanic sway.

12

The shutter swung against the granite wall, banging and slamming in the wind and echoing through the swirling mist. While up from the wet bog and moorland loomed the dark silhouette of Bog Inn, wild and desolate, the grey fog writhing around its chimneys.

From chinks in the rotten shutters of the lower windows, shafts of light glimmered out into the black night. The hail beat heavily upon the rain-soaked figures making their way between the tussocks of reed across the treacherous bogland.

Zach was the first to reach the door and hammered urgently on it with his fist. Immediately the light from the windows vanished.

He beat on the door again shouting, "Trewin!" into the wind. The bolts were slowly pulled back, and the boy at the door was thrust aside as they pushed their way into the room.

"Took yer time!" grunted Zach, flinging off his wet waterproofs.

"Boy – light," came a harsh voice from inside. "Who's that with you?"

"Seth - Truscott - Casley - Treloar - an' a wild night 'tis too."

The room lightened again with candle-flame, and the men drew near to the fire that threw out warmth from a knotted log.

"Boy! Brandy . . ." growled Casley.

"Set to, boy - an' fer the devil's sake go an' fix that shutter!" the hoarse voice shouted above those of the other men in the room.

The only female sat in the corner, her grey head nodding as she rocked to and fro, her beady eyes going from one to the other as she tried to lip-read their talk. Now and again they called out to her "Ain't that so, Granny?" and she would cackle and show her toothless gums.

Truscott brought a stoppered jar from beneath his jacket and opening it, swung the neck up to his mouth and drank greedily. Then he slammed it down hard on the table, "Brought m'own, Black Jack," he said.

"Gut-rot," grated the voice, "Parson'll soon smell it on 'ee."

Black Jack stood up from the bench where he'd been sitting, his head having to bend sideways beneath the blackened beams. He rose six and a half feet in his stockings, his muscular arms swinging below his knees and his legs as thick as tree trunks in his great thigh-boots. He lifted his tankard and emptied its contents, banging the vessel down on the table and roaring for the boy.

The timid youth came scuttling from the kitchen with a stone jug. As he grasped hold of the tankard to fill it, a large hand descended upon the neck of his jerkin. Black Jack swung him high into the air, bellowing with loud gusts of laughter at the thin legs dangling frenziedly, then with a swoop hung him by his collar upon the hook in the beam of the ceiling.

The men shouted with delight at the boy jerking upon the nail like a joint of ham, clapping each other's shoulders and quaffing great gulps of their liquor.

"Jack – put 'im down!" screeched Granny, waving her stick and clawed hands in the air.

"Put 'im down – poor devil!" called Zach, who didn't go along with Black Jack's rough ways.

Black Jack reached up and unhooked the hapless lad. He landed on all fours like a stray cat and ran in fright back to the kitchen.

The boy hid beneath the table, but not for long before he was shouted for, to scurry to and fro with liquor, keeping as far as he could out of the reach of Black Jack and the sly cuffs of the men.

"I 'ear the revenue men are out an' about," said Seth.

"Where?" Treloar swung round to face him.

"Pendeen."

"Tcha!" Black Jack spat onto the stone flags.

Others beat on the door of the kiddly-wink to pass the night in drunken brawl, supping Black Jack's liquor.

His lone windswept dwelling, far from the seeing eyes of the parson and village elders, huddled in the middle of the boggy moorland of Bostraze, where the wild Bartinney Forest once stretched for miles down to the rocky shores of the Celtic sea.

There were still copses of the forest where sturdy oaks had been felled for the church of St. Just, the small mining village on the seaward side of the marsh.

On the other side rose the hill of Bartinney, the hill of the rings of fire, where the circular rampart of earth and stone of the ancient hill fort stood starkly against the sky. Here the Celtic warriors had fired their beacons at the first sign of vessels approaching the shore.

Northwards reared the bleak hoary cairn of Kenidzhek, the hooting cairn. Its black crags harsh against the moonlight, it uttered haunting whistles in the wild winds.

Bog Inn was desolate indeed, where many in their cups who took a wrong turn on the treacherous track disappeared without trace beneath the mire.

When most of the men had departed and the heavy snores of Black Jack eventually began, along with those who were too far gone to leave, the lad would creep wearily out from beneath the table and climb the ladder in the corner, to a broad shelf that ran high along the wall. This served as his bed, where he could stretch his aching limbs beneath an old blanket. It was warmer here, where the granite fireplace glowed all night with furzy-stogs than in the chill scullery.

Black Jack had exchanged him for a flagon of dark spirit, from an acquaintance at Madron workhouse. All Black Jack's boys came from there but they didn't last long.

"What's yer name?" Granny Jack had asked.

"Boy!" growled Black Jack, and giving him a cuff sent him to pull water from the well. "Tha's what they're all called."

But Clem had seen his mother die of fever at the workhouse, and his father had been buried in a fall of earth at the tin mine, the year before.

The following night when many of his customers had left, Black Jack gave a shout, "Boy! Take a look-see."

Clem hurried to the window and peered through the cracked shutters. The moor appeared pitch black, but then he caught sight of a faint light winking across the marsh.

"They're coming," he called.

"Set to, boy – set to," Black Jack pulled himself up from the bench and lurched towards a small door set in the recess of the wall. This led to a cellar tucked behind the outhouses where he kept his two pigs and some poultry. Clem ran into the scullery and lifted the latch, turning his head against the rain and rounded the corner of the house.

The flicker of light showed twice, thrice, in the darkness, and upon the wind came the rattle of bridle-bit. He could see the sway-backed shapes as they neared the house and hear the calling voices. Then the line of ponies were passing him, and he ran to the back of the inn to help to unload the merchandise into the cellar.

"Rough night," greeted Black Jack, as he heaved at boxes and barrels.

"A good 'n . . ." said Zach.

The dark-clad figures toiled in the rain, then as suddenly they re-mounted and swiftly disappeared into the wild night again. Black Jack slammed the door and Clem followed him back into the house. Here he scurried to and fro again with tankard and liquor until drunken snores allowed him at last to creep up the ladder to his bed. As his eyes drooped, he stored in his mind the direction the smugglers always took across the marshes. He'd heard that they came up from the rocky Priest's Cove where Cape Cornwall jutted out into the sea, and this was where he would head for if he could ever slip away.

The old granite stones of the inn whispered and groaned with the gusts of the clamorous wind. The very walls seemed to sway with the gale like a grey ship sailing on the reed of the bogland, where the grasses rippled in wild waves.

With the grey light of dawn Black Jack roared the boy awake, while the last lingerers from the night before were sent on their way, sore in head and pocket.

The day's work was always heavy, with moving barrels and getting rid of empty containers. This was simply done by piling them on the cart, and hitching up the moor pony to pull them along a track which led to a spongy area of bog. Clem then heaved the barrels over the side and they slowly sank beneath the soggy swamp.

It was while he was leading the pony back that evening, that Zach came striding up in great haste.

"There's rumour of customs men over Pendeen way," he shouted.

"Ha! Where they'll stay, most likely . . ." grunted Black Jack, "Boy!" - and so that night began with the inn soon filling with thirsty men.

Later, Clem was in the cellar tapping a barrel when he heard shouting. He ran up the steps and saw Seth rushing into the room.

"Officers – heading this way!" he cried.

Black Jack leapt to his feet, his chair toppling backwards. He reached the half-opened door, and there was a sudden explosion and part of the door-frame splintered beside him.

Granny Jack screeched with fright and he jumped sideways, slamming the door shut.

He drew his guns from his belt, as some of the others scrambled up the stairs and began shooting out of the windows.

"We're gettin' out of this!" Seth pulled Zach by the shoulder. "We've no truck with fire-arms!" They ran through the side door and clattered down the steps to the cellar.

There was a volley of firing from outside followed by painful cries and shouts from within. Black Jack roared in anger as he flung the shutters aside and fired at random into the night.

Then a great rush of men burst through the door, firing as they came. As Clem stood open-mouthed, the huge hulk of Black Jack teetered backwards onto him and they both rolled down the steps to the cellar floor.

Black Jack let off another explosion from his gun, and Clem, wriggling from under his legs, ran out into the yard.

He heard the pony whinnying in the stable and he slipped in and caught hold of her tangled mane. She bolted in fright with Clem clinging on to her, and took off over the moor.

Then there came a sudden bellow and a hefty hand seized his jerkin, dragging the pony round, with the voice of Black Jack snarling in his ear.

There was a flash of cordite and as Black Jack staggered, loosening his grip, Clem kicked out at him. The pony leapt free, rushing frenziedly into the darkness.

He clung onto the animal until she eventually slowed. But as he slid off her back, his heart sank in fear when his foot slid into the soft morass of the bog.

As he stood there, the lurching shadow of Black Jack holding a painful shoulder, caught up with him and reached out to grasp the pony. But she reared up nervously and threw him backwards, his feet sinking into the sucking ooze of the marsh.

He gave a terrified roar and reeled from side to side, trying to drag his great thigh-boots from the clinging mire, but at each step they sank deeper.

Then the heavy bulk of Black Jack toppled back into the bog, until the pale oval of his face disappeared into the black morass.

Clem stood petrified, but the pony began to move, seemingly to know by instinct the path she had often taken with Granny Jack. She picked her way over the treacherous heathland until her hooves struck firmer ground.

Two figures appeared from the darkness, of Zach and Seth struggling to catch one of the officer's horses.

" 'Old onto 'im!" cried Seth.

Zach snatched at the bridle, "I'm 'aving a 'ard job," he panted as he clung on.

But they both scrambled up onto its back and followed the ground that Clem's pony was taking.

The sky was lighter here and when they made out the hunch-backed mass of Cairn Kenidzhek rearing up against the sky-line, they knew that they were riding the haunted way over Truthwall moor and Woon Gumpus. They hurried their steeds on the faster, for fear of meeting the arch-fiend who was said to ride over the heath at night and hunt lost souls.

The wind grew stronger the higher they went, and as it whistled around the hoary crags of the cairn, the voices of the ancient ones hooted and cried out to them. Then they were drawing away and galloping down the other side.

Zach looked anxiously back over his shoulder for fear that he should see their shadows following, but what he did see was the glint of armed officers riding after them. He shouted out and they urged their mounts on to a greater pace towards some lights showing in the distance, which they guessed were those of Pendeen village.

They neared a cluster of buildings, swerved through the gateway of a large house and pulled up inside the yard. A young girl carrying a water-jug, stopped in amazement as Clem slid wearily off the pony's back. But before he could greet her the customs men arrived with a great noise, leaping to the ground and running with shouts and firing of weapons towards the house.

The girl gasped, dropping the jug, and seizing Clem's arm, pulled him across the yard. He looked back and saw Zach and Seth leaping off their horse and following them. They ran, hearing screams and cries as the residence was searched and set on fire, the tongues of orange flames shooting high in the dark night.

"Who lives 'ere?" he panted.

"Tha's Trezise," she said, and he remembered Zach saying that the customs men were watching the Pendeen moors.

The girl led them to a hidden opening in the wall, an ancient vau, a cave. They hastened along its passage-way for some length, until she slowed to a halt and sank breathlessly to the ground.

"We'm be safe 'ere," she whispered, "this goes right down to the shore."

Clem lowered himself beside her and found that the floor was strewn with large flat stones, and he'd heard it said that the vaus had been used as storehouses by the Celts.

Seth squatted down leaning against the granite wall, "That was a near one." Zach groaned, "Haw! I'm getting' a bit long-toothed fer this lark."

They sat together throughout the long night, and when the

glimmer of dawn broke in the sky, crept cautiously to the entrance.

A heavy silence hung over the building before them, one side blackened with grey wisps of smoke still rising, and not a soul to be seen.

"You come wi' me," said the girl, and took them towards her mother's cottage.

After many weeks had passed Trezise began to restore his house and Clem was taken on at the farm.

On one occasion, when he had to visit one of the moorland farms overlooking the heath of Bog Inn, he reined in his horse and surveyed that barren landscape. It was said that a giant of a man, now haunted the ways of the bog and the shifting marshes. "Black Jack," he thought with a shiver.

The inn had fallen into a ruin, its roof sagging and its crumbling stone bleak against the lowering sky.

The windows gaped across the moor, with the hollow slamming of a shutter swinging against the wall, echoing eerily through the swirling mists that rose up from the treacherous bogland.

13

The black hull rode the mounting back of the wave in a corkscrew silhouette. She raced the stormy swell, her bows leaping to the dark sky and then plunging deeply into the sloping troughs.

She was drifting ever nearer to the jagged teeth of the reef that ran out from Polpry's rock-strewn shore.

"Wreck!" echoed the shout from the watchers on the high cliffs in the swirling rain.

"Wreck!" echoed the shouts from cove to cove, as the wild seas in a thunderous roar beat the cliffs in cascading spray.

The ship reeled and listed sharply, slipping it's cargo – a cargo of timber, in a floating mass, tossing and turning, striking the boulders, spinning, up-ending, of mahogany, pine and sweet smelling cedar.

Zach ran, knocking on doors and there was a whistling and rousing from bed, and a hurrying and scurrying of a hundred feet of those running and clambering over the cliff paths and rocks down to the shore.

They came with ropes and grapnels, peering through the driving rain for any sign of life.

Not a soul stirred on her decks or clung to rigging, or floated nearby in the sea. She wallowed empty and bereft.

They fired a bright flare in the dark dawn sky, but there came not a sign of movement.

Then through the foaming crests, she rushed the reef and with a shuddering crack, struck and keeled over onto her side.

The tide had begun to recede and the fishermen managed to launch one of the boats in a short interval between the wind-tossed waves.

With four hands on the oars helping the engine, they were

away, thrown up on the surging wave one minute and disappearing into its depths the next.

Many times a sea rose up and broke over them, so that they were soon baling out, before they reached the lurching hull of the wreck.

Zach caught at the tangled rope festooning her side, with Seth and Ben joining him, climbing up and over onto her sloping decks. They clung onto stay and rail, searching and calling into the cabins and holds, the doors and hatches torn away, or wide open and slamming into the wind.

When they struggled back down the ropes to their own boat, they shook their heads, shouting into the roar of the sea of their failure at finding anyone. Only her name, Southern Maid, painted on her reeling side, told them anything.

The tide swept beneath their bow, racing them to the beach through the tumbling surf, and they jumped wearily ashore, pulling the boat high up the slipway.

A message went out from the customs to the lifeboat crew who searched the area for survivors, and meanwhile, men, women and children were combing the shore.

As the tide went out the beach was littered with lengths of timber – twenty-foot builder's lengths, square baulks and short lengths.

The whole coastline was bristling with hundreds of figures, the timber lifted across shoulders and backs, pulled and levered over slippery kelp and carried over boulders and stony tracks, as they dragged it from the sea.

Climbing and stumbling over heath and gorse, by arm, by hip, by shoulder, by thigh, loading tractor and trailer, cart and horse, away went the timber to barn and cottage to hide from the sight of the customs officer.

Up and down all day in the rain and drizzle, to beat the turning tide, with the children stacking great piles, trundling wheelbarrows, shouting and laughing, and the dogs barking. Women and wives came with pasties and heavy cake and flagons of tea and ale.

All night they toiled by flickering lights bobbing and weaving in the pale moonlight. When the rain came down heavily, they sheltered in the mine adits, talking of plans they had for using the timber.

Young courting Simeon, renovating his cottage, found long lengths for rafters, beams and floor, almost new, hardly scabbed by the sea and rocks. Another lad, wood for his goathouse and pigeon loft, the fishermen, for repairs to their old boathouse store.

Farmer Pender found hardwood for his leaking barn roof, for field gates and gate-posts, fencing stakes and new sides for the trailer. Zach carried off cedar for beehives, and Seth found wood to make slats for windbreaks.

Each dropped bundles of wreckwood at the widow Lizzie's gate, adding to her pile as she collected smaller pieces for firewood. Old codgers carried off planks for a new seat in the sun, and the children began building a treehouse in the copse.

Early next morning, Leah Tregurtha was resting against a boulder, from carrying a heavy timber up the cliff path. He looked over to the reef and the half-submerged wreck, as the surf still surged around her hull.

He suddenly saw a movement – at one of the portholes. There! he saw it again!

He leapt to his feet, blinking his tired eyes, thinking that being up all night had played tricks on his vision.

But there! He saw it again – a pale image – a face – a hand! He gave a great roar that echoed all round the cove.

Each one stopped transfixed, staring up at him, at his fist wildly pointing and stabbing the air, running and stumbling over the rough path until he reached the shore.

"I saw – a face it were!" he hoarsely panted.

" 'Old on there, boy," old man Jacob grasped him by the shoulder, bringing him to a halt.

"What?" others crowded round him.

"A face – 'orrible white – at the porthole!" Leah's eyes rolled in fright.

"After all this time – 24 hours?" scoffed Jem.

"Naw . . ." grunted Zach, "you'm seein' things. Anyone'd be drowned by now."

"An' we searched 'ard. There's nobody on that vessel," Seth poked him in the chest.

"I saw 'im – I saw 'im!" insisted Leah.

They looked from one to the other, undecided, then Zach said, "Right, we'll 'ave to go out there ag'in."

They muttered between themselves, but there was no help for it. They had to make certain that there was no-one there, and the Lord help Leah Tregurtha if it was all for nothing.

Leah felt guilt-ridden as he watched them struggle into their waterproofs, not yet dried out and wet and stiff with salt water.

"We're one short, young Ben's gone home to milk the cows," said Seth.

"I'll go," Leah snatched an oilskin from the seat, "I saw 'im, so it's me ought to go out there."

He gulped at the waves still angrily washing the rocks. He worked on the land and didn't have good 'sea legs.'

They pushed the boat out, leapt in and headed for the reef. A clash of thunder split the heavens and the tossing craft soared up the crests and disappeared into the troughs.

"You'm lookin' green," shouted Zach above the roar of the waves.

Leah miserably nodded his head, he certainly felt like it. His eyes peered through the curtain of rain trickling down his face, as he grimly held on.

They saw no-one as they neared the wreck, and it was clear that she was very low in the water and would soon heel over and be gone.

Leah clambered over her side with Zach and Seth, clutching at the flailing ropes and sliding across her slippery angled deck.

They went from end to end, searching through the wrecked hatches and cabins and where Leah thought he'd seen somebody.

"We've looked 'ere before – all over," shouted Seth.

Benches, bunks and bedding were thrown and tangled into sodden chaos. They searched everywhere, throwing aside clothing and splintered fittings.

Then Zach caught hold of a rubber boot rolling in the rising water, the matted blanket pulled away and the bedraggled body of a man sprawled at their feet.

His face was bleached blue-white and his lips salt-encrusted by the sea-water, but the staring red-rimmed eyes suddenly blinked up at them, and his hand trembled out to them before falling away.

"Dear life!" cried Zach jumping back.

They rolled him in one of the blankets, hauled him over the ship's side, and lowered him into the hands of Jem.

As they pulled away from the reef, a breaking sea struck the wreck and she reared up, heeled over, and disappeared from sight.

The Southern Maid was seemingly unknown and nobody knew where she came from, or where she was going.

The rescued seaman couldn't tell them, or say what happened to her crew, for though he recovered in body, his mind remained vacant.

Old Jacob took pity on him, and took him to live with him in his cottage, "He's company – a mate," he would say.

14

The last time that Zach had visited his widowed sister Lucille at Tredinney had been in the late autumn, a quiet time of the year, with few people venturing out onto the moors.

This week however, was in midsummer and was also a festival week in the village in celebration of the church's saint, and the old granite house was full of guests.

He'd promised to stay for a couple of days, to help to repair part of her roof that had lost some slates in the last gale, and followed her up the narrow flight of stairs to the room at the end of the panelled passage.

"You're welcome to 'ave this room," she said, opening the door. "It's the only empty one left – but not a lot of people take to it."

It was attractive, low beamed, with two small windows opening out onto the purple heathered moors, with the granite cliffs and the blue of the sea in the distance.

"If you find you can't sleep in it, you'll 'ave to make do on the sofa in the back room," she added, pulling back the quilt on the bed.

"It's fine," he assured her, and leant out of the window, as she hurried off down the stairs again.

Later that night it was also by that same window that he lingered, looking out across the wild moor as the pale moonlight lit the deep blue of the heavens at the end of the warm summer's day.

He'd spent long hours climbing the ladder with hammer and slates, with Jervis his nephew. Lucille's sloe wine had been rich and heady, so he soon crossed to the bed and lay back against the pillow, sinking swiftly into sleep.

It was some time before his conscious self became aware of the rhythm of sound that had been weaving in and out through the threads of his slumber. An uneven echo becoming louder and louder. The hollow tremor of muffled hoof. Nearer and nearer it grew, coming over the moor and heather, through the sifting shadows and the clement night.

He opened his eyes slowly, and saw the waning sliver of the moon shining through the mullioned window. The thudding sound of a horse ridden hard galloped up to the house and slid over the small stones in the yard, and as he looked he saw his window swing open into the night. Its panes glinted in the gilded moonlight, as the gentle rustle of the breeze brushed the evergreens at the corner of the manor.

A small white hand appeared on the sill and lifted towards the sound of the rider coming nearer. In the pale moonlight a soft shadow leant far out, a lithe figure of a young girl, her arms reaching forward expectantly, her dark hair tumbling around her shoulders and over the windowsill. With a sparkle in the almond eyes and her lips parted in a slow smile, her laughter came whispering on the air.

In one hand she fluttered a lace handkerchief, sending it floating like a white leaf down towards the rider passing beneath.

"Zelma . . ." came a call echoing around the eaves, as the steed pawed the ground.

Zach flung back the covers and went slowly towards the figure at the window, but she took no heed of his presence. He stood beside her and looked out into the night and watched as horse and rider disappeared again into the shadows of the moor, the sound of hooves on the turf gradually fading away.

Then from the long track winding up from the sea there came a creaking of belt and leather and the clink and rattle of bridle bit. Shifting shapes blurred together, straining and lumbering up the stony way. Sturdy, laden ponies plodding one behind the other. There was a whispering rustle of bracken and thorn, and the shuffle of hurrying feet. A flicker of light of will o' wisp lanterns that danced and winked, sliding and slanting across the mullioned panes of the window. Shrouded forms streamed by in a straggling cavalcade, with low murmuring voices calling softly, and sibilant echoes rising and falling.

Brandy for the judge, for the priest, for the squire and for his Lordship of the Manor, full and fiery for the drinking. Lace and ribbons for his daughter with sparkling claret with which to court her. With bolt and barrel, bottle and saddle, all wending their way to their Lordship's cellars.

And the lingering shadow beside Zach watching at the window, singing her love-dream, gazed out across the heath, her song weaving its melody upon his ear, her breath like a cobweb brushing his cheek.

Then suddenly, upon the windswept cliff rose a dark silhouette, a massed group of figures, swarming quickly across the rock-strewn slopes.

There was a startled gasp at his side, breaking the low humming, and a rustle of skirts as the shadow at the window turned. She hurried to the oak wardrobe, taking from it a long cloak, then crossed to the door and Zach heard her light footsteps swiftly going down the stairs.

He followed her as silently as he could, but even when he stumbled against the banister in the dark, she gave no sign that she'd heard him.

She crossed the yard and disappeared into the stables, then re-appeared leading a mare by the rein, and leaping lightly onto its back, she set off at an urgent pace across the moor.

Zach ran to the low wall and climbed up it, trying to see in the shadowy night in which direction she was going. It seemed as if it was the same as that of the lone rider, with the intent to warn the long caravan of laden ponies.

Then he saw her riding beneath the pale light of the moon, with her dark cloak flying behind her, thundering swiftly over the springy peated heather.

There also, to his right, he heard another sound of thudding hooves, those of the group of figures that now were sweeping past him. Grey coated, a dozen in all, their boot and buckle creaking noisily as they gave earnest chase to the fleeing shadow.

Zach called out to her in alarm, but no sound came forth from his lips. He stood on the crumbling top of the dry-stone wall and cried his warning out to her again and again, but it was to no avail, his voice being sucked away into the stirring breeze and his limbs flailing weakly as he jumped down and rolled into the bracken.

He tried to run, stumbling over boulder and ditch, stabbed by the sharp needles of gorse, and his breath panting in panic as he struggled across the moor. The ground rose steeply as it neared the cliffs, and he climbed up to the craggy cairn at the edge of the dizzy height that swooped in a sheer drop to the shore.

Here he could look down upon the racing figure and those gaining upon her.

There came a flash of light, a crack, that broke the stillness of the night, and her steed stumbled and slowed but she urged it onwards. Along the side of the sloping bank she sped, weaving in and out of the treacherous blackthorn, dipping down into the cutting to be hidden from sight for a moment, then flying out again from the copse of swaying withies.

She followed the winding watercourse of the tumbling stream, the white fluorescent flecks of the water shining in the dark from her mare's hooves, until she came to a deep pool swirling between high boulders. Then she leapt up the bank and galloped along the narrow track going down to the sea.

There came the flash and report again and she slewed sideways upon the mare's neck, clutching frantically at the tangled mane. The acrid taint of cordite, bitter and strong, wafted by Zach on the breeze, stinging his nostrils.

But although she had felt the bullet's impact, she spurred her mount forward with greater urgency.

The long string of burdened ponies could now be seen plodding ahead, and with sharp ejaculations of voice and the slap and rattle of straining rein, the pursuing riders whirled and turned their mounts towards them. They spread out across the black heath with the intent to bar any way for escape, with the thudding of hooves, rasping breath and specks of foam whipping from the horses.

To the right they swerved to sweep up upon the labouring beasts, but at the sound of the fire-arm, a dire warning in the night, the train of ponies and men had quickly scattered and was no longer visible. Horse and rider galloped at random over cliff and coomb in a frenzied chase at any shape or shadow that seemed to move.

To the left went those scurrying through the thorn and wallowing in the boggy marsh, but all sign of their quarry had disappeared, melting into the darkness, each according to his own way, until not a trace of man or beast was seen upon the rugged heath.

Save one, who turned and rode to meet her, flying like an arrow over the heather. He leant forward to grasp the mare's rein, and racing onwards side by side with her, they sped towards the shore.

Then the moon shone fitfully upon her swaying form as her hood fell back and her dark hair tumbled around her pale brow, which was damp with the beads of moisture. The cloak slipped from one shoulder, and from the height of the cairn, Zach could see glistening upon her white muslin clad breast, a dark stain.

The rider caught her up upon his own steed as her blood spread and flowed, dripping in a scarlet stream upon his hand. He slowed to an easier pace as they came to an area of flat rocks and ford in the swift flowing brook. The sound of their followers gradually faded into the night as they searched further and further afield across the moors. He brought his mount to a stop and slid awkwardly off its back, carefully holding his wounded companion, and carried her down to the water's edge. Here he laid her gently against the bank of thyme and bowed his head in anguish, and she slowly lifted her hand and lay it against his cheek, smiling faintly.

Then he rose and took out the lace handkerchief that she'd thrown to him from the window, and went to the stream and dipped it in the running water.

He came back to her and held it to her lips and stroked the cool linen over her brow, then pressed it against her breast to try to halt the scarlet flow of her blood, as it spilled in bright specks upon the smooth rock.

Her hand trembled and fell weakly as its weight became too much, and she lay her head wearily against his shoulder. Her voice ebbed faintly to a whisper, until only her shallow breath stirred the chill air.

Then in the distance, there came the muted thudding of hooves, gradually drawing nearer, and the low mutter of voices. The horsemen had turned back and were now hastening their search towards the stream.

He caught her up in his arms and placed her carefully on his horse, then leapt up into the saddle and hurriedly clambered up the bank. He kicked his heels, urging his horse the faster, as their pursuers came nearer. He flew across the moorland with his companion held tightly against him, his steed striking the loose stones as he dipped again into the valley leading down to the shore.

The rearing cliffs hid him from sight as he sped like a phantom through the soft dunes with their tall waving marram grasses. Then out onto the wide yellow sands he flew, the wet grains scattering from the threshing hooves as they skimmed across the newly washed beach.

The slight figure against his shoulder murmured his name into the night, and as he looked down he saw her eyes smiling into his. He neared the long curve of the moonlit bay and the following horsemen ploughed into the soft hillocks of the dunes, then thundered forward onto the hard compact sands. They saw the pair silhouetted against the dark sea in the moonlight and with hoarse cries, set their mounts in a frenzy after them.

The granite cliffs soared upwards to the night sky, throwing their craggy shadows upon the beach, and the swell of the waves swooped upon the riders, breaking into scattered showers of spray.

Again she murmured his name, and as he looked into the wide dark eyes, they closed, and she drew her last trembling breath before his stricken sight.

With a piercing cry he pulled cruelly on the rein and bit, the forelegs of his stallion pawing at the air, then set its head towards the creaming surf.

Together they plunged into the coming tide, and as the restless seas broke upon the shore, they vanished beneath the surging waves.

The pursuing horsemen raced along the wide sands in a ploy to bar their way, but as their captain reined in his steed, not a sign or figure was to be seen upon the shore.

When morning dawned, Zach opened his eyes dazedly in the warm glow of the sun rising above the hill and shining through the window of the room.

He swung himself from the bed and looked out, seeing the moors and cliffs basking in the early light of the day.

When he saw his sister, she remarked, "There are many who don't sense anything – untoward that is …"

But Zach spent the following night on the sofa, not being able to bear to live through the tragic story again on another night.

Lucille told him that when the night falls softly and the moon slides silently across the sky, there comes to some who stay in that corner room the sound of a cantering horse, the jingle of bit and leather, riding over the moor and heathland.

And a gentleman comes riding beneath the waning sliver of moon, thundering swiftly on iron hoof. The corner window opens, swinging widely into the night. A white hand trembles upon the sill, and laughter whispers upon the cool breeze.

A shadow leans against the window, a figure of soft delicate light, and a lacy cobweb of a handkerchief flutters down like a white shimmering leaf.

Then together they ride over the purple heather and down the winding path to the shore, side by side, their voices floating away on the cool night air, as onward they plunge into the coming tide.

15

Mists shrouded the restless seas, dark vapours swept the cliff and shore, and the ghostly moon lit the coiling trails that swirled over bracken and heather on the moors.

The windblown vessel came sailing the wave, surging onwards in the racing tide, her masts reeling in the stormy swell, her bow flinging aside the white salt-spray.

Jedd Penrose leant into the wind, his cap cocked on his weathered brow. He stood six feet four in his great thigh boots as he swayed with the roll of the deck. His rough voice roared aloud into the night as he drove the boat hard into the gale and cursed his labouring motley crew.

Then a light flickered through the billowing mists on the towering cliffs, where by the lookout, old man Zekel had fired the furze, for Ferris his only son sailed with skipper Penrose.

Zach had been fishing from Porthgwyna for many years and on bad weather nights he would climb the cliff path with him, to light a fire as a warning of the reef of black rocks.

Zekel strained to see through the windswept rain for the crabber, with a prayer of fear, for he was a goodly Wesleyan man, a lay preacher at the small chapel nearby. He both prayed and cursed the scoundrel Penrose for enticing his son away to the sea, but then he muttered a prayer of thanks when at last he saw the ship coming safely into the bay.

Penrose also favoured his daughter Amy May, dark-eyed, lithe and carefree. But she shunned the skipper's rough ways, caring little at all for his fervent courting, and so he angrily passed his time at the inn with the women and in riotous drinking.

Though Zekel was well-known for reading the skies with ready omens of good and bad weather, Penrose would jeer at his sayings and signs, pouring scorn on his prophecy and wordy prayers.

Ferris and Matt were sorting out one of Seth's long lines which had been entangled in the seaweed in rough weather, when Penrose, getting ready to go to sea to put out a fresh line of crab pots, called out to the boys to join him.

They eagerly pushed the rest of the line and hooks into the bin and went aboard, as the boat was getting ready to sail.

Zach dropped the rope and tackle that he was bringing down when he saw them on the Mermaid, and shouted at them.

"Matt – come off! Not with Penrose!" but the noise of the engine starting drowned out his voice.

He ran along the quay and leapt across the widening gap onto the boat as it moved out into the bay.

"Penrose! Turn round - the boy's not to be goin' with you . ." he slapped the skipper's arm.

"Ha! Too late. No goin' back now. We'll not be long, just goin' to put out a few pots," roared Penrose.

Zach turned and glared at Matt, but he gave him a cheeky grin and went with Ferris to help the crew to bait the stack of crab pots.

Zach would have threatened Penrose and made him turn for shore if he'd known that the previous evening the skipper had come to blows with Zekel.

When the setting sun had begun to cloud over, the preacher had climbed the high cliff path to make a fire and say his prayers of grace. Penrose followed with taunting jests, mocking his virtuous and righteous ways, and leapt in spite on the errant flames to stamp out the bracken that Zekel had set alight.

He scoffed at his warning of a coming storm and threw him aside into the prickly blackthorn.

"Nobody'd ever earn their livin' at sea with you fore-tellin' of bad weather all the time!" he shouted, then he set off down the path intending to coax the fair Amy May to keep him company.

But she coldly rejected his forward ardour, so he drowned his frustration all night at the inn, and when the morning came he went down to the quay, and now Zekel watched with foreboding as the Mermaid set out to sea.

He set off again to light the fire for the day was close and he could feel that thunder was in the air, but he'd sprained his ankle when Penrose had thrown him, so he painfully made his way up the steep cliff path, having to rest every few paces.

Slowly the heat haze became colder and dense, lifting up a heavy swell, and ranks of hunch-backed waves rolled the boat into deeper troughs. Then a high wave struck the craft and she shuddered and then heeled onto her side.

Zekel's boy was thrown down onto his knees and he prayed with a great dread in his heart, but Penrose roared at his pitiful fright, shouting out to him in the teeth of the wind.

Zach pulled both boys towards him and held them huddled against the hatchway. Dark mists fell and hid all sight of the land while Ferris prayed again more fearfully, and Penrose now cursed that he'd smothered Zekel's fire, for unknown to his crew only he knew that the warning light from the blazing furze wouldn't appear.

Awe seized his heart as a roaring sea towered over the swaying masts, and he too cried out his own hurried prayer for a signal to save them from the reef.

Then suddenly a shaft of light pierced the black clouds in shining relief. Zekel had succeeded in climbing the cliff path in the sweeping rain and had tried to light the furze again, but it had become soaked in the storm and smouldered in miserable wisps of smoke. So he now stood in the shelter of the wall of the lookout and held up his light, peering through the mists to watch for the boat.

But the bright signal came too late for the stricken vessel as her plunging bow drove forward onto the reef, her mast falling across the jagged rocks at the foot of the cliffs.

Penrose seized hold of the huge timbered pole upon his broad shoulders, and shouted to his crew to climb over it and haul themselves along the stays to try to get to the shore.

" 'Old on tight!" cried Zach to the two lads. "Pull yerself over – I'm right behind yer!"

He pushed first Matt and then Ferris in front of him, as he inched his way along the wet slippery mast, clutching at the flailing ropes swirling in the water.

Each man struggled through the seething surf, while the great strength of Penrose held steady the mast against the surge of the waves that threatened to tear it away from his grasp.

The undertow sucking at crevice and ledge, threw up fountains of showering spume that shattered against the cliffs and cascaded in torrents over them. A myriad flurries stung and blinded them from the sight of each other and of Penrose and the boat.

Dark waves lifted in a groundswell and crested in a thunderous roar, rushing along in the wild tidal race, climbing and breaking asunder onto the rocks.

When the boys managed to reach the foot of the cliff, two of the crew caught hold of them by the arms and dragged them up onto a ledge with them, out of the wash of the sea. Zach scrambled up after them, with the tide flinging salt-spray over him, and he gave thanks that the timber had stayed fast.

He looked back for skipper Penrose to follow, but the waters rose up in a tumbling whirl, plucking mast and man away with the spate in the race of the swirling tide.

Through the night and the following morning when the winds had died away, the flotsam and jetsam of splintered wood and rope littered the surface of the sea and floated here and there on the current.

And on the jagged rocks at the foot of the cliffs, wedged upright in a fissure of the granite stood the mast with Penrose still grasping its timber, frozen in the icy grip of the sea.

The men of the cove climbed down the cliff with ropes and prised Jedd Penrose away from the mast, and brought him up to the headland where they carried him on their shoulders to the chapel.

Here they laid him to rest, with Zekel saying the last prayer over him and thanking him and God for saving his son and all those on the boat.

The rays of the rising sun shine on the walls of the old lookout, sending a golden light glowing through the apertures, as if Zekel was there showing his light, and the men of the sea are warned of the rocky shore, which Zekel guards with fire and prayer.

When Seth sets out to sea he feels in the air the warmth of Zekel's words when he sees the light shining on the mast still standing there, wedged in the granite cliff, and remembers the bravery of big Jedd Penrose who saved his crew from the clutches of the sea.

16

The letter came – dropping onto the granite wall, sending up the garden midges in the already increasing heat of the morning.

"From Penzance," the gruff voice of Jacca the postman, inquisitive, "official stamp too."

Zach's youngest, Josh, coming out through the doorway turned it over, "Chanells Solicitors – it's for Dad."

He strode back into the house and put the letter on the table, as he reached for the teapot. Zach and Clarissa were at breakfast and his father picked up the envelope.

He read it and grunted, "M'brother Rueben's passed away," and pushed it back to his son.

"It asks you to go over to clear up his house after the funeral," said Josh, looking through it.

"No! not I," Zach stood up, "m'brother Abe can do it."

"You're the eldest now," Josh pointed out.

But Zach and Rueben had fallen out over money matters, the latter being a spendthrift, while Zach, out fishing many hours at sea, had been trying to hold the family farm together.

Eventually, he had set off with Clarissa Rose for Porthgwyna, vowing never to set foot in Trevarrick again.

Clarissa put her hand on his arm, "Abe is ill – he can't go anywhere."

"I'm not settin' foot in that place ag'in – let the solicitors an' auctioneers sort it out. It's probably in ruins by now anyway," his dark brows knitted together in a scowl.

"I'll go," suggested Josh. "Seth's too busy out at sea, he can't leave the fishin'. But he won't mind me goin' off for a few days. Jem'll crew fer 'im for a while."

Trevarrick was a few miles outside Penzance, on the moors near Zennor, so at the end of the week Josh set out to find a bus going in that direction. It was full, noisy with the gossip of farmers' wives going home with bags of groceries, and mothers with chattering children.

The bus swung round the tight corners of the lanes, the gorse on the stone walls scraping the windows.

He was dropped off at a rough lane in the middle of the moor. This was the way to Trevarrick he was told, the inquisitive passengers gazing out at him from the bus windows as it pulled away.

The lane wound on higher and higher up the moor with Greenbarrow engine house solitary on the skyline.

Eventually he could see the roof and chimneys of the old house silhouetted against the sky, surrounded by walls and stunted trees.

There was a farm and a couple of cottages just before he came to the entrance, the rusty gates leaning half open.

He realised that he should have found out the time when the bus returned before coming up here, but he'd been eager to see Zach's old home, and he clambered over brambles and nettles, peering in through the dark windows.

The house was of dressed granite and was a fine building, but in need of repair. He strode around the wild jungle of the garden, one part paved with a sundial but covered in creeping weed.

He wandered out towards the nearest cottage, but there was no-one around, so he went on to the farmhouse and found an open window.

"Hello there," he called. There came the barking of a dog and footsteps on the flagstone floor. A woman smiled out at him as he asked her when the next bus passed the lane for Penzance.

"I think you've missed it," she said, "but if you wait a while,

Jim'll take you when he comes in from milking."

She looked intently at him, "You're a Trewin – I recognise that brow and jaw anywhere."

He laughed, "I'm Josh. My parents, Zach and Clarissa Rose, are still in Porthgwyna."

"I remember them both. We was all upset when they went from 'ere. The place hasn't been the same since," she turned and he followed her into a sunny kitchen. He sat at the scrubbed table and ate scones just out of the oven, and heard tales of the rundown of the farm and house.

Jim Treneer came home, followed by his daughter Wenna who was beginning her training in the council offices. She gave Josh the keys which she held, to keep Trevarrick dusted. Jim took him back into Penzance and left him at the bus stop to wait for the bus going back to Porthgwyna.

The following morning Josh paid a visit to his uncle Rueben's solicitors, who made arrangements with Davis the auctioneers to visit Trevarrick with him later that day, to make an inventory of its contents for auction.

They spent that afternoon going through the old Victorian furniture of heavy chairs and tables, which Davis valued quite highly, but the moth spotted paintings were mostly beyond repair. The drawers and cupboards revealed useless bills and papers, and some good silver cutlery and silverware.

In the attic they found children's toys, a train set, a rocking horse and some clockwork toys too, which were now unusual collector's items.

At the end of the afternoon they went back to Penzance, Davis saying that as the next day was Saturday, they would come back on the Monday.

When Josh returned home, Clarissa Rose wanted to hear all about the old house and farm.

"Zach worked hard on that place, Josh," she said, "an' we were happy until Rueben fell into his spendthrift ways. There was little left then to put back into the land again."

Josh didn't mention anything about the house to Zach, fearing it would annoy him.

Martha Treneer had invited him to lunch with them the next day, so Seth lent him Matt's bicycle, and he rode through the narrow lanes and panted up the long hill through the villages of Heamoor and Madron, until he climbed the heights of the moors, passing the ancient stone kyst of Lanyon Quoit, the granite burial tomb of a Cornu-Briton king.

Wenna joined him in going round the rest of the house. They sorted through trunks of musty velvet and satin gowns and old photographs, some of his father. He put aside a couple of large photograph albums of his ancestors to take back home.

Josh came upon a box filled with bundles of newspaper. He unwrapped one and inside was a dark metal chalice. He carefully took out all the newspaper from the box and found similar goblets, nine in all.

Wenna stood them on the sideboard and noticed the initials BM on the base of each.

"I know what these are!" she exclaimed, "BM are the initials for the old Botallack Mine, that closed down some years ago. It's on all of their pewter plates. They're pewter wine goblets from the mine that the managers used for their business dinners, and they're part of the dinner service, all made of tin from the mine."

Josh smiled, "I remember great Grandfather was one of the managers at one time."

"They're very valuable," whispered Wenna. "There's nine here, and there's probably more around the district somewhere."

"I've seen somethin' like this before," Josh stroked the

100

curved shape in his hand, "I know – the christening mug! Uncle gave one of these each to my brothers an' I when we were born!"

"Where are they now?" she asked.

"In the cabinet at home," said Josh. "I'll ask Mother to get them out. They must come back with these, where they belong."

"That'll make a dozen," Wenna said.

"Yes," he excitedly caught her hand and laughed into her eyes. They were the colour of the summer sea. He knew then that his future was Trevarrick.

Davis became very excited when he saw the set of goblets.

"They're unique," he said. "Not only for their antique value, but because of their historic connection with the local mine here."

"Then they ought to go to the County or Geological museum," suggested Josh.

"You'll get much more if you auction them. Collectors worldwide will bid for them," urged Davis.

"They must stay here in Cornwall – where they belong," insisted Josh.

Davis sighed at losing such an exciting item, but agreed to notify the museums.

Josh was full of news when he got home, giving his parents the gossip of the area, of the house and the description of the pewter goblets.

Clarissa took out the three that were still there in her cabinet and even Zach admired them.

"You'll 'ave to ask Seth and Ezra if they want to give theirs up," she said.

"Ha! Well, somethin' good's come out of that place then," grunted Zach.

101

The County Museum was eager to obtain the collection and made a good offer. The goblets would then be loaned on show to many other museums.

"I think," Josh said to Zach, "that I want to stay at the old house. I'll be able to renovate it now."

"You mean – there'll be once more a Trewin at Trevarrick?" his father seemed pleased.

"That'll be good," smiled Clarissa.

Wenna was so enthusiastic over the gardens, that she'd already started clearing the sundial courtyard.

Together they decided they would like to turn the house into a guest-house, for those who wished to spend time walking the moors and cairns, birdwatching, and discovering the old mines and ancient stone circles.

17

The heavens opened with a blinding flash of lightning streaking to the earth with a sharp crack. A thin pillar of smoke spiralled into the veil of falling rain and a loud clap of thunder rolled across the clouds. Long swathes of heavier rain lashed the windows of the car, beating on the roof and door.

Zach clutched tightly at the wheel as the car slithered in the swift rivulets running across the road. He and Clarissa Rose often visited Trevarrick now, their interest becoming more and more involved as they watched Josh and Wenna bringing the place to life again. From the old house on the moors they had got caught in the thunderstorm, just as they were coming to the top of the steep hill that dropped narrowly into the village of Gulval. The road was strewn with pebbles and gorse roots and had become a river rushing down between the high granite walls.

The car bucked and shuddered and the rain swept the windscreen in a wash so dense that all he could see was a white shimmer of milky water. The wheel hit a fallen branch from the trees lining the road, and the car slewed suddenly round and tilted over into the ditch.

Clarissa Rose clutched nervously at the hanging strap above her head, "We'm goin' to be swept away!" she cried out.

The car was a recent purchase and Zach was none too familiar with the gears as yet.

"Hold on to me, Granma," Matt held her arm against his side.

Zach opened the window a little way to see where he was and the rain blew in, stinging their faces. Rushing waterfalls were cascading over the sides of the stone walls onto the road in front of them, welling into a tumbling river coursing down the steep hill. He quickly wound up the window and dried his face on his scarf. All the catchment areas and streams from the upper fields were filling and racing down the sides of the hills into the valley bottom.

Zach tried to re-start the engine. The car slithered, then gripped the gravel and lurched forward out of the ditch. He pushed his foot down on the pedal and rounded the sharp corners coming down into Heamoor ford.

Two other vehicles were abandoned with the water lapping their radiators. He slowed to a stop, ready to start a long walk home.

Then he heard the throb of a heavy engine behind him. He thrust his head out of the window and saw the blurred shape of a lorry lurching down the road.

It was going too fast to stop at the water and forced its way through, pushing large waves of wake to each side of its high wheels.

Zach hurriedly started his engine and followed behind the big vehicle, taking advantage of the shallower centre of the road cleared by the lorry. When he glanced back he could see the foaming wash of the waters closing in a surging swell behind him.

The lorry rumbled on and he kept closely behind it. The rain lessened against the windscreen and he could see the number plate on the mud-spattered board in front of him. It belonged to one of Chirgwin's drivers, going to and fro from the tin mine.

The rain had suddenly stopped but pebbles, furze and debris hit the windows and flew past in the howl of the wind, as they came out onto the main road going through Newbridge. Here they met a torrent of brackish water, but the lorry pushed forward relentlessly, although the water each side came above the hubs.

Zach clenched his teeth and Clarissa and Matt gave sharp cries as walls of water gushed by at window height against the car. Blue smoke poured out of the lorry's exhaust, but the big vehicle thrust onwards through the racing swirl, to the curving hill that climbed up from the bridge. An arm shot out of the cab window and waved to him and Zach signalled grimly back.

They went on up the hill, floodwater pouring off the fields in gushing waterfalls, and the cottages and the small Post Office were up to their windows in the swollen streams.

"Dear life!" exclaimed Clarissa.

The crossroads appeared where the north road swept across the moors. Here, with another arm wave, the lorry branched off, the wind buffeting its sides. Zach grasped a firmer hold of the wheel as the stormy gusts plucked and lifted the car.

At the corner of Jericho farm the twist in the tight bend warned him that he was now on the downward slope to a deep cutting which always flooded in a heavy shower. But it was too late to slow down and he hurtled down the hill and hit the wall of water head on.

A great spouting wave shot over the whole car, stones and gravel raining down with a noisy clattering. The windscreen was awash with a wall of dirty brown flurries as the car crabbed its way under water.

Clarissa shrieked, clutching Matt's shoulder as he was thrown forward.

Then suddenly the debris cleared and they were roaring up the hill to the clayworks of Bostraze. The car coughed and spluttered, veering on three wheels round the tight bends above the Blue Pool and up to the cemetery on Carn Bosarven.

Here the wind whooshed and wailed as they took the Brea road and coasted down the twisting Crippas hill to the narrow Kelynack Bridge. A wide rushing current swept down to the bridge, spurting high into the air. Zach stamped hard on the pedal and the car disappeared into the swirling waters, coughed and shuddered, drifted sideways onto the far bank, then

105

gripped the tarmac and struggled clear of the flood.

The rising hill was swept with a tide of stones and earth. He took the lane going alongside the open heathland where the old people still dug furze and turf to burn for fuel. Here the wide arena of cliff and sea opened out and the wind roared across the great expanse. The car veered drunkenly as the gusts caught the sides going down the steep hill into Nanquidno valley.

The trees bent over into a canopy of swaying branches. Huge limbs lay fallen at the ford and a trunk floated in the swollen river. From here to the lower valley the stream, the road and the scrubland each side had flooded into a wide lake rushing into the fast flowing river. The brackish waters were rising rapidly, whipped up by the wind.

The lane was slightly raised, but after a few yards the rising waters became too deep and the car began to float sideways on the surge. It was swept past Nanjulian farmhouse and cottage and Zach wrenched the steering wheel over, as he neared the rising ground of the leat and millpool.

He felt the car jar against a rock and then he came to a shuddering halt by the bank.

"We shouldn't 'ave come down 'ere!" cried Clarissa. "We should 'ave gone straight home."

"Ah, but Aggie is expectin' us – an' we better see how she's copin' with this gale," Zach pulled up the hood of his oilskin, then thrust open the door with all his strength against the rage of the wind and a furious onslaught of lashing rain. The frenzy of the falling night fell upon him and screamed around his ears. He clung onto the car until he reached the lee of the thick granite wall and peered through the bracken.

The mill stood in turbulent waters that gurgled to the top of the lower windows. Gorse and furzy stogs had been washed downstream and were now piled up into a dam which blocked the small bridge. The waves broke against it, flinging spouts high into the air. The old leat had filled, surging over and turning the huge millwheel.

Swirling pieces of furniture, garden tools and odd boots and shoes swept past. Then in the howl of the wind he heard an eerie whistling and a faint cry.

He struggled along in the shelter of the wall until he came to the cottage. Here, a dark figure wrapped in a wild flapping cloak swayed precariously out of the upstairs window, with the water now risen half way up the lower windows.

The high whistle came again as he clambered and pulled himself along the hedge to the windowsill and clung there by his fingers.

"Z – a – cch – ae - us . . ." screeched the voice, thrusting a whistle between pouting lips, and blowing a high piercing wail. He dragged himself over the sill into the dark warmth of the cottage.

Aggie Annie had the peaked hood of the black cloak tied witch-like and tight under her long chin and peered out with her toothy grin.

"Don't!" shouted Zach as she put the whistle again to her mouth. "That's enough to frighten me out of m'wits."

He took her hand and led her, cackling at the lapping water on the stairs, to the window looking over to the barn.

Here he left her and held onto the drainpipe to reach the barn roof, then slithered into the gaping window of the hay store. He looked down into the darkness and saw almost every loose object and tool afloat. Aggie's late husband's cove boat, still upturned, was slamming against the wall with the wash. He climbed down the ladder and with the hay fork, managed to hook the painter and drag the boat towards him.

The boat was heavy and awkward to turn over, and he was soaked through by the time the craft flopped over with his final thrust. He searched for the oars and found them still standing upright just showing above the surface. He stepped into the boat, grasped hold of the oars, and manoeuvred the craft out through the open doorway.

Here, the strong current threatened to suck him into the vortex towards the racing river. But he stemmed the tide with his oar and scraped along the wall until he was under Aggie's window.

She clambered unsteadily into the boat, shrieking with alarm. He lifted the oars to make way, but she hung onto the sill and dragged at the lead of her dog and pulled it in with her. The terrier's eyes showed white, rolling in terror, and its legs splayed out and went all ways as it hid under her cloak.

Zach bumped and yawed along the length of the wall to the car. The white faces of Matt and Clarissa stared out of the window at him.

"Get in!" he shouted to them. They struggled with the car door against the wind and scrambled into the boat. Zach used the oars to make way along the hedge to the farmhouse.

A light wavered from the dark blob of the window. He pulled towards it and they saw the figures of farmer Rowe and his family leaning out.

"Hurry!" Zach cried up to them, "I can't hold the boat steady."

Frank Rowe climbed into the boat, then turned and helped his two children as his wife handed them down to him, Frank grunting and stamping his feet so that they rocked unsafely.

The craft was now full and it took all Zach's strength to row. Boy Billy and little Bessie clutched at the sides and Nellie Rowe held onto them for fear they would all overturn.

Zach headed for the high ground of the cliff where Frank kept his flock of sheep, and they came to a grinding halt as the boat bottomed on a huge boulder. Water gushed through as they jumped quickly out and climbed the rocky bank.

From here they hung onto each other, staggering against the sudden gusts of wind that tore at their hair and clothes. The children shrieked in excited fright, clinging to their parents' hands as they stumbled into ditches and waterlogged holes.

Zach and Clarissa held onto Aggie's arms as they half-lifted and almost carried her across the gorse and furze stumps, her black cloak whipping across Zach's face and billowing out in the gale, like a ship's sail. She had a firm grip on the dog's lead, winding it two or three times around her wrist, as she screeched and cackled at the terrier, dragging it unwillingly at her side.

When a white flash of lightning zig-zagged across the sky, the little dog stopped in his tracks and refused to move a step further. Matt took pity on him and scooped him up, carrying him under his arm.

They began to climb higher, the ground rising until Zach shouted, "The track to Penhale's farm is 'ere somewheres."

But although they struggled over boulders and bigger slabs of slippery rock, they didn't find it until Clarissa saw a light ahead.

They clambered over a stone wall, Aggie Annie shrieking and almost taking off in the wind as Zach kept a tight hold on her, and stumbled to the farmhouse on the top of the cliff.

Here he thumped on the door with his fist, shouting above the howling wind. Old Job Penhale appeared in the doorway, pitting his strength against the gusts threatening to take the door.

They crowded into his warm kitchen, thankful for the heat coming from the glowing range, his wife Biddy hurriedly making great mugs of tea and finding dry towels

"I've never seen anythin' like it," Clarissa told her. "We'm lucky to 'ave got here at all, without bein' swept away down river an' out to sea."

Matt grinned, "I thought Aggie Annie was goin' to take off with the wind!"

Job drank his hot tea down, then declared he had to check his sheep, as some of them were heavy in lamb, even though they were on the higher ground. So the men turned out into the night again to look for the sheep, and to drive them into the higher barn. They took Job's collie with them and followed the granite walls from one field to the next.

At the dog's sudden barking, they found the flock huddled against the lee of a high wall. Job took a count, then counted again, but found one missing out of the thirty ewes. They searched the cliff face, the collie scurrying hither and thither in the wet bracken, then giving frenzied barks at a shadow lying on a ledge, just below the cliff edge.

In its fright of the storm, the ewe was giving an early birth to its offspring.

"Little beggar!" shouted Job and slithered down to the ewe. Zach leant over the edge, peering through the stinging rain and shone the light onto the ledge. He could see the long front legs and the head of the lamb. Job grasped the legs and gently eased the lamb from its mother.

He wiped the nose and eyes and moved one of the front legs up and down to stimulate its heart. They saw it give a great intake of air, shake its head and begin bleating. The ewe bleated back to it, licking its face with her large tongue. Job leant against the cliff face to steady himself as a strong gust of wind swept up from the raging sea below.

He pulled a length of rope from his pocket, thrust the end at Frank, and made a harness over the ewe's head and shoulders. He picked up the lamb and pushed it up the cliff edge. Zach caught hold of it under his arm as Frank pulled on the rope. When the ewe saw her lamb above her, she scrambled up the cliff with Job pushing her from behind.

He then climbed after her, carrying the lamb under his arm in front of her nose, so that the mother could see it and begin to follow closely. Every so often she would lose sight of it in the darkness and in a panic would turn back and head for the cliff again, where she knew she had given birth.

Zach and Frank waved their arms to head her off, and Job called and sang out, bleating like the lamb, so that she would swing back and see its white coat and begin to follow again. They came to the rest of the flock, rounded them up and herded them into the shelter of the top barn.

Finding water for them was easy, but the hay had to be fetched from the storage barn across the next field. They trudged through the wet grass and burst thankfully into the doorway of the hay barn.

There was a hoarse muttering from the dark corner of the building, and when Zach shone his light around, it lit up the sleeping figure of Ephraim, the local tramp.

His bleary eyes blinked in the sudden light and his breath came in startled snorts. He was huddled between the stacked bales under a worn tattered grey blanket.

"Catch yer death 'ere, Ephraim," scolded Job.

"Naw," the slight figure hitched at the blanket.

"Come back wi' us to the farm," Job heaved a bale onto his back.

"Naw . . . "

" 'Yu," greeted Zach, as he and Frank each took another bale and they struggled across the field again against the howling gale.

They filled the feeding racks and the ewes pulled hungrily at the hay. The newborn lamb bleated and kept close to his mother's side, drinking her milk as she ate.

When they reached the farmhouse again, Zach sank back into a deep chair and supped gratefully at a bowl of hot soup. But his mind flickered back to the old tramp huddled in the corner of the barn.

"It's no good," he sighed and got wearily to his feet, and when Job looked questionably at him, he reached up to a large flask on the shelf. Then he poured the remainder of the soup into it.

"You're right, he's on m'mind as well," Job reached into his cupboard for his whisky bottle and put it in his pocket.

"We can't leave 'im out there in this weather I s'pose," he said as Frank put a half loaf and meat pie into a bag and struggled into his oilskin again.

Once again they bent their heads before the wind and made for the hay barn.

"Ephra'm!" bellowed Job, swinging the light he'd brought.
The tramp watched the sodden figures swaying wearily on their feet, coming towards him, holding out food and the whisky bottle.

"Aa-ah," he sighed and reached for the bottle. But Zach made him take the hot soup and bread before they broke open the whisky. They'd just put the first dram to their lips when an enormous gust of wind hit the barn roof with a roar, sucking and drawing at the timbers, until with a splintering crack, the rafters on one side peeled away.

The men dragged the tramp with them and dived for cover under the tarpaulin covering the stack of bales. Timber and slates came crashing down on them, and dust and pieces of rafter flew about their heads.

Rain swept through the wrecked roof, running in rivulets along the floor and the wind howled through the exposed beams and battered the double doors of the barn, bending and rattling at the hinges threatening to hurl them into the night.

Zach and Frank crawled out from their cover and searched for long pieces of wood or iron, and jammed them in the fastenings of the doors hoping they would hold. As they were doing this, they saw water pushing its way underneath, widening into a steady stream.

"Ephra'm!" shouted Job. "Get up the ladder to the loft – quick." They pulled him out of the tarpaulin to the ladder, but his limbs didn't have the strength to climb.

"I'll go first, an' pull 'im up. You push from behind," Zach climbed up halfway, then hauled him up by the scruff of his neck. Frank pushed from below and between them they reached the hayloft.

"Gaw – 'tis worse'n getting that sheep up the cliff," gasped Job as they sat back, getting their breath.

Zach looked down to the floor and could see the water still rising.

"We could save most of those bales," he said, "if we throw them up 'ere."

So Frank clambered down again and heaved bale after bale to the ladder, pushing them up so that Zach and Job could get a grip on the bailer twine and roll them into the far corner of the hayloft where it was dry.

Frank also threw up bags of barley and grain that the sheep would need, before he was conscious of the water swirling over his boots and around his knees.

"Best come up now," shouted Zach and caught his hand to help him as the ladder began to sway sideways with the surge of the current. Frank poured water from his boots and wrung out his socks.

"Where's m'whisky?" demanded Ephraim suddenly.

Frank looked at Job, "We've left it down there," he groaned. But Zach smirked at him and pulled the bottle out of his large waterproof pocket.

113

"Not likely," he laughed. "We'll not get out of 'ere till the mornin', so we might as well make the best of it."

Between them they drank the bottle dry, guffawing tales far into the wild night, with the hoarse snorts and wheezes of Ephraim in their ears rumbling with the roar of the storm.

18

They were down the old Wheal Hermyn tin mine, burrowing in the dark, shovelling out barrows of rab and stone. Ezra and Simeon had brought Zach and Seth down with them, Matt tagging along behind, with their belief in the rumour that the last miners had left rich tin ore in the last lode, before they'd abandoned the mine.

Simeon's fellow miner Jory was wielding the pick, strong and willing even though he walked with a limp, for one foot was lame and slow in movement.

They were like moles working through the earth's heart, with the lamps burning yellow, setting the shadows flitting in the air that hung heavy in the warm red dust.

The vein had faltered and ceased to show much sign of tin, and the old mine had failed and had closed down.

They'd been working for three days, from early in the morning until late in the afternoon, but hadn't found very much worthwhile. When it was time for crowst, they all sat around munching pasties, leaning their backs against the damp walls.

"We'll give it one more day tomorrow," grunted Ezra, "then give up."

Zach laughed, "I reckon yer rich tin is long gone."

They went on digging with pick and bent back, hammer and gad, Matt enthusiastically using the banjo, shovelling the waste rock into the barrow, and the men hacking away at the vein that was poor.

Jory was working up ahead, moving back the fallen stone and rab. He came back, his ear cocked questionably, asking who was that who called out to him.

But neither Seth or Matt had uttered a word, except to pant and grunt with the heavy work, and nor had the others when he asked them.

With a puzzled mind he went back to work, while the rest of them chaffed him.

But an hour or so later, again he appeared, "Who's calling out an' havin' me on?"

Then it was that uneasiness grew on them, as Zach muttered, "Well – all stop an' listen."

They stood silently, trying to hear any unusual sound, but all was still, except their laboured breathing.

"I hope it ain't they Bucca spirits we hear about, who give cries of warning when there's danger," said Ezra nervously.

"You've bin at this job long enough to knaw not to believe in they tales," replied Simeon.

Ezra snorted, and they began working again, but their senses were alert for the slightest strange sounds.

Time dragged by as they toiled away in the ground, each hoping it would soon be time for when they'd down tools and be off home.

Then Ezra noticed Jory's shadow going down the sloping level and saw his light bobbing up and down.

"What's up?" he shouted. But there was no reply, so he followed him until he slowed his stride.

"I heard 'em," Jory cried, "I heard 'em clear and plain, down 'ere somewheres."

They looked all around, shining their lights, when suddenly Ezra caught sight of something that made him cry out excitedly.

"The pick," he shouted, "give me the pick – an' call the others to come down 'ere."

Jory scurried off as fast as his limp would allow, while Ezra peered at the vein which none of them had known about. It was rich with tin ore, and it set his heart glowing.

When the others arrived they gathered round in awe, for this would mean a new lease of life for the old mine.

"Them was lucky voices you heard, Jory," said Zach.

"I can't b'lieve it," exclaimed Seth, "but let's get clearin' this lot 'ere an' get up to grass fer home."

Even as he spoke, there came a gust of rushing air, a warm blast of wind in their faces, and as they flattened up against the granite wall they heard the dreaded sound, the rumble and roaring of an underground fall.

The dust and rubble choked them until they could hardly breathe, dimming their lights so that they could hardly see each other.

"You all right Matt ? – Dad?" shouted Seth.

"We're over 'ere," cried Zach, his arm sheltering Matt's shoulder, "Ezra?"

"I got Simeon and Jory 'ere with me," he replied.

None of them had suffered any injury, but now they were afraid.

"They Buccas warned us," moaned Jory, "an' we didn't take heed of them."

"Them's unlucky voices, lad," said Zach, "we should've got out the first time you heard them."

When the noise was settled they ventured down the level, and they saw the fall, a solid wall of rock. They retraced their steps but the fall had caused an avalanche of stone and blocked their way back to the entrance of the adit.

Simeon cried out, "That lode could be the richest vein, the best in all the world, but it's no use to us if we're buried underground."

There they were entombed, for no-one would hear their cries and no-one would think to look before night had come or until the following morning.

They sat quietly, conserving their air, putting out their lights until they were really needed. Matt leaned against Seth, trusting his father's judgement that he would soon find a way out, and wishing he was now safely at home.

Then Jory suddenly sat up, alert, his grimy eyes gleaming in the dark.

"There's they voices again!" he cried. He rose to his feet and turned back to his right.

The others scrambled up, and holding on to each other slowly followed him, their hearts sinking in despair as they stumbled along in the stone rubble of a long abandoned level.

Then he gave another shout, raising their hopes with, "Come quick, come quick – I c'n smell a different air!"

They hurried to catch up with him, finding they were breathing great gulps of air that was fresher, and coming from up ahead.

Jory scrabbled upwards to a small niche in the granite and began pulling away loose stone.

"That's bin shaken down by the vibration of the fall," said Zach joining him, passing the rocks to the others behind him and hand by hand they began clearing a passage.

On and on Jory went, and they just crawled after him, squeezing through the old miners' tunnels made years before.

Simeon brought up the rear and made signs on the wall every few yards, in case they lost their way, but that young Jory, he seemed to go right through that warren's maze.

They went on hour after hour, taking rests and encouraging each other to keep going, when gradually the blackness began turning to a shade of grey.

"I c'n see some light!" cried out Jory, and soon to their loud shouts and cries of relief they caught the sight of daylight.

Morning had dawned upon the outside world when at last they broke free, and there they were right on the cliff above the sea.

The old miners' adit path shelved away and led down to the shore and they stumbled forward, thankful to be out in the open air.

Red from the dusty earth, bruised and grimy, they made their way along the cliff path, and it was then that they noticed that Jory's limp had almost disappeared and he was walking upright even though he was weary.

"Tha's just uncanny," said Zach to Clarissa, when they got back to his cottage.

"I reckon so – but I dunno what Hannah Jane's goin' to say to Seth, takin' Matt underground," she scolded. "Out all night too – an' look at the state of you!"

"Ah, well – we got held up," he mumbled, winking slyly at Matt.

Pengegon said that it was the strenuous climbing that had set Jory's foot straight, but the old folk whispered that it was the Buccas that had helped him.

Many of the miners at the Wheal Venton mine were always eager to work shifts with Jory, believing they were safe with him. They were reluctant to exchange places with anyone else, for word had spread that he had ear to the hidden world of the Buccas.

19

"Ginger!" The call rang out across the cove and a tawny head jerked up from the rocky pool.

The small blenny that had been idling near his hand darted away beneath the weed.

"What you got?" Matt ran up panting, and peered into the pool.

"Nothin' now, you idiot! I was just right to catch it."

"There it is," Matt pointed under the weed.

"You won't get it now," Ginger frowned at him.

Matt gently lowered his arm into the warm water, careful not to make any ripples. But the fish saw his shadow and disappeared into the weed again.

"Told you so," Ginger gave him a push.

"Hey, watch out!" Matt plunged the other arm into the rocky bed of the pool to steady himself, then flung both arms around his friend, and they went rolling over and over on the sand, shouting and pummelling each other.

Matt pulled away and scrambled to his feet.

"I got one anyway," Ginger shook sand out of his hair.

Matt ran over to the tin propped up beside the pool. "It's a big one."

"Yeh."

"You goin' to eat it?"

" 'Course not. You can't eat them."

"Let's look fer mackerel then."

"Okay," Ginger tipped the blenny back into the water and it darted away beneath the weed.

They went over to Matt's small boat.

"You got any feathers?" Ginger picked up a length of line lying in the bottom of the boat.

"Ask Jacob. He's got some."

The old fisherman was sitting on the wooden seat by the door of his boathouse, dozing in the sun.

"Jacob, you got any feathers?" the boys leant over him.

He squinted up at them and nodded towards the door. They went inside and found half-a-dozen on the bench in there.

"Want some bait?" he mumbled and nodded again towards a row of rusty bins. Matt went over to them and lifted the wooden crate that served as a cover and looked inside.

"Phaw! It's stinkin'!" he pulled his head back quickly.

"Aye," Jacob gave a toothless grin.

"What is it?" Ginger leant over.

"Squid – smell it!" Matt pushed his head down.

"Cor . . . !" he leapt back.

"We don't need it fer mackerel anyway."

"We might catch a conger with it."

"You keep off them – give you a nasty bite them do," Jacob struggled to his feet and went over and covered the bin again. "Go on – scarper!"

"Thanks," the two ran down to the boat with the feathers and squatted beside it, tying them to the hooks on the line.

Then they pushed the boat down to the water's edge and clambered in.

Matt rowed out into the bay, and they let down the line and took it in turns, whiffing and jiggling it up and down to attract the fish.

They had drifted a little way by the time Ginger had two mackerel on the hooks. When Matt looked up he saw that they were near the caves.

"Let's go in the cave of many colours."

"Yeh. We can row right in it."

"If there's enough water."

"Just," Ginger took up the oars and they rowed into the

largest opening until the boat grounded on the sand.

They leapt out and pulled it up from the water and then went exploring. It was cool and clammy inside the granite cliff, and the colours glistened along the roof and sides of the cave, caused by the veins and outcrops of tin and copper trapped in quartz crystals contained in the rock, especially when the sun's rays shone through the apertures.

Their voices and footsteps echoed from the crannies as they shouted to each other. For although they and most of the children around, had clambered along the boulders and rocks from the cove at low tide and had been there many times, there was always something new to be found.

At last they came back to the boat and pushed off to try for mackerel again.

Tamsin met Leah coming in with the milking herd and followed him into the yard. She looked hard at the last cow which was heavy in calf.

"In a couple of days, that one," he said, following her gaze.

"I should think so – she'll be glad to be over it in this hot weather."

"Aye, she will, what wi' that thunder and hot wind we 'ad a short while ago. It's a wonder that didn't start 'er off." Leah began milking, showing Tamsin the routine, moving around the herd quietly and talking to them.

He'd almost finished when a motorcycle drew up, scattering the gravel outside. Zach came into the parlour.

"Boy Matt 'ere?" he asked.

"I was wonderin' where he'd got to," Tamsin straightened up.

"He's still out then."

"Out?"

"Fishing. He and the boy Williams got feathers off Jacob

122

Pendrea and the boat's not back yet!"

"You mean they were out in that squall that blew up?" asked Tamsin.

Zach seemed to age in a second, the flesh falling away from his cheekbones, as he leapt onto the bike and roared off down the lane.

"Start the van!" Leah shouted at Tamsin and swung open the gate to the paddock for the herd to wander out, and then ran across the yard.

They were driving down the lane when Seth came hurrying across, followed by Hannah Jane and Clarissa. They climbed into the back and Tamsin set it racing down to the harbour.

When they pulled up at the top of the slipway, they could see groups of fishermen and villagers huddled round the boats.

The sea was coming up to high tide and was breaking in a surging wash upon the beach. They made their way down to the Pollard's boat, where Rob was re-filling his engine with more fuel.

"We already bin out an' made a search," he told Seth, "but didn't see a sign of 'em. We're waitin' now fer the tide to go down a bit afore we try ag'in. It won't be as rough then."

"Aye," Pete joined them, "the sea's got up a bit."

Seth scanned the bay for a sight of anything on the water, but the continuous swell of the waves made it difficult to see. He turned and walked slowly to Jacob's bench and sank down on it with his head in his hands.

"Matt - Matt - Ginger . . ." breathed Clarissa anxiously.

"Matt - Matt . . ." echoed Hannah Jane and went hurrying up the cliff path to the end of the point, searching the white-flecked sea.

Tamsin stood despairingly, shading her eyes against the glare as they combed the water, the rocks, the cliffs - and - of course, the caves.

The boys were always in and out of them, across the rocks or by boat when the tide was half way. But the sea had to be watched, because with high spring tides the water surged into the openings and inlets.

The forecast had not been good that morning. If the boys were sheltering in the caves they would have to try to get out now, or wait perhaps for a day or two until the seas abated. The boats must look for them now. She turned and ran to Zach's boathouse and pulled down the waterproof smock and boots.

As she was struggling into them, Zach and Leah came to the door, "They are in the caves!" she shouted.

"You can't go," Zach stayed her with his hand on her arm.

"It's got to be now – before high tide an' before it gets rougher," she fastened the smock.

"You ain't goin' where I wouldn't," Leah said, "I'm comin' with you."

"You're no sailor, Leah."

"Now's the time to learn . . ."

"An' I know the caves."

"Let's push out afore Clarissa sees us," urged Zach.

"Or Hannah Jane," added Seth rushing in and unhooking another waterproof.

They hurried after Tammy down the slipway to Seth's small boat, shrugging into their oilskins.

"You goin'?" shouted Rob.

"Aye. Tammy reckons they're in the caves. We'll 'ave to get them out before high tide."

"You're right – we'll follow."

The boat was run down to the water and they pushed off in a lull in the surf. Other boats followed, spreading out, searching the area. The rising wind threw up short choppy waves on the surface and they were tossed about uncomfortably, the spray coming over the bows and into their faces.

As the boats were pulling out, there was a screech of brakes from a vehicle at the top of the slipway. The door swung open and Jem Morgan jumped out.

He'd been on the way to the farm to return equipment that he'd borrowed, but had heard the news from the Laity's before he'd reached there. He saw the boats moving out in the bay.

"They're out in this sea!"

"Aye," Jacob nodded and spat from the corner of his mouth, "they reckon the boys are in the caves."

"Where's Tamsin?" he looked round at the groups of villagers.

"Out there – with Seth – 'twas 'er idea."

"Good grief – who let her?" and he was running down to the Pollard's craft that was just pushing out and leapt in.

Zach and Seth, being the first launched, reached the caves ahead of the others and shouted at the top of their voices. The surge tumbled noisily around them, making it difficult to hear anything. They called again and again, searching all the mouths of the caves but there was no answer.

Tamsin looked up at the cliffs soaring above them, scanning the ledges, the crannies, the outcrops – all that her father had shown her as a child. Then she caught a glimpse of the islands surrounded by the white surf of the breakers.

She shouted to him, "The Brisons – there's caves there too – Smuggler's Hole . . ."

Zach turned the boat and they headed for the islands. He knew the Hole had mooring rings in the side of the largest cave and were used by smugglers in the old days, a long dark secret tunnel.

As they changed direction, some of the other boats came within hailing distance, indicating that they had found nothing, and Seth pointed to the islands with his hand.

Zach opened up the engine and they bounced from wave to wave, and roared round to the leeward side of the islands, shouting Matt's name.

"D - a - d!" the sound came back over the hiss of the waves. "D - a - d!"

The white blur of Matt's face appeared from a ledge at the side of the cave. There were tears, salt or otherwise coursing down Seth's leather-skinned features.

"Please Lord – help us to get them off," muttered Tamsin.

"Pull your own boat to the back of the cave – tie it there," he cried.

"We've done that," Ginger's head bobbed beside Matt's.

Zach brought the boat as close as he could to the rocks, as Seth steadied himself in the bows and leapt onto the ledge.

Zach kept the engine revving against the roll of the surge, while Seth passed Ginger over the gunnels to Leah in the boat.

They pulled out before the next wave rushed towards them, coming round again to draw level with the ledge as Seth pushed Matt into Leah's arms, then he himself jumped into the boat and they roared back out to sea.

Ginger crouched down as the waves drenched him, and Matt fell on top of him, both soaked to the skin, the salt water stinging their eyes.

"Take her out!" shouted Seth, watching a wave banking high to the left of them. Zach opened up the throttle, and they roared up the steep roller and smacked down into the trough.

"Hang on! Here's another," he cried. The Pollard's boat appeared behind them – then two more, and Seth gave them the thumbs up, pointing at the half-drowned pair hanging onto the sides of the boat.

Jem lifted his hand to them indicating the shore and they headed back towards the harbour.

It was becoming more blustery as they approached and Jem shouted to them and they slowed down, letting a series of racing breakers go thundering by.

Then there came a momentary lull on the surface while the sea gathered itself to build up again, and the engines opened up and the boats surged in, one after the other.

Many hands caught hold of the gunnels to drag the boats up the slipway before the next onslaught of waves. Even so, the last boat was slewed round near to the rocks by the turbulent surf, before it was dragged back to safety.

"Matt!" the voice echoed over the roar of the waters, and looking up, they saw the lone windswept figure of Hannah Jane stumbling and running down the cliff path.

Matt ran up to meet her and they clasped each other, his mother panting and tearfully laughing at his safe return.

Theo Williams threw his arm around Ginger, "What 'ave you bin up to, son?" he said, squeezing his shoulder.

"Come Mother - sit down," Seth helped her into the boathouse and onto the seat. The boys had a blanket flung around them and were handed a hot mug of soup that Wendy from one of the cove cottages had made ready for them.

"Tammy!" Jem caught her arm and pulled one of the blankets over her shoulders, as she struggled out of the wet oilskins.

"You're the craziest – in this weather!"

"I didn't think – it was so rough . . ." she trembled, more with reaction than with the wet.

"Here," he held a mug to her. The soup tasted good and she sank shakily down on the bench, drinking it thankfully.

"It was fine when we went, Dad," Matt turned to Seth.

"I know."

"Our boat's okay," added Ginger.

"One of us'll get it back in a day or two, when the sea's gone down a bit," answered Pete.

"We'd 'ave bin alright – the tide doesn't come up to the top ledges in the cave."

"You'd 'ave bin there several days, though," Tamsin wiped the salt water from her face with the back of her hand, "with the forecast being what it is."

"Aw, crumbs – we'd 'ave starved!" cried Matt.

Zach gave him a playful cuff on the side of his head.

20

Where frets the sifting tide upon the pale and yellow sands beneath the morning haze of the sky, and where the tufted grassy dunes hump in the hollow bays, the granite mill stood overlooking the rugged shore.

Beside the tumbling water rill that rippled down to meet the sea, the great wheel turned on creaking cogs. Here Ebenezer Viddicomb, the staunch miller lived with his son Mewan, toiling hard from dawn to dusk grinding the dusty grain.

He was sitting in his open doorway, resting from the morning's labour with a husky sigh, when Zach drove into the yard.

"I've come fer some flour, Ebenezer," he called out.

"Zach," the miller nodded his greeting.

"Clarissa Rose is bakin' tomorrow an' needs more, an' I'll take some fer Hannah Jane."

"Mewan'll get it fer 'ee."

Zach climbed the steps and sat down beside him, looking out towards the sea where the clouds were low, and a sea fog was swirling in.

The great mill wheel was turning behind him, ever clanking with a loud grating and scraping rumble.

"Looks like that fog is gettin' thicker," grumbled Ebenezer.

The mists coiled round their limbs and swept round the towering cliffs in chilling strands.

Both men rose to their feet and turned to enter the mill, when looking back, Zach caught sight of the bow of a boat.

"Who's that comin' ashore?" he asked.

There came a momentary break between the drifting wisps of mist, and Ebenezer saw the craft and cried out to Mewan.

The mist closed over again, but they'd all seen the boat and heard the grating of its keel as it pulled up onto the sand.

"Revenue men!" gasped the miller, and they ran into the mill and bolted the door.

"What're they after?" panted Zach.

"Brandy came ashore last night from that wreck," said Mewan. "Truscott and Casley brought some barrels up 'ere."

"I've told 'ee before not to leave 'em 'ere!" ranted Ebenezer, his eyes glared angrily at his son.

"Didn't 'ave time to put 'em anywheres else," Mewan shrugged his shoulders and looked cautiously out of the small side window. "They're comin' up 'ere alright!"

The officers beached their boat, leaping into the shallow wash. They firmly strode up the sloping dunes, their booted footprints in the sands swallowed by the eddies, and through the maze of the sea fog came to a halt before the mill.

The miller beckoned to Mewan, "Fetch m'musket!"

"That old thing'll never fire . . ." spluttered Zach.

Ebenezer thrust the barrel through the large keyhole of the door as the revenue men came nearer.

"Don't shoot!" shouted Zach, "You'll start 'em off . . ."

But he was too late, Ebenezer pulled the trigger, taking the officers by surprise so that they scattered amongst the gorse.

"Now you've done it!" cried Mewan.

The miller's glance fell on his rick of furze-stogs stacked outside the back wall, that he used for fuel.

"Ha . . ." he said to Zach, "Pick up yer flour an' ready yerself to get out the back door."

"What're you doin'?"

"Mewan – set fire to they furzes!"

So, hidden by the mantled fog his son set light to the thick stemmed furze-stogs. Ebenezer hefted a sack of flour onto his back and waited for the furze stack to get well alight.

Swallowed by the billowing smoke they hurriedly started up

130

the hill, each carrying a flour sack over their shoulder.

The favourable wind blew the blinding smoke downwards keeping the officers back.

Zach was half way up the track when the revenue men pushed through the smog and began firing. But the miller and his son were saved by the sacks they carried, which were being pierced by stray bullets.

They reached the highest point of the hill and floundered over the top to hide in the gorse and heather, where they lay still.

The officers, vexed at losing their prey, spread out searching the moor, then worked their way down the hill again to ransack the mill, scattering every item abroad in order to find the barrels they'd heard had been landed.

For the rest of the day they sought out each track and ditch, but finding nothing they eventually departed on their way, climbing into their boat and pushing off out to sea.

Zach quietly stretched his cramped limbs, afraid to make any noise or movement in case they'd left a lookout behind. When he ventured to peer out through the prickly gorse bush that he'd painfully thrown himself into, there was no-one about.

Then in the heavy silence he heard the miller's voice, "Mewan – you there?"

There was the sound of stones rattling down and the dishevelled figure of his son crawled out of a pile of waste rubble from a nearby derelict mine.

Zach pulled himself slowly out of the gorse, "Ebenezer, where are yer?"

A thicket of blackthorn quivered, its stark two inch thorns ready to ensnare anyone coming in contact.

"I can't move . . ." Ebenezer's voice quavered, "I'm caught on these darned thorns – you'll 'ave to get me out!"

"How the hell did you get in there?" queried Mewan. "Give us yer arm."

They had to pull away each branch, one by one, that had hooked into Ebenezer's clothes, as he gasped and yelled painfully at them to proceed with care.

Eventually they lay quietly in the softer heather getting their breath back.

"Well – where is it?" Ebenezer glared at his son.

"What?"

"The brandy – after all this palaver I certainly earned it!" his father demanded.

"In the well!"

"Haw – haw . . ." laughed Zach. He got to his feet, "Come's on – let's get to it . . ."

They made their way down to the mill as a breeze started to blow and the sea fog began to clear.

Mewan hauled one of the barrels out of the well and tapped it - and never had the golden nectar tasted so good.

They sat on the steps in the open doorway of the mill in the setting sun, while Zach searched his sack of flour, trying to find the stray bullet lodged in there, before Clarissa Rose came upon it when making the bread.

21

The gales came, and in the fierce weather with thick fog eddying around the Land's End and the Brisons island, a ship appeared rounding the reef, heeling and wallowing in the raging storm.

Zach and Seth with a group of fishermen stood in the shelter of the boathouse watching the vessel, her bows racing the mounting seas and riptides, as the rearing waves tossed her hull ever nearer to the jagged rocks.

They could see the crew struggling with ropes and stays and trying to alter course, lashed by the windswept rain, as the turbulent waves relentlessly drove her forward.

Mountainous ranks of hunch-backed waves struck the craft as she rolled and fell, and the tall masts reeled in the storm, her bow flinging white spray aside, as she surged onwards. Her captain, swaying with the trembling roll of the prow, roared aloud to the black dawn and his crew, as his ship drove hard into the gale.

Dark mists hid all sight of the land, and awe seized him as a roaring sea rose over the floundering vessel, and he cried out a prayer to save them from the storm.

But the stricken ship plunged onward and she struck the reef between the twin peaks of the Brisons, her pitching bow shattering on the jagged teeth. Her mast fell across the broken crags as the waters rose up in a tumbling spate, plucking mast and men away in the race of the swift swirling tide.

The crew struggled in the heaving seas, then were thrown upon a ledge of the larger Brison. Two figures, still clutching desperately to the rigging of the mast were swept onto the rocks nearby. With the surf breaking over them, they remained huddled on the ledge, frozen in the bitter wind as the dawn broke into grey morning.

Faint shouts blew on the wind as the fishermen on the shore tried to launch a boat to the rescue, but the sea was too rough and they were driven back.

When they looked harder at the island rocks, they could see the waterlogged figures of the seamen clinging haphazardly to the crags, while being pounded by the ferocious seas.

Soon the headland was dotted with watchers, but it was impossible to render any further assistance. The storm gained even more strength, the waves roaring with the shrieking of the wind around the crew in their wretched condition, as they tried in vain to avoid being swept off the ledge.

But with a desperate cry, the frozen fingers of one of the men slipped from his hold, as he clawed at the wet rock to save himself and he disappeared into the angry seas. The seaman near him flung out his arm to help, but the surf swirled around his waist and he was carried away with him.

Suddenly a tremendous wave rose up, towering over the remaining crewmen, sweeping them all from the rock. For a while the watchers on the shore could see no-one in the waters, and thought all was lost. Then Seth gave a shout, pointing at some splintered debris whirling by.

A boy, floundering in the tumbling tide had caught hold of a shattered timber and managed to stay afloat. He was engulfed and tossed by the racing tide for many hours, but by grasping the piece of wreckage kept afloat in the boiling surf.

Zach cried out, "We'll try again!" and with Seth, Jem and Rob, decided to take a chance to launch their boat through the breakers.

Watched by the crowd of villagers on the shore, they struggled against being dashed by the riptide, but reached the deeper seas beyond the surf, and began to make headway against the wind.

They were thrown and spun all ways, having to bail out the water flung into the boat by the waves, and trying to keep a lookout for the boy. Many times they thought he'd disappeared beneath the waters, but then they'd see him on the next wave.

The seas drove them forward at a tremendous pace until suddenly they were almost on top of the wreckage, as Zach shouted, "Get hold of 'im, Jem!"

"Haul 'im up!" cried Seth, and they leant dangerously over the side, being buried in cascades of salt sea, as they dragged him into the lurching boat.

There were ragged cheers from those anxiously watching as the fishermen neared the shore, riding the tumbling surf into the safety of the cove. Here they took the boy into one of the cottages to revive him with warmth, clothing and food.

There came a great deal of shouting from the watchers again, one of whom had seen some-one on the smaller Brison island. Through his spyglass, Seth could see two huddled figures clinging to the wet granite rock.

"One is a woman!" he declared. Jem snatched the glass from him, " 'Tis true – I see her long hair."

The pair had been swept off by the huge seas, and were engulfed by the undertow, then washed up on the Little Brison. Here they clutched at the rocky crevices, keeping a desperate hold on each other, until they found a ledge to protect them from the stinging spray.

During the day the lifeboat arrived, but after several attempts to near the Brisons, was forced to return. The storm continued its fury, so nothing more could be done until the following day. The revenue boat from Penzance slowly made her way around Land's End to a safe distance from the islands. A small boat was put off from her but had to pull back, so they let out her anchor chain and flew her colours to let those on the rock know that they would stay there and not desert them.

The night was long, without food and shelter with the salt spray cascading over the pair with each successive wave, and the wind bitterly cold.

On the following morning the wind had lessened and the lifeboat and several boats put off, but could not come near enough to the island because of the great surge of the tide.

Then the coastguard boat joined them and sent a line by rocket, which fell short of the rock and was then taken away by the current. The second line fired however, landed nearer to one of the shipwrecked figures who grasped hold of it and attempted to tie it around the woman's waist.

Zach watched from the boathouse, ready to try to launch again to help them.

"She's not going to jump!" he shouted. "She's afraid."

They could see the man encouraging and pleading with her, and she obviously came to realise that her only hope was to give herself to the angry waves, for neither of them would survive another night on the rocks.

With a despairing cry she leapt into the creaming surf and was pulled towards the boat.

The rocket was fired again and the man was successful in seizing it and tying it around himself. He was drawn towards the boat and over the side to join the woman, both lying bedraggled and exhausted in the bottom of the boat.

Seth had taken the boy home with him, and after a good night's sleep in the warmth of the cottage, he and Matt struck up a friendship.

The ship was bound from Bristol to the Spanish coast he told them, and he was Drew, cabin boy to the captain, and also sailing on the voyage was the captain's wife.

Drew had tried to comfort her when the storm broke upon them, but she'd crouched in terror in the corner of the cabin,

136

with dread in her heart at each shudder of the vessel lurching in the heavy swell.

"Poor woman," sighed Hannah Jane.

"But the worst thing is," said Zach, putting his hand quietly on Drew's shoulder, "that we've heard that the two people who were rescued from the Little Brison rocks was the captain an' his wife . . . "

"An' the officer said when they reached the shore," added Seth, "the captain turned to help his wife. Then he threw back his head and gave out a heart-rendin' cry to the wild wind, for she had succumbed to the icy waters, her spirit departin' on the turbulent seas."

The following weeks became calm and sunny. Drew joined Matt and his friends in their activities, until it was time for him to go back to his home in Bristol.

Then one evening as the wind started to blow strongly again, Zach was closing up the boathouse and in the darkness that had fallen, he saw a light on the Brisons and what seemed to be a shadow moving on the rock.

"Jem – Pete," he called, and they joined him on the slipway.

Rob said, "We'd better launch the boat again an' get out there, an' see who it is."

"There's nobody there – all the boats are in," replied Zach.

But he went out with the Pollards and they took the boat all round the islands, searching and calling out to anyone on the rocks.

They found no-one and came back to the cove to the group of fishermen that had gathered there.

"There's the light again!" cried Seth.

They all stood and stared, watching where the wild wind blew on the Brisons - and where the curling mists drifted by there appeared a flicker of light, lingering here, hovering there, and the shadow of a woman gliding from ledge to rocky ledge.

Zach uttered the words that were in the minds of all who were there, " 'Tes the captain's lady, hauntin' the night, searching fer her captain."

22

Across the dry barren landscape the relentless blaze of the African sun beat down in a shimmering haze, scorching the dry dusty earth.

Lisa Treggedda leaned against the doorway of the wooden cabin, weary of the heat. She longed for her father to come up from the small mine that he and Tremayne worked, finding enough gold now and then to have kept them there for the last few years.

Without warning, there came a loud roar from beneath the earth and a yellow cloud of dust blew out of the mine entrance. The cabin shook and the door was wrenched off its hinges. She was flung aside. She leapt to her feet, gathering up her skirts and ran out to the mine.

"Dad!" she shouted, "Dad!" She could see nothing in the dust that hung in the air.

Tremayne pushed past her, "In there," he coughed and rushed by.

She picked her way through the mine tunnel to the shaft, where lengths of ladders fastened to the shoring went down to the level being worked. The only sound came from showers of debris settling.

"Dad – can you hear me?" she cried.

There came an answer from the right of the tunnel and a movement.

"Where are you?" she groped forward, coughing with the thick air.

"Lisa Lyn? – it's alright – I can't move m'leg . . ."

"Can I make a light – is it safe?"

"Aye – come over 'ere an' see what you can do."

She took matches and candle from her apron pocket and lit it anxiously.

He was lying with one leg free, but the other disappeared under rubble where part of the roof had fallen in. He began to pull away stones and earth as she wedged the candle in a crack. He groaned as the weight shifted, then worked his limb free.

"That fool Tremayne lit the round afore I told 'im. He's always doin' that – where is he?"

"Up top."

He hobbled and climbed painfully up to the mine entrance.

"What a shambles!" he exclaimed as he saw the leaning cabin. He sat in a dusty chair and patted his bruised thigh.

"I think m'mining days are over. They were the end of yer Mother – she couldn't stand the heat, dear soul – an' near on the end o' me by the looks of it."

"What are you going to do then?" Lisa sipped at her mug of tea.

"We'll go back home, that's what."

"Home? – this is home."

"No, no. Though it's only one of many you've known. No, your real home. Treggedda – Cornwall."

"Cornwall – that's across the sea!"

"Aye, it is Lisa Lyn – an' it's yer home," he leaned towards her. "Yer Grandmother an' m'sister live there. They haven't very much – that's why I came out 'ere."

"What about the mine?"

"Let Tremayne 'ave it – the vein's almost petered out anyway."

He picked up one of his old books from the shelf and opened it. "There!"

"Dad!" Light sparkled from the stones that rolled out of the cut out pages.

"I bin gradually changin' the gold we've mined into these diamonds. They're easy to carry an' don't lose their value.

140

Now, you 'ave half of these an' sew them in your clothin'."

She protested, but he wanted to safeguard against loss. So she found her needle and thread and stitched a pocket into the inside of his shirt and did likewise round the waist of her shift.

Hannah Jane looked up from the letter she was reading, "Callum's comin' home," she declared to Seth, "after all this time."

Seth grunted, "Ha – he'll find the old house in a right muddle. Yer Mother's past tryin' to keep it fitty."

"I know, an' that Ambrose Liddicoat she keeps on, grows more ancient than they standin' stones up on the moors," she pursed her lips.

"They say he's gone a bit doo-la-li in the head an' all," he laughed.

Hannah sighed, "Well – he does his best fer Granny Treggedda, an' I know you an' Zach 'ave given a hand 'ere an' there, Eli too, but you all got yer own work to do."

"Are 'ee writin' back to Callum?"

"He's already on 'is way – daughter Lisa too!" Hannah hurriedly rose to her feet. "I'll 'ave to go up an' warn Mother, an' see if she's had a letter from him."

Lisa had never seen the sea before. The expanse of moving water astonished her, and she revelled in the fresh breeze that blew in her hair and in the salt spray.

One morning she awoke to a thick white mist surrounding them, unable to see the sky, and even the sound of the wave was muffled to her ears.

For three days they moved through the dense curtain, when those on watch suddenly saw the dark mass of another bow surging towards them, slicing hard into their port side.

Callum Treggedda flung Lisa's cloak over her and they

stumbled to the companion way, climbing the tilting deck.

He clutched at a hatch cover as the vessel rolled further and further onto its side and they were thrown into the sea. They held onto the cover as they came to the surface and lay there floating in the dark night, frozen to the bone.

As the hours went by he found it difficult to breathe.

"Hold on Dad – it'll soon be light enough to see," Lisa gasped through her clenched teeth, hearing his wheezing cough. But the accumulation of dust from the mines and pneumonia from the chilling cold, took its toll and he slipped away into the dark sea.

Lisa cried and called to him throughout the night, but found herself floating alone.

Momentarily, as the morning lifted the cloud, she heard a calling in the fog and thought it was him, but she couldn't see anything. Then again the crying came over her own, and as she raised herself, she caught a glimpse of a low shape in the trough of the wave. When she rose up on the next crest, she saw it again nearly on top of her, coming through the water.

She flung out her arm and grasped hold of it, almost wrenching her arm out of her shoulder, and saw that it was a large float on which small forms were huddled together.

They were children, five of them, she discovered later. Her limbs were numb and stiff, but she forced herself to move onto the sturdier raft.

Her strength began to weaken and she was giving up hope, when there appeared lights through the mist. A ship was bearing down on them. Lisa waved and shouted, until her voice started to falter, but the skipper of the fishing trawler had seen them and had already slowed his engines. A boat was lowered over the side and rowed towards them and they were hauled into it, and found blankets and hot drinks.

She found out from Emily that she, along with many others,

were on the other ship going to Canada, their families seeking work in the mines and on the farms, because of the scarcity of work at home, but Lisa knew that very often they were poorly paid.

They stared at her with large dark eyes, knowing that they couldn't go back and would have to begin the journey all over again.

The trawler was due in to Penzance, and early one morning they woke up to hear the gulls mewing above them in the bay.

While the children sat on the harbour wall watching the crew unload the fish, Lisa walked around the fishing town with its houses of beams and granite stone, and the even more huddled cottages of Newlyn and Mousehole.

She found herself going up the hill to the cliffs where she could see the magnificent sweep of the land going down to the sea. How her father would have loved to have seen this again. Her eyes misted over in grief for him and she wondered whether she should stay in this strange country or return to Africa.

She felt a touch at her side. She looked down and saw a small child gazing up at her and felt a hand in hers.

"Stay with us," Emily whispered.

There was a movement on her other side and a raised face looked up into hers.

"Stay with us," he breathed.

She turned round and found that they had all followed her. She looked at them sadly, homeless and lonely, like herself – but she had the means to help them, sewn around her waist.

"Come on – we'll go home together," she said, and they went with her down the hill.

With much ado and fuss she managed to obtain some money on one of the stones with a Penzance banker, and they had pasty pie at the harbour inn. They all clambered into a hired cab and set off for Treggedda, spending the entire journey gazing and leaning out of the window, looking at the splendour of the wild moors.

They approached the outskirts of Porthgwyna, and turning down a lane, came to a large iron gateway set between two granite pillars. As they halted, they could see they were closed and rusty and the driveway was overgrown and weed ridden. The house stood silent and seemed to be empty.

Lisa sent the driver away and pushed at the gates, and as they managed to squeeze through, the children exclaimed with delight at the wild jungle the garden had become and went whooping off to explore.

Old Ambrose Liddicoat heard their excited cries. He peered over the crumbling granite wall, his eyes darting from bush to briars. The garden had sprung alive with small life, running, jumping, leaping everywhere, and high pitched voices that shouted into the air.

He drew in a quavering breath and closed his eyes, and when he looked again, there appeared a figure standing by the leaning sundial, wearing a faded green cloak. The hood was half thrown back and from it tumbled a mane of tawny red hair, and he knew that it couldn't be, but it was a Treggedda.

His old heart fluttered and he climbed shakily down and set off to the village, his bowed legs stumbling along the road.

He met Zach and Seth loading up the van with Hannah Jane's fresh linen and Clarissa carrying pots and pans.

"What's up?" Zach caught hold of a tottering Ambrose before his legs gave way.

"Gypsies! In the garden!" he gasped.

"Gypsies?" Seth wondered about Ambrose Liddicoat's forgetful mind.

"Gypo's," the old man's head went up and down in his agitation.

"At Granny Treggedda's place?" Zach and Seth caught each other's eye.

"Gypo's!" Ambrose shouted, his eyes brilliant with excitement.

"We'd best go an' see," Clarissa pushed Hannah into the van as the men climbed in and they started up the hill.

Ambrose waved at Zach to stop when they came to the place by the wall where he'd been. They stumbled over the loose stone and brambles and looked over the wall.

Children were chasing and darting between the bushes, shouting and laughing, and Lisa stood there with them enjoying the sun that had broken through into a bright day. Her auburn hair, lifting from her brow by the breeze fell about her shoulders.

"Gypo's!" snorted Ambrose.

" 'Tesn't," retorted Seth.

" 'Tesn't Gypo's – 'tes a Treggedda," argued Zach, "I recognise the red hair!"

" 'Tes Callum's daughter – Lisa Lyn," laughed Hannah Jane. Clarissa began climbing over the wall. "Give us a lift up, Zach."

They clambered along the top and down the other side of the wall, calling out to Lisa.

She turned and saw the familiar tawny hair of Hannah Jane, so like her father's.

"Aunt!" she shrieked and flung herself into Hannah's outstretched arms.

Clarissa looked around for Callum, "Where's yer Father?" she asked.

Lisa's eyes filled with tears, "He's drowned at sea. We got run down by another ship in the fog."

145

"Oh, love," Clarissa wrapped her arms around the girl's slight frame.

"So, Callum never made it back home," Hannah said sadly to Seth.

"Seems so," Seth looked over his shoulder at Pengegon coming round the corner of the house towards them.

"Uncle?" asked Lisa.

He came up to her smiling, "I'm Andrew Pengegon, local doctor - not related to Hannah or Seth. I was with your Grandmother when your letter came." He looked at the playing children, "These all yours?"

"Yes – I mean no – but they're with me."

He laughed, "Come with me to the side entrance. Your Grandmother only uses a few rooms. The rest has been shut up for some time."

They went in through a small door which opened straight into a large kitchen. It was full of villagers who had heard the news of her coming. They came forward, welcoming her, smiling and chattering.

In an adjoining room, in a large winged chair sat a small elderly figure. Her white hair was drawn back and she wore a fringed shawl around her shoulders. She looked very frail, but her eyes were still bright and twinkled with tears when she saw the red hair of her grand-daughter.

"Lisa Lyn!" she pushed herself up free from the chair.

"That's what Dad used to call me!" cried Lisa, flinging her arms around her.

"Callum?" her grandmother looked over Lisa's shoulder for him.

"He's not here," Lisa's eyes too filled. "Sit down – I'll tell you."

So with both joy and sorrow, Alice Treggedda heard about the collision at sea and of the loss of her son and the gaining of

146

a grand-daughter.

"What's that noise outside?" she asked.

"That's the children."

"Children?" her head jerked upright.

"Yes. From the other ship. I brought them with me – I couldn't think what else to do."

"Good gracious! How are we going to keep them?"

"Look!" Lisa wrenched open her bodice, forgetting about the doctor, and tore out the pocket sewn in her shift. She emptied the stones into her grandmother's lap. The old lady gasped.

"It's part of Dad's savings. There's enough there and more for all of us," she hastily fastened her buttons. "Perhaps we can make this the children's home?"

"My dear, that'd be wonderful. It would bring the old place to life," her grandmother was delighted.

"You won't mind?"

"I can't live in this place on m'own. It's just going to ruin because I can't afford the repairs. Besides, you're family – you belong here."

Lisa laughed, "Wait till we've been here a few days – you'll wish for some peace and quiet."

"I've had all the peace an' quiet I need. Now I'm goin' to enjoy myself. Andrew, take Lisa Lyn round the village while we get some rooms ready fer m'new family."

Andrew led Lisa out into the kitchen. There was Milly, the blacksmith's wife, who used to cook at the house, and Morwenna, Fay and Sarah, the baker's daughters. There were the wives of nearby farmers, the vicar Glyn Owen, and gaunt Ambrose the gardener of course. There was also a tall gray-haired gentleman with a wide forehead, who bent to shake her hand.

"You'll be needed here, Paul," said the doctor. "This is Mr. Borlase, our schoolmaster."

"Yes, indeed," the schoolmaster nodded his head, "I shall be pleased to help you."

Andrew ushered the women into Alice Treggedda's presence, where she happily took charge.

The excited children milled around Zach as he turned to Seth, "Where's Lisa got to? Call 'er to put these kids to order."

Ambrose shifted on his creaking joints to a quiet corner, "Aw, – she's gone off."

"Gone off with the doctor," grinned Seth.

"Haw! He ain't wasted much time!" Zach winked at Clarissa Jane.

She flapped her apron at him, "Go an' do somethin' useful yerself – bring in some fuel fer the range."

"Shall we ride or walk?" Andrew asked Lisa.

"Walk, please. I can see everything then," and they set off down the lane that came out by the blacksmith's shop.

Crantok was there with his boy Luke, shoeing a horse. Lisa watched fascinated until the shoe was fitted, then from across the street came Manny Trehare with his two daughters, who kept the grocery store.

"It'll be nice to 'ave more youngsters around the village," he said.

They came to the Black Knight inn, and were pulled inside to a "welcome ale" by the host and his wife, Peder and Gwenny Pengelly. Here, there were farmers from the farms around and also fishermen from the cove. Faces, reddened and weathered by the wind and salt sea, with their firm handshakes and warmth, their voices filling the bar room with topics ranging from sheep to boats.

"You'd stay here all evening talking, if they had their way," said Andrew as they came out through the side door.

Lisa smiled happily as she looked back on the village, and

she knew it would be good to live and love and raise a family here.

Andrew took her arm, "It's growing dark. We must be getting back to your Grandmother or she'll be after me for spiriting you away from her."

The garden was strangely quiet, the children having been called in. But the house now glowed with light, and as they entered the kitchen it was full of bustling women and girls and delicious smells of cooking.

The doors to the hall and reception rooms were thrown open and a great noise of voices burst from them. The low beams were hung with hastily put up holly and ivy and brightly berried branches, as a welcome to celebrate this special occasion to one of their own. Almost the whole of the village was there and as they saw Lisa they raised their glasses to her.

Alice Treggedda stood amongst them, spritely and smiling, "Welcome home, Lisa Treggedda," she declared. "Welcome home."

Benna the fisherboy, sat on the busy quay, his fingers working the wands of withies in and out, coaxing them into the shape of the round lobster pot, that would soon join the others stacked in rows behind him against his workshop wall. He would make pots and mend nets, as the quay bustled with voices and footsteps passing by.

All day and every day, he would be there in his place, hearing the noisy workings of the fishing boats landing their catch, and the loading of boxes and crates for the fish market.

But although he knew each voice and sound, his world revealed only the blind darkness that he was born with.

However, he liked to work on the quay where he had all the varied sounds of the day around him, instead of remaining indoors at home.

Here, he could hear the different cries of the seabirds, even though he couldn't see them. He could hear the sound of the waves, whether they were calm or restless, feel the wind and sun on his face, drink in the rain, and hear the hollow calls from the seals as they played in the surf, or lay on the rocks nearby.

The school children brought him shells and seaweeds so that his fingers could explore the flutes and whorls of each variety, and he would hold them to his cheek and smell their salty brine. The children chattered with news of the village and he enjoyed their play and teasing.

His little neighbour, Jessica brought him flowers and leaves and would try to describe to him the colours of the birds and trees, and of the brilliance of the rainbow in the sky. It was then that he felt a great sadness, and wished that he could see her face as she laughed and the beautiful world around him.

At the end of each day when everybody had gone, he would make his way home to the nearby cottage, where he lived with his brothers, his mother Naomi and father Phineas Ladner.

Phineas and his brothers went out in their boat, the Gwylan, at dawn each day, sometimes with lobster pots to catch lobster and crab, and sometimes to throw the net for pollack and cod and sometimes for mackerel.

Quite often Benna would go with them, but he couldn't help them as much at sea as he could by making and mending the pots and nets for the boat. In this way he felt useful to everyone and he was soon making nets for the other fishermen as well.

He was working late one summer's evening, the sun setting into a glow, when he heard a low sighing and whimpering from beneath the quay wall. He crept cautiously to the edge and knelt down, feeling the stone with his hands and leant over to listen.

The whimper rose up again – a murmuring of woe, from below him, and there came a soft shuffling. He stretched out his arm and his fingers touched the damp skin of a young seal, where they often liked to lie basking in the sun on the ledge that ran along the side of the quay.

The seal lifted its head, uttering small cries as it squirmed and wriggled along the ledge. Benna knew that the tide was out and the sea would only be lapping the far end of the quay, quite a way for the small seal to travel on the dry stones, and it was a long drop below to the empty harbour seabed.

"Silly seal," he chided, as the soft mouth nuzzled his hand, "the tide has caught you nappin' this time."

He clambered carefully down to the ledge, then half-lifting the seal with his outer arm, he edged his way along the wall, feeling the stonework and guiding himself with his other hand.

The height that he couldn't see didn't bother him, so he only halted here and there to rest his aching arm, or when the seal began to wriggle too much.

He came at last to the end of the quay and there he could hear the tide washing around the foot of the wall. The seal could also smell the salty spray as it spattered against the boulders, and it began to thump its tail.

"Hold on," cautioned Benna, "or you'll take me with you."

He balanced himself against the wall, then urged the seal along the ledge which now sloped down at the end of the quay into the water. He heard the seal flopping excitedly down the slope, with little cries, to slide into the waves.

Benna wished that he could swim with the seal in its play and see its gleaming eyes as it bobbed up to the surface. He heard its soft breath sighing on the summer air, and shook his head as the longings that he often had flooded through his mind.

There came the whispering again and his surge of thought-waves swirled around him until he felt dizzy, and he shook his head once more, but he couldn't resist the call of the cool water.

Benna turned his head towards the sea, trying to pierce the darkness of his sight. He felt his way cautiously to the sloping end of the ledge, and flung himself into the water towards the seal. He could hear the sigh again on the sound of the waves as he swam towards it, breathing quickly with excitement.

A wavelet tossed its briny spray into the air, and the salt-laden droplets fell, stinging his upturned face and eyes.

He gasped as the droplets washed away the dark curtain from his sight and he saw – the brilliant colours of the rainbow arching in the cascading spray, the last dying glow of the sunset, the bright shiny eyes of the seal – and he cried out with joy, gazing in wonder at the sleek head in the waves.

He swam, splashing and turning in the water, and when he climbed up again onto the quay, he leapt and skipped high in the air, throwing his arms out to the coming night. He turned round and round, and saw the quay, his workshop, the huddle of cottages, the cliffs and rocks and sand in the rising moonlight.

Then he dived into the sea and swam up to where the seal hooted with excitement, flipping her tail and rolling over in the waves. They chased each other through the foaming surf, tumbling Benna in the water into the dark depths below and up to the surface again, until the dawn sky began to break and the sun threw its warm rays across the heavens.

The seal darted away and while she fished for her breakfast in the harbour, Benna sat on the quay gazing around him at the sunrise flooding the cove with golden light, and he thought he'd never known anything so beautiful.

As he watched, he saw his father and his brothers go out to sea in their boat with the rest of the small fleet, and though his mother came down to him with some food, he didn't want to go home, but wandered about the cove and cliffs, drinking in as much of the world as he could.

His friends were used to his wanderings, as he had learnt every step and turn of the village. But this time he saw the colours of the earth, the green of the grass and trees, the grey granite cliffs and the purple heath and wild flowers, and the blue of the sky and sea.

Then as he sat on the quay again, a lithe figure of light with wind-blown hair and sunny smile came running up to him. She flung herself breathlessly down beside him, putting her hand in his and offering him a spray of fern and flowers, and by her touch he knew it was Jessica.

She began to tell him the village news and describe all she could see going on in the bay around them. She often helped her mother Hannah Jane, in the chandler's when she was not at school, selling jerseys and smocks, rope, net and waterproofs and all items needed for working at sea, and she was contented just to sit quietly beside him, savouring the rosy glow of the sunset at the end of the day.

He listened to her happily, for although he could see it all he liked to hear her voice and watch her eager face.

Her eyes were the clear blue of the sea and creased at the edges when she laughed, and as he gazed deeply into the pupils she clutched excitedly at his hand.

"I sometimes think that you can really see me," she cried, "I can almost feel you can."

"Not really," said Benna, guiltily turning his head to the harbour, reluctant to spoil the moment.

She followed his gaze and cried, "The seals are here . . ."

Benna looked and saw that a group of sleek heads had joined the little seal in the water. He could see the myriad colours in the falling droplets of spray as they played and dived in the waves.

They sat and watched the seals for a long time, Jessica describing their antics to him, until she felt a chill breeze suddenly blowing across her shoulders. She shivered and Benna looked up and saw that dark clouds were gathering closer across the sun, and a wind was whipping the waves into white crests.

There on the horizon, he could see the small cluster of fishing boats lurching and surging home through the mounting seas. The wind began to whistle through the masts and rigging of the boats in the harbour, and they jostled and swayed against the quay.

"We're in fer a blow," warned Benna, and leapt to his feet, pulling Jessica with him. They began to carry the unfinished pots into his workshop, gathering together net and rope, and bolting the shutters on the window.

As they worked, they could hear the seas breaking against the quay and cascading over in fountains of spray.

One by one the boats came in, landing on the slipway with the winch labouring noisily, pulling them up out of the reach of the tide, and the bigger boats tying up to the lee of the quay.

"This squall came up from nowhere," shouted Seth, making fast the ropes.

Zach watched the last few boats rushing in on the creaming surf.

"Are we all in?" he asked, "I can't see Phineas . . ."

The dark clouds suddenly split asunder and the rain thundered upon the roof of the workshop in a noisy deluge. Benna and Jessica stood in the sheltered side of the doorway, peering out, trying to pierce the curtain of driving rain.

The vision was gradually fading from Benna's eyes as he saw the dark shapes of the seals appearing now and again on the surface, turning and swimming out to sea. He could see the green mass of water and the white whorls of the tossing waves as the seals dived.

Then in the distance he could just see the pointed bow of a vessel, its masts reeling against the stormy sky, and he knew it was the Gwylan, plunging vainly against the wind and tide to gain the safety of the harbour.

He could see his father hunched at the wheel, struggling to bring the bows round before the racing swell swept them onto the black rocks that reared their pointed teeth on the far side of the quay. He could hear the cries and shouts of his brothers, as they seized rope and line when the rushing waves smothered the deck in a welter of foam.

Then as the sky grew darker, Benna ran from the doorway, shouting into the shrieking wind. Jessica cried out to him as he neared the edge of the quay and ran after him, calling his name, while the icy rain drenched them both to the skin.

She caught up with him and pulled at his arm to stop him, but he stumbled on the faster, so she ran with him, hanging on to his shirt tail.

"Jessica!" shouted an alarmed Seth, going after them.

They reached the end of the quay and Benna shouted into the storm, waving his arms to the wallowing craft.

His father, flinging all his strength upon the wheel, strained to see ahead, but the murky veil of streaming rain that beat down on the waves blotted out all sight of the slipway.

As Benna watched, the boat rolled and drifted towards the reef and he screamed frantically into the darkening night. Jessica shouted with him as she searched through the swirling gloom for the boat.

Then suddenly, the rearing bows were racing towards them, Benna tore off his shirt and the wind seized it, whipping the white linen like a sail from his grasp.

To the crew plunging through the blinding storm, the shirt billowed out in a ghostly wraith and they cried out in fear. But Phineas wrenched the wheel over as hard as it would go towards the white signal and the boat heeled violently, sliding swiftly past the craggy reef and into the safe waters of the harbour.

With Benna's sight ebbing fast, the light of his vision blurred with the cool green of the deep as he saw the seals swim away out to sea. He clasped Jessica's hand sadly as the darkness came down again, covering his eyes.

But he discovered in the following days of the summer, that there were times when he dived into the sea and swam with the wash of the salt spray in his eyes, that for a short while he could see the rainbow in the surf, and the colours of the sky and sea and earth. The seals would come to play in the harbour and also bring their young, and Benna would hear their calls and watch them chase each other beneath the waves.

24

She walks the bleak moors in a long grey gown. She walks where she once walked aeons ago, where the winds are wild on the heather and gorse, and where the summer suns turn the bracken yellow and burnt amber. Where the breaking seas surge against the land, and the terns and gulls soar and swoop with their mournful cries.

Many still see her spirit as she walks where she once walked, from village to village of round crellas and huts of rugged granite walls, with roof covers of poles and reeds and dried brackcn.

Here she cooked with the women, baking bread ground from the ears of corn and baked on gredles of heated stones. Or cooked venison, fowl or fish on beds of flaming fern covered with steaming blackened stones and more layers of fern. The air was filled with the smoky fires and aroma that rose from the sides of the scorching segh, the savage deer.

Many enclosures were surrounded by gurgos, the fences that held their herds of beef, and flocks of sheep with the curling horn ranged over the moors.

And there too was the vau, the cave. Here they would lay their corn, cutting the ear from the stalk and storing it in the many recsscs of the cave. They smoked and dried fish, beef, fowl or venison, and stored and hung it to preserve in the cool subterranean caverns, against the hunger months of the year or times of danger.

The vau was a secret world of chambers and passages, going on and on and on down to the sea. With spaccs to secure cattle and sheep from marauders, to store food and water, and safe areas to hide groups of fighting men and the people of the village.

The vau was in every villagers' sacred oath to each other, to die with its secret place locked in their hearts.

She slept with them on skins of beasts, she talked with them, she tended their hurts and sickness. She washed their wounds from tribal battles and prayed over them when in death.

She followed the hunters through thicket and forest as they ran with their dogs after the bear, bull and boar. Over the moors, hunting the savage segh, the moose deer, their segh-dogs racing and giving tongue as they hurled themselves upon their prey.

She was with them in all their hunting, fowling and hurling. She stood with them silently in the dawn light, in the circle of standing stones of their ancient ancestors, and spoke with them when a council was pending and they made their vows to the rising sun.

As she calmed their fevers and bound their wounds, she drew them slowly from their idolatrous ways. She listened to the bards who spoke and sang their praise-songs, playing the harp, in praise of their heroes in prose and song.

And they followed her and walked with her over all Belerium, the Land's End, where the wild winds blew on the moorland and the shores were washed by the waves of the Celtic sea. The fame of Beriana became known far and wide.

So it was that King Gerent sent his chief warrior to her hermitage, with word of his much loved son Mark, who had long been sick with fever. To come quickly before his death, so that he may have her prayers spoken over him and so take them with him into the next life.

She walked many miles across the windswept heath where the granite cairns rose darkly against the skies.

When she knelt by the king's son she spoke her prayers and tended his trembling limbs. She stayed at his side day and night, washing his hot skin with the pure dew-water gathered from the rock basins.

Then one morning, as the dawning half-light began to move across the sky, his fever broke and he spoke his father's name. Gerent's joy went up in a great shout, waking and bringing his people hastening to his side, and an even greater noise and jubilation erupted from the thankful villagers.

As Mark improved each day, until he was himself again and running with his fellow warriors to the hunt, from far and near they came to pay homage at her hermitage.

And when she came to the end of her life, they laid her to rest in her long grey gown, and from that time they called that same place St. Buriana, after her name. And Elwyn the bard, took his old harp and sang a Celtic lament to praise her fame and deeds in melody and song.

For years many came to her shrine to worship her, to pay her homage with gifts and flowers, to pray and ask for her help.

And when the grey clouds sweep across the heath, there is seen her spirit in the long grey gown, walking the moors and merging with the haze of the swirling mists.

Tamsin and Jessica would walk over the moors and meet Gwennol who lived near the old hermitage, and in keeping with the custom, they would gather the wild flowers and herbs and bring them to the shrine as an offering. Gwennol would relate the legend to her friends as they sat on the grassy bank and gazed out over the cliffs that ran down to the sea.

It was when Tamsin was leaning against the gnarled elder tree talking with Matt and Jessica, at the same time keeping a lookout as instructed by Zach, that she looked up and saw in the distance a large group of men, running and silhouetted against the skyline.

"Run!" she cried, leaping to her feet.

"What's up?" Matt looked around.

"Run!" shouted Gwennol.

They ran across the heath to the village where the local men were hurriedly bolting the doors, and the women were running to and fro carrying coats and snatching up any morsel of food on the way.

"Hurry!" cried Gwennol's mother, thrusting a bundle into the arms of each child. "To the cave – hurry!"

They ran clutching their burdens, breathless with apprehension, Tamsin pulling Matt and Jessica along at her side.

She could see Seth and Zach coming up from the beach with some of the other fishermen, but when they saw the officers, Zach shouted a warning and they swiftly turned and disappeared below the cliff.

The pursuers were slowly advancing into the village, bursting through the cottage doors and barns as they went, looking for the contraband of which they'd had word had come in from the wreck of the ship two days before.

Gwennol's older brothers, Cadar and Gawen were amongst those staying behind to hide the rest of the wrecked ship's goods under floorboards, in cellars and under hay in the barns. They were joined by men from villages around, rolling the larger barrels into the recesses inside the vau, and then each man scattering over the moors and into the valleys.

As she passed by the hermitage, Gwennol sent up a fervent prayer to Beriana for her brothers' safety. Her mother pushed them into the throng of villagers disappearing into the hidden mouth of the vau, where they ran and scurried through the dark passages as fast as they could to reach the shore. There they would find hidden, numerous craft of every shape and size, in which they could escape out to sea. They could land in some of the coves farther along the coast, or even sail as far as the Scilly Isles, twenty or so miles away.

For a long time they could still hear the shouts and noise of the search, but it gradually faded as they went further into the bowels of the earth. They passed chambers hewn out of the rock where barrels and boxes were stored, and small recesses with seats for resting awhile. The further they travelled, a heavy silence began to fall around them, except for their hurried breathing and the shuffling of many feet.

Above ground, some of the fishermen reached Castle Treryn, where the towering rock rose up high from the breaking waves, with the three embankments that formed a defence on the fortified isthmus in ancient times.

But onwards pressed the officers and the fishermen disappeared quietly across the moorland.

Gwennol and Tamsin walked for a long time through the earth's darkness with Matt and Jessica, following others before them, until gradually they saw the blackness lifting. Shadows became figures and soon a clouded sky filtered into the sea entrance of the cave, that was washed by waves sweeping up against the granite sides.

The tide was high and surged quite a way into the cavern, so hiding it from the outer world. Each one waded up to the waist in water to clamber out onto the rocky boulder-strewn beach.

Low cloud and rain swept down on them as the craft were pulled from the concealed crevices and ledges, and were pushed out to sea.

Gwennol and her mother ran to where their father had hidden his boat. As they dragged it down to the surf, her mother suddenly gave a cry. She sank down onto the wet rock, the tears beginning to fall onto her hands. Gwennol rushed to her side, while the others held onto the craft.

"What is it – what is it?" she held her mother's arm.

"Your father – he might 'ave bin taken!" her mother started

to run back towards the cave, stumbling over the boulders.

"No – no!" cried Gwennol, "I'll go. Stay with the children," and she thrust her mother into the boat, lifting each child up to her and pushing them out through the surf.

"We'll both go," shouted Tamsin.

"An' me!" added Matt, eager for more excitement.

"You stay with Jessica," Tamsin held him back from leaping into the water again.

The spray splattered and tugged at their skirts as the girls turned and waded back through the cave's entrance, struggling against the tide of villagers still making their way out.

They walked wearily through the dark caverns again, keeping to the dank walls to avoid being pushed aside. Soon the crowded passages gradually emptied until they met only a few stragglers.

When they reached the entrance of the vau it was empty, and they saw that the last man had swept the earthy rab with bracken to hide their footsteps.

It was late in the day and dusk was falling. From the distance there came the sounds of cattle, but here it was quiet.

They went out beneath the darkening skies, looking for Gwennol's father and brothers in the village and over the moors. For a long time they searched but they met only those from other villages, and eventually they turned to go back to the cave.

As they neared the entrance they heard a rustling in the heath, a gasping sigh, and saw a slow movement on the ground. Tamsin drew her short knife, a blade she used for gutting fish, and she stood still, watching as the figure dragged itself along on one arm.

Then she moved towards it – and recognized the jacket. He looked up, saw the drawn knife in her raised hand and fell back into the bracken.

"Tamsin! It's me!"

"Jem?" she touched his shoulder which made him wince, and her hand came away warm with blood.

"It's Jem – from the cove," she called to Gwennol.

"What's the matter with yer arm?" she asked him.

"I fell on the sharp scythe as we were comin' out of the barn," he got to his feet and they helped him into the entrance of the cave, sweeping the ground after them, and on into one of the chambers to rest for the night where Tamsin tied her scarf around his wound.

In the morning they came out into the light and could see that he had a deep slash in the shoulder. Tamsin walked to the sanctuary, and sending up a prayer to Beriana, collected the pure dew-water from the rock basin.

Then she returned and cleansed his wound and Gwennol bound it with the freshly washed scarf.

"That feels much better," Jem seemed to gain his old cheekiness, and grinned at Tamsin when she found food for them to eat.

Later, they made their way together along the tunnels towards the sea. They came upon many people resting in the recesses with their children.

"I was with yer brothers," Jem told Gwennol, "but we separated on the moor. I didn't see them after that."

"An' m'Dad?" she asked.

He shook his head, "He went over Boscregan way with Zach I think."

At last they reached the mouth of the cave and came out onto the shore. They found room in one of the boats being pushed out to sea, and they watched the cliffs slowly recede into the mists as they rounded the headland.

"Hsst!"

Seth spun round and dropped down into the bracken, then cautiously raised his head. He couldn't see anything at first, then caught a faint movement in the heather.

He crept quietly, halting every now and then until he was near to the clump of heath, then sprang forward.

"Aw!"

"That you, Zach?" he cried.

"Who d'yer think – yer numbskill!" groaned Zach trying to move out from under Seth's weight.

Seth rolled off him and lay back in the bracken.

"I think they've given up," he panted, "they 'aven't got anyone, we'd 'ave heard the shoutin'."

"We're lucky then," Zach rubbed his unshaven chin, "I 'ope Tamsin an' the others got off."

"They're not interested in the women anyway. I don't think they found anythin' either."

Zach spat out leaf debris from the heather, "That silly codger, Truscott - asleep on lookout - till it's too late!"

"Here's Ellis," Seth watched him coming towards them.

"Casley and Treloar are behind me," Ellis told them, "an' Cadar and Gawen are down in the stream – in the rushes."

"Matt?" queried Seth.

"They're with m'wife in m'boat, an' Tamsin's with Jem," answered Ellis as they trudged over the moor, then each went their separate ways.

Seth and Zach came down the cliff path to the back lane of the cottage yards and gardens. Hannah Jane was hanging out the washing.

" 'Ave yer seen Tamsin?" she asked anxiously, "Jessica and Matt are with her, they took a picnic, but they bin out all night! Are they at your place Zach?"

"They're with Jem."

"I b'lieve they're comin' in now," Seth slyly caught Zach's eye.

"Ah," Zach winked at him. "Comin' in by boat."

"Dear life!" she exclaimed. "What'll they get up to next?"

25

The air hung close – no breath in the mizzen, and the blue of the sea met the blue of the clear heavens. The sun's rays glittered upon the wave and the restless tide raced swiftly along.

Zach pulled the line in strong quick strokes, eager to turn the boat towards the harbour, for the sea was unsettled – one moment still – the next a rolling mountainous curl.

There came a fitful breeze that sighed and stirred the canvas sail, and Seth could see the wreathing haze banking slowly into cloud.

"Ah, blast it!" he cried. " 'Tes comin' in quicker than we thought."

Zach flung the last of dripping hook and rope into the skip, while Seth, glancing at the sultry sky, turned the boat and set a course for the shore.

The curving waves changed a sulky grey and broke in crests of creaming froth, while the flutters of wind came in gusty spells that funnelled around the mast.

Then lightning flashed in a crackling streak and the heavens glowered over the sea, while the rumbling thunder split the air above the heaving waters.

A hooded wall of arching wave reared up with over-hanging spume which turned inward, then swept down, shrouding the deck in icy foam.

The boat reeled from side to side, shuddering through the tidal race, then rose up to meet the surge of the following rush of deep groundswell.

"Hold on!" shouted Seth, as they sank in a wallowing trough.

A shattering tremor ripped through the hull, amidst the white confusion of seething surf.

"We've hit Shark's Fin!" yelled Zach, searching for the hidden rock of the devil's make.

"No – we aren't that far," Seth turned the boat. " 'Twas Kettles Bottom!"

He leant towards the side in a moment's respite, and above the roar of the swirl he shouted and pointed downwards.

Zach, clinging to a spar, followed his gaze, and to their amazement there appeared a slender spire of sculptured stone rising above the waters.

He was spellbound, "We're above the sunken isle of Lyonesse!" he gasped.

" 'Tes an old myth," Seth braced himself against the swell, "I wonder what's thrown that up?"

There came a deafening sound and a vaulted wave of sheer momentum spilled over, blotting out the world around.

Zach thrashed about, but couldn't fill his lungs with air, and thought his last had come. He opened wide his water-logged eyes but all was blurred in a hazy light, the furious noise of the storm closing over in a silent void.

He felt his feet on rock, and looking down he could see he was standing on cobblestones. There rose up tier on tier, tall monuments and dwellings of gilded towers and graceful spires of a great and splendid city, set amidst a range of mountainous peaks.

Spires carved with fruit and flowers. Statues mused in wall and arch, encrusted with a thousand shells and garlands of sea daffodils. And all the myths that the old folk told of the beauteous vales of Lyonesse submerged beneath the stormy waves, were lying here in the ocean's depths.

The winding stems of sallow thorn and waving seaweeds, writhed and swayed around his limbs with curling tentacles of green. It seemed that he couldn't tear free. Their clinging tendrils pulled him forward towards a tumbling spate which foamed and fretted about his ears.

He cried out and wildly struck at the gripping fronds which held him, and heard through the rain of salt spray, Seth's furious voice.

"Leave off beatin' m'head !"

Seth had him by the scruff of the neck, struggling in the surf, to haul him over the side of the boat. The sea had calmed away and was its early quiet roll.

"I saw . . ." spluttered Zach, "I saw . . ."

Seth propped him up, with his great hands on his arms, against the hatch.

"What?" he exclaimed.

"I saw . . ." began Zach again, "I dunno what I saw!"

The boat had come through the sudden squall and was now drifting with the tide. They both sat back, spent, trying to regain their breath, before uttering another word.

"Well," said Seth at last, "when I shout 'hold on' – you hold fast, or you'll end up swimmin' ashore."

"Yeh . . ." Zach began, "but I saw . . ."

26

The west wind howled down the chimney and rattled at the shutters. Tamsin opened her window and leant out into the wild night. The rain wetted her hair and arms, but her curiosity was so intense that she felt nothing of the cold damp seeping into her skin.

She could just see lights moving through the driving rain, coming along the track that crossed the moors, and she heard Kathy calling out to her.

"Come away – you'm be drowned . . ."

She leant out even further as vehicles came to a halt and horses clattered into the yard, dark figures leaping down from their backs.

A tall head glanced upwards towards the window, and Tamsin saw the piercing glare of Rob Pollard's eyes as they swept over her. She stepped swiftly back, pulling the window closed.

"Isn't it exciting?" she said breathlessly. "There'll be a whole host of people here fer Feast Day supper tonight."

She rubbed her hair dry and peeled off her wet garments, wrapping the towel around her and shivered by the small furze fire. Tredinney Manor was very draughty.

The door opened and Hannah Jane appeared, "Aren't you ready, Tammy?"

"Yes, yes," she pushed her arms into the dress that Kathy held up for her. "Who are they – will they be at supper?"

"Don't be nosy, remember we're Aunt Lucille's guests 'ere," her mother turned to go, "and put a comb through yer hair, Tammy."

Kathy snatched the comb off the side table and pulled it through the chestnut tangles.

Tamsin shrieked as tears sprang from her eyes.

"Hoyden!" exclaimed her mother, hurrying from the room.

Suddenly, there came from outside harsh shouts. Tamsin ran past a bewildered Kathy and flung the window open again, and from the same way over the moors, came vehicles lurching into the yard, and another group of riders.

Her door was thrown back with a crash. She gasped as Zach stood in the doorway. He strode urgently up to the window and peered out.

Then he seized Tamsin by the shoulders, clapping his other hand over her mouth and backed into the drapes of the long curtain. She struggled, pulling her mouth free.

"Is it you they're lookin' fer?"

"Aye, an' they'll soon be lucky, me thinks," he growled.

Her eyes alighted on the old linen chest through a gap in the curtain, "The chest – quickly . . ."

He released her and she ran swiftly over to it and lifted the heavy lid. "In 'ere – hurry!" she could hear the pounding of boots on the wooden floor.

He leapt in and she closed the lid, draping her shawl over it, and sat on it. She beckoned to Kathy to pass over the hand mirror, and continued to comb her hair.

"Can he breathe?" queried her friend anxiously.

"S-sh . . ."

The boots thudded up the stairs and into the room. Two men burst through, searching with their eyes every corner of the room. Tamsin lowered the mirror.

"Nothin' 'ere," one muttered, and they ran out and along the landing. The two girls giggled and could hear them going to all the other rooms, then up the stairs to the next floor.

"They've gone," breathed Kathy. Tamsin began to rise, but immediately sat down again as another figure appeared in the doorway. It was Rob Pollard who'd glanced upwards at her window.

"Where is 'e?" he hissed. Tamsin twirled her hair round her finger, pointing at the chest.

"What!" he pulled her from the seat and flung it open. "Zach – Zach . . ."

Her grandfather started to rise up from the interior, "Sh! Pollard – I'm doin' well . . ."

"There's somebody comin'," cried Tamsin, and shut the lid down again. Rob looked quickly around the room, then pulled her urgently with him into the closet amongst the hanging clothes.

Kathy dragged the shawl over the chest again and began to shake out Tamsin's damp dress, humming an unsteady tune beneath her breath.

This time, four men reached the top of the stairway and burst into the room, rushing from wall to bed, to window drapes, to the large settle.

Then there came shouts from the hallway, and finding nothing of interest, they hurried down to the ground floor.

For a second time a large hand was clamped over Tamsin's mouth. She could scarcely breathe, and out of vexation bit the hard flesh.

"A-ah!" gasped Rob. "Vixen!"

She struggled to free herself but he held her tight.

"Wait," he whispered, "they're not gone yet." For a long time they stood listening to the tuneless humming of Kathy. Then from the window they heard the noise of the vehicles starting up and the clatter of horses riding away.

"There they go," breathed her captor. He pushed the closet door open and in the shaft of light, looked down from his height at her upturned face.

"Well, it's my little Cornish rosebud," he smiled.

"It's Tammy. Let's get out of 'ere," she replied, impatient to

171

be out of the stuffiness of the cupboard.

"Ah, Tammy," he smiled his slow wide smile again, "nice to meet up with you Tammy, on this Feast Day," and bending his head he touched his lips to hers.

She dimly heard Kathy calling and began to push against the strong arm that had encircled her waist. Rob inclined his head and looked deeply into the blue eyes with a steady glare. She drew a sharp breath and fumbled her way out of the closet.

She helped Kathy to lift the heavy lid of the chest, and the figure inside climbed out and stretched his legs. Rob strode across the room, "Zach, are you -?"

"Not a word, you girls!" warned Zach, he peered cautiously out of the door.

Rob laughed, "Rosebud, you'll be the only one who's ever sat on yer grandfer – an' survived! But – not a word . . ." he winked wickedly at her, then followed Zach out into the passage way.

"You'll hear strong words when Clarissa Rose hears about you pushing Zach into that chest," laughed Kathy.

"An' sat on top of him!" shrieked Tamsin.

"Quick, my shoes," she straightened her dress as nimbly as her nervous fingers could manage, and then they hurried down the stairway to the hall.

Clarissa and Hannah Jane were mopping up water and wet footprints left by the men, and Tamsin saw her aunt and cousins grouped around the huge granite fireplace that glowed with burning logs.

Then they sat down at the long oak table to eat, and as Tamsin lifted her glass of wine to her lips, she glanced towards the end of the table. There sat Rob Pollard, and she became aware of his hard stare and hastily dropped her eyes to her plate.

172

When next she stole a look that way, she could see how tall he was, head and shoulders above the men around him. His thick hair flopping over his forehead and his pleasant mouth in a wide smile.

During the meal a fiddler and two accordion players came and began to play, so that eventually some left the table to dance jigs and reels.

Tamsin recognised many of those who were talking to Seth and Zach, Truscott and Casley among them. She realised they must be up to something devious, but there were many informers about. Thus the searching of the house that very evening.

She became aware of Rob standing before her and he took her arm to dance.

"Tammy," he whispered, as they met in the middle of a turn.

"Rob," she returned and smiled up at him.

At the next step when his hand touched hers in mid-air, he clasped it tightly and leant closer so that she could feel his hot breath.

She hurriedly moved away at the end of the music, but he quickly drew her arm through his and sauntered towards the long window.

"Thanks," his eyes smiled down into hers, "Zach an' I."

She tossed her head, "I don't like bullyin' customs men!"

He laughed, "A loyal spitfire!" He led her back into the dancing, and by the late hour when she met up with her aunt she was breathless.

Lucille rose, "I want a word with you," she said, drawing Tamsin with her and bidding goodnight to their cousins.

"Now – I want to hear – all," she demanded when they reached her aunt's room.

"Nothin' – nothin'," Tamsin turned away.

"Rubbish! You'll do well to encourage 'im. He an' his

brother 'ave got their own boat an' I hear they 'ave savings in the bank."

Tamsin gasped indignantly, "I'll not be fobbed off onto any uncouth fellow!"

"Good!" smiled her aunt. "He's well known for his prowess in getting on . . ."

"With women, no doubt," replied Tamsin, "besides, he's at least seven feet tall. How can you pass me off to a – a – giant?"

"Easily! Your father has no money to speak of, an' your brother'll need the house when he's older, so then where'll you go?" she peered at her closely.

"Oh!" Tamsin pulled the door open and ran out.

During the next day, however, she found herself being sought out by Rob. He spent much of his time following the hunt and competing in the shooting contests.

He would find her in the gardens with the dogs and walk along with her, and Lucille would smile encouragingly.

She might have had second thoughts if she had known that Tamsin had demanded to know how to use one of the fire-arms.

Rob's eyes flashed humorously as he instructed her as to the aiming of the weapon, holding her lithe form against his while he steadied her arm, she giggling with a high shriek when the shot soared up over the trees.

In the afternoon he came towards the house with his own stallion, a Cornish cob, one of the Guinnilly breed, that he called Samson, and a small dapple-grey mare.

"We'll ride up to the moors," he shouted up to her window. "There's some good trout in the valley streams."

"I'll be down," she called back excitedly.

"Tammy . . ." Kathy wasn't sure whether this was 'proper', but Tamsin was already being helped onto the mare.

"I c'n lift you up with one hand," he jested.

"Don't dare," she cried, and she set off at a brisk pace. He leapt into the saddle and rode up level with her, watching her hair blowing freely in the breeze.

He led the way along the twisting path on the banks of the moorland stream, where the seagulls swooped and called and the wild hawks hovered and mewed their haunting cry.

"We'll find trout here," he slid out of the saddle and lifted her off the mare, holding her against him.

"I think I love you, rosebud," he said. Tamsin jumped back from him.

"No," she declared firmly. "Not so – an' I've a fearful temper!"

"Haw – haw," he laughed, "I'm glad you've warned me!"

He put his finger to his lips, "S-sh!" and crept quietly along the bank of the stream, being careful to lean over the water without casting his shadow upon it. Tamsin leant over his shoulder as he gently lowered his arm into the water. For several minutes he didn't move, then his hand slowly floated with the water and with a quick flip he scooped out a lively trout.

Tamsin shrieked as both water and fish cascaded over her, but fortunately it was shallow, wetting only his trouser legs and her shoes. She scrambled up the bank and surveyed a wet foot. He caught it in his two large hands and pulled off a shoe, setting it to dry in the sun.

He stroked the wriggling toes and the slim ankle, "Tamsin," he kissed her – and she kissed him in return, then she suddenly stumbled to her feet and ran for her horse. She climbed hastily up into the saddle and was galloping away into the wind.

He slipped the gasping trout back into the stream, shouting boisterously after her, and leapt onto his mount, racing with her across the moor.

At last, they came to the narrow pathway and she slowed her pace. She turned as he caught up with her and laughed at his wet trousers. He grinned and held out her shoe, which she'd forgotten in her haste, and he leant over and slipped it onto her foot. Then away they rode along the track, back to the manor.

That evening the festivities began to draw to a close, and Rob found her in the garden and drew her into the shade of the sycamore.

He twisted off the gold signet ring that he always wore on his small finger and dropped it into the white froth of her blouse.

In return she pulled from her wrist her lace 'kerchief and gave it to him as a keepsake, and he pressed it to his face, breathing in the perfume of her skin where it had lain.

Later, when she heard sounds of their departure she ran to the window and leant out.

As Rob passed beneath her, he pulled a red rose from his tunic and threw it up to her, and she stood there watching until they had disappeared over the horizon.

After the bustle of the last couple of days, she and Kathy were packing their belongings, getting ready to leave for home, when they heard shouting and the firing of weapons from outside.

She looked out cautiously from behind the curtains and there were men in the yard. Then from the corner of the house came a strange glow, and she realised that the kitchen wing had caught fire.

"Quick, Kathy – warn grandma! The house is on fire!" She snatched up her jacket and ran from the room. There were men now inside the hall, and thick smoke came swirling up from tables, chairs and panelling, making her eyes stream.

She burst into her mother's room, but it was empty. Hannah Jane and Seth had already left, so she turned to follow them but men were running up the stairs. She whirled round and sped to the end of the corridor, to the back stairs.

When she reached the kitchen she heard the ominous crackling of flames, and in front of her was a wall of fire. She searched from corner to corner for a way out, but the walls were blistering in the heat.

Then she saw the small pantry window and opening it as wide as it would go, squeezed herself through, falling into the rosebushes. There were people running everywhere, fighting with hoe and hayfork and anything they could find.

"Tammy!" Kathy caught her hand and they both ran out into the darkness of the moor.

Tamsin pulled her friend into a low cave that travelled into the granite wall and cliffside. After going some way they slowed and then sank wearily onto the ground.

"We're safe 'ere," she gasped, "Aunt showed me this a while ago. 'Tis a fougou, it goes right down to the shore."

Zach had decided to take a different route on their return home. This would throw off anyone following them and they disappeared into the valley that cut through the hill. Tamsin and Kathy were to be making their own way on their bicycles.

Rob and others with him who had come on horseback went across the open moorland, and it was from these heights that he looked back and saw the bright glow in the sky. He knew then that the manor was on fire.

He shouted to the men and they turned and started off for the manor. But although they rode far into the night, the grey dawn was breaking when they came upon a group of officers heading their way who gave chase, and they scattered and disappeared over the moorland.

When they eventually arrived at Tredinney the place was silent and part of the kitchen wall was blackened in the swirling mists that had come down.

Rob searched through the house, throwing aside the burnt timbers, calling Tamsin over and over, until his clothes and hands were stained with the grey ash.

Then he hunted through the outbuildings, and on one of the pathways he saw something gleaming. He picked it up and recognised the ring that he'd given her, fastened on a thin chain whose clasp had broken.

"Tamsin!" he cried, "Tamsin!"

She heard his call and crept towards the entrance of the cave and looked out on a scene of the smoking house wall.

There standing in the middle of it was the figure of Rob Pollard, shouting into the wild wind.

She shrieked at him in a mixture of tears and relief and he ran across the rough pasture and swung her up into his arms, kissing her smoky hair and ash-grimed cheek as she clung to him.

Kathy came up to them and held out Tamsin's jacket, "The villagers are comin' to help."

They turned and Seth appeared with his arm bound with a torn cloth, as some of the men began to throw aside the burnt timbers.

"Dad!" Tamsin ran to him.

"Follow Rob," her father urged her, "before they come back. I'll bring Kathy and the rest of the family."

Rob was suddenly alert. There was renewed shouting coming from the village. He caught her hand and pulled her along to the stables, and there they found the mare unharmed.

He helped her onto the horse, and leading the mare to where his own tired cob waited, he leapt into the saddle and urged it through the breached wall and out onto the moor.

There was an explosion and Tamsin felt shots flying past her, and they could hear vehicles and the thudding of hooves thundering after them, but their mounts sped into the wind that howled about their ears.

On the heights of Cairn Kenidzhek, with the wild hawks circling above them, they paused for a while behind the huge rocks.

"A gypsy, you are!" laughed Rob, and he grasped her tangled hair, entwining it round his hand.

Then, as they saw the dark figures of men still moving over the heathland, they set off again across the moor and their fleeting shadows were swallowed in the swirling mists.

27

Jem Morgan with the help of Casley, dragged his boat down the slipway, throwing in rope and tackle, making ready to go to sea. Behind him followed the Pollard brothers, pulling their boat down next to his.

"Fine mornin'," called Rob.

Jem scowled at him. He'd heard all about the festivities at Tredinney, with Rob making up to Tamsin, from her brother Matt.

"Sea's quiet," added Pete, looking from one to the other out of the corner of his eyes. He hoped they weren't going to resort to 'fisticuffs.'

"I'll give you a hand," offered Rob.

"No thanks – I c'n do without – an' so c'n Tammy," muttered Jem.

"Ha – Tammy's got a mind of 'er own," Rob replied.

"Leave 'er be," warned Jem.

"She's comin' fer a trip with me this afternoon," grinned Rob.

Jem swung round and caught hold of Rob's shirt front.

"Hold on!" shouted Pete, "That'll do no good!"

"I'll race you round the Brisons an' back," taunted Rob, "the one who gets back first, takes Tammy out fer a trip."

"Right!" agreed Jem, and he began throwing out pots and ropes to make his boat lighter.

Rob did the same, tackle and bait littering the slipway.

"Here – this's stupid!" argued Pete. "We're supposed to be pullin' pots. We'll miss the tide."

Jem pushed his boat into the water, Rob doing likewise and both leapt into their craft, started the engine and were cutting rakishly across the bay.

"You're both out of yer minds!" shouted Pete. He sat down on the nearest crabpot in frustration to wait until they came to their senses.

The early morning lay cool and swathed in silence, except for the wash of the sea that lapped and licked along the granite quay, and the call of the gulls. The first rays of the sun spread outward as each boat roared their vibrant discord to the morning.

They churned and scythed their way through the shallow water, and turned out towards the Brisons isle accelerating in sporadic tremors, skittering from flurried wave to wave-top.

First one, then the other, thrusting forward, skimming through the iridescent salt-spray, the creamy surge racing in their wake.

The sun's rays fanned into a murky dazzle, pulling cloud and moistness to the land, hanging in a swirl of misty tendrils and clinging everywhere to straining coil and spar.

Each could no longer see the other clearly, nor tell how far the distance marked between them. A brief respite would bring a hazy shadow that dispersed again into the wispy air, and through the leaden fog that was descending, an engine throbbing that waxed and waned above the harassed swell.

The mounting banks of green sea rose around them, falling steeply into deepening troughs, and the white plumes flecked the broken surface, throwing flying specks into the wreathing mists.

There came a low and muffled furore, growing with the agitating currents, whistling harshly by in spiteful rasps, lifting up and whipping round the waters and flaying boisterously against the heeling boats.

The writhing mists let fall their heavy showers, raking with their chilling icy grains. Flailed by the funnelling wind that soared and swooped, the climbing wave clawed along the bucking bow, while erupting mountainous seas arched their yawning chasms to plummet down upon the wallowing craft.

As the streaming cascade drained and parted each saw the other listing with the wind, a tangle of rope and cordage as the hulls veered sidewards in the roaring cavalcade of tumbling water.

The raging whirlpool swept the boats together, tossing them from frothing crest to frothing crest, and each caught sight of the other as the wild cross-current sped the craft away.

The black rocks of the island pointed upward, showing jagged teeth above the surf. The thunder of exploding groundsea broke and shattered against the towering cliff as the two boats rounded the end rock and raced for the shore.

A small group of fishermen were standing on the slipway, watching the two boats coming in, neither one giving way to the other.

"What the 'ell are they up to?" Zach muttered.

"Gone off their heads," snorted Seth.

The two boats swept into the cove and up onto the slipway.

"A tie!" shouted Pete. "Now p'rhaps we can get out to fish."

Tamsin ran along the cliff path and down to the shore.

"You're both crazy!" she shrieked.

"You comin' fer a trip wi' me, then?" smirked Rob.

"Not with 'im – I'll take yer," Jem leapt onto the slipway and moved towards her.

"Boil yer head – both of you," she swung round and stalked off.

Jem and Rob grinned slyly at each other.

"That'll learn yer!" laughed Zach.

28

Clarissa Rose sat staring into nothing, her mind and body frozen to a sudden chill, scarcely able to take a breath.

"Ah, no! I don't b'lieve it!" she whispered, as she listened to the sombre voice coming from the wireless, declaring a second war between England and Germany. "Not again!"

Zach stood, leaning against the dresser, his mind darting between thoughts of his sons and relatives who would be caught up in a second catastrophe.

Josh had brought some fruit over to his mother from the greenhouse at Trevarrick.

He leapt to his feet at the news, eager with the thought of going off to foreign parts, wearing a uniform and brandishing a weapon.

Zach glared at him to stay quiet, as Clarissa gazed at her youngest with an anguish that brought tears to her eyes.

"I'm too old," muttered Zach, "but I c'n do a desk job."

"Oh, Zach," she sighed, "all the fishermen'll be needed to bring in food for the country."

"Seth'll be alright then. They won't want 'im at his age anyway."

He opened the kitchen door, "I'll be off down the cove – see what's goin' on."

"I'm with you," Josh rushed out after him, keen to hear what others were going to do.

They found some of the fishermen standing in groups at the top of the slipway. The younger ones pacing around each other, waving their arms with the excitement of having a chance of leaving home for a while, and going to far off places.

Zach joined the older men, all who had been through the previous war, and knew it was far from what the younger men imagined it would be, the latter being children at the time and had only heard about the hardships second hand from their elders.

Clarissa hurried into Hannah Jane's kitchen where she found her solemnly sitting in the fireside chair.

"What're we to do?" she murmured.

"I can't b'lieve they men in Germany are so stupid as to 'ave another war!" exclaimed Clarissa.

"Or ours," Hannah pushed herself up to pace from room to room. She glanced out of the window and saw the figures of the village women and girls worriedly talking around the cottage gates.

Nearing the end of the month, Zach came back from Penzance with the news of queues of young lads from all over the area, signing on for the services.

"An' you?" asked Clarissa anxiously.

"Not even for a desk job," he said gloomily.

"So it should be. I don't know what yer thinkin' of. You know what it was like last time."

She breathed a sigh of relief, but when Josh came in later in the day, with "I've done it – signed on," she listened to him with a heavy heart.

"We've all got t'do our bit," said Zach.

Most of the lads in the cove had enlisted for the navy, but those from the farms around were signing on for the army.

"But what about Trevarrick and the farm?" cried Clarissa.

"Wenna and her mother'll look after the house," Josh replied, "and her dad, Jim Treneer, will carry on workin' the farm with his son."

"Oh, Josh, I'm feared fer you," she sighed.

"I'll be fine," he grinned, "the Pollard brothers are goin', an' Jem, Truscott an' Treloar were signin' on there too."

184

"An' what about Wenna, what does she feel about it?"

"She'll wait fer me. An' the pay'll come in just right fer us."

"There'll only be us old'uns left in the cove," grumbled Zach, "Leah is goin' fer the army, an' so is Mewan an' Cadar. Ezra's Simeon is staying. Both of them'll be needed down the mines fer a while."

He swung round as Hannah Jane burst in through the door.

"Where's Tamsin?" she cried.

"Oh, dear life! Not 'er too," gasped Clarissa.

"Don't be daft, both of yer!" Zach pressed Hannah into a chair. "She's too young."

"I'll make a pot of tea," stated Clarissa, "or we'll all end up nervous wrecks."

When brown envelopes were delivered by Jacca, trudging up and down the lanes from cottage to cottage, each contained orders for those enlisted to report at Penzance railway station.

The platform was crowded with families and friends wanting to see them off, many with tears and dread in their hearts.

Zach shook Rob and Pete Pollard by the hand, wishing them luck and flung his arm round his youngest, Josh.

"Keep yer head down, lad," he said, remembering the old saying of the last war.

"See yer, Dad," Josh grinned at him as Clarissa held him tightly against her.

"Get back home safely," she said sadly as he turned into the embraces of Hannah Jane, Tamsin and Jessica, while Seth clapped him on the shoulder and Matt took his hand and held on to it.

"I'll be alright, Ma." He turned to Wenna and held her closely, whispering to her, then climbed into the carriage and leant out as others pushed their way passed him.

Jem stood stiffly, facing Tamsin while his parents went to

185

have a word with Clarissa and Zach.

"Well – this is it," he said, suddenly feeling bereft in spite of the crowds.

"Look out fer yourself," she touched his hand.

He hesitated, then asked, "Er – will you write to me?"

"If you want."

"I'll send my address when I know it," he said eagerly as doors began to slam and the train slowly started to move.

"Get on!" she cried.

He leapt aboard, pulling the carriage door shut and hung out of the window.

She kept pace with the train, then impulsively leant forward and kissed him.

He suddenly smiled, and she waved until he was gone from sight as the train rounded the corner out of the station.

"It's alright love, they say it'll be over by Christmas," Seth let his arm rest warmly across her shoulder.

29

Everyone could see that it wouldn't be over by Christmas however, and for many it was a bleak festivity with one or more of the family and friends away.

Clarissa Rose had received one short letter from Josh who had headed his letter, 'Somewhere in England', though they all knew that it must be Portsmouth. She had replied back with all the local news, but had been warned not to mention places.

"It's impossible!" she declared. "How am I to tell 'im what's goin' on without sayin' anything?"

Zach laughed, "You know everythin' is read through an' they'll only block it out!"

Tamsin had heard from Jem, but he didn't say very much and she would stand at the gate waiting hopefully for the post if she had a late start at the farm, when Ben took over the milking.

There were rumours on and off during the next year that troop carriers and shipping had moved out onto the high seas, so any letters and news were delayed by months.

She was shading her eyes with her hand against the bright sunlight one morning, while the wind tangled her hair and wrapped her skirt about her. The cottage, tucked away under the granite cliff was partly sheltered where the breezes from the sea whistled around the eaves.

She could see the small figure of Jacca trudging along the winding path, and as he came nearer, could hear his panting breath.

"These lanes are getting steeper every day," he grumbled as Hannah Jane appeared at the door to take the post.

"I've the kettle on fer some tea," she said, "I expect you could do with it."

She held out a letter to her daughter, smiling, "For you

Tammy," guessing who it was from, as she and Jacca went into the cottage.

Tamsin took it with her up to the top of the cliff, and sat in a sheltered nook overlooking the cove with its variety of fishing boats.

The sea in the bay sparkled blue in the bright day with the lighthouse silhouetted against the sky, as she leant against the granite rock and opened the letter . . .

' . . . this shore, Tammy, is all barren rock an' the sun is burning. Just a yellow orb in the sky - it's scorching.

A hot wind is blowing over sea and land, sweeping the dust across the plain – I can't tell you where I am – but the sand dunes ripple and shift like the waves on our shore.

As I walk along the deck - I can't tell you the ship's name - the air is all shimmery.

I think of the cold white surf of our Celtic sea, throwing itself against the granite cliffs, an' the cool winds blowing across the quay.

Tammy, will you write to me soon an' tell me if you still think of me - I don't know when I'll get your letter, when we're at sea.

Though I'm hundreds of miles an' more away, write an' tell me if you'll wait for me.

The noise of guns are like thunder. The shells scream overhead, ripping the skies with flares and fire.

We carry the wounded down below on stretchers an' I c'n hear their cries from below in the sick bay.

When it goes quiet for a moment I think of our little fishing fleet out on the Atlantic swell, pulling line an' net an' lobster pots in the fresh westerlies.

I wonder if my boat with Howie in charge, is fishing well, while I'm out 'ere . . .'

Tamsin looked up, "Good grief!" she whispered. "He must be 'aving a bad time – to write all this."

Her heart grew heavy with sadness as she read on, but there was the glimmer of hope that he was still alive to write to her.

She walked down to the quay and watched the boats unloading and taking on board bait for their next trip.

Zach and Eli had been made air-raid wardens, each doing a turn on alternate nights.

"I'm goin' to wear m'legs out, trooping up an' down these lanes," muttered Zach who was just used to walking the length of a deck, "though what planes are goin' to come over an bomb us 'ere, I dunno. They'll all be concentrating on Plymouth an' Devonport docks."

Seth snorted, "You still got to check that everyone's got blackout curtains at their windows, an' ain't showin' any light."

The women of the village had been into Penzance and practically cleared the shelves of black dye, and were busy in the kitchens with dying old curtains and any pieces of cloth that they could find, swirling, dubbing and boiling them in tubs of the black liquid.

Tamsin ended up with stained hands and dark streaks in her hair, from the bubbles that splashed out.

"The enemy's not goin' to see you in the dark, that's fer sure," laughed Zach, escaping from the rancid smell that filled the kitchen.

The garden washing lines were festooned with the black flapping material during the following weeks.

The whole village was blacked out at night, looking empty and desolate thought Zach as he made his rounds.

Lights or oil lamps as some still used, showing from the cottage windows and from farmhouses scattered around in the distance, always brought a warm feeling to those coming home at night. As he made his way through the dark lanes, his thoughts wandered to all those young lads who'd gone to join the services and were now in foreign lands.

Half way up the hill he saw a glimmer of light, "Winnie Harvey, I'll be bound," he guessed as he went through the side gate and tapped on the back window.

"You're showin' a light, Winnie," he called out as he opened the door.

"Zach! – You sure?"

"Come out 'ere an' look," he answered.

She followed him round to the front of the cottage, "You'm right," she said. "It's that old cloth I dyed black, it's got a split in it."

Zach sighed, "Well, pin it up fer now or shut yer light off altogether."

"I will an' I'll darn it in the morning," she promised, "g'night."

" 'Night," Zach went on up the rest of the hill and headed for home down the back lane.

"I'll be glad to get off m'feet," he grumbled, "Ah – not another!" as he saw specks of light coming from behind old Gracie's window.

He quietly opened the door which she never locked, for being nearly ninety she was hard of hearing, and her neighbours would come in at any time of the day and help out in the cottage.

"Gracie," he called, "It's Zach 'ere." He went up to her where she was dozing over her knitting and put his hand gently on her shoulder.

She raised her head and smiled at him, " 'Ello – you'll 'ave a drop o'tea?"

"You got a light showin'," he said, miming with his hands so that she could understand.

"What's zat? Oh - dratted curtains are fallin' to bits. A darned nuisance 'aving to put 'em up, all 'cause of they foreigners," she grumbled.

"I'll see to 'em," Zach went to the window and pulled at the curtain to close the tear, which only widened the rent next to it.

"Gor 'elp me - this is hopeless, 'tis lit up like a Christmas tree." He tried arranging the cloth in different ways, but it came away from the top.

" 'Aven't you got anythin' else?" he asked.

"Only got m'black skirt," she cackled, "but I 'ave to wear that tomorrow."

"Where is it? Give me some pins an' I'll pin it over the holes fer now," he stood on a chair, "Clarry'll be in tomorrow – I'm sure she's got somethin' you c'n 'ave."

And when he got home in the early morning as the dawn was breaking, he stumbled into bed, glad of a few hours sleep.

30

"I'll 'ave to look in the attic again an' dig out the rest of they old curtains," said Clarissa, when Zach told her of the state Gracie was in.

"She'll be arrested by that group of Home Guard that's settin' up," he warned. "They're itchin' to get their hands on somebody."

Clarissa and Hannah Jane began the rounds of their neighbours, getting them to have another search for spare curtains.

"Any old pieces'll do," they were told, "we'll die 'em and there'll be plenty fer anybody else who's in need of 'em."

So the boiling up of boilers began again and she and Hannah Jane went round to Gracie's to hang better blackout materials in her windows.

"You'm angels," sighed the old dear, "I can't get up they steps no more – but I c'n get 'ee a pot o' tea."

Tamsin would come home from the farm, tired out at the end of the day since Leah had joined up, as she and Ben were doing much of his work as well, but there was news of a couple of Land Girls coming to join them, which they both welcomed.

When she had time and the evening was fine, she'd sit at the cottage window looking over the bay and write . . .

' . . . I'm sitting here, Jem, at the window with the sun going down in a lovely sunset. I'm always thinking of you. My thoughts are winging over the sea for you to come safely home.

I still walk the cliffs and hidden creeks that we knew and where we walked along the rocky shore. The purple heather and yellow gorse are out early this year on the cliffs and on the steep banks of the moor and heath.

This morning the blustery west wind was blowing with the seagulls crying their mournful calls, swooping and generally making a racket in the harbour.

The boats were out fishing, but yesterday Howie in your Seamaid came in well-laden, as the mackerel are now shoaling. The bay was full of swaying masts rigged with yard and rope as the boats rounded the headland of Pedmendhu on their way back.

Dear Jem, I'll wait for you . . .'

Seth pushed himself up from the table and settled the khaki cap on his head.

" 'Ow's that?" he asked.

Hannah Jane straightened it, " 'andsome," she remarked, "yer m'andsome soldier boy."

"Well, got to do m'bit," he smirked. He'd joined the fishermen, miners and farmers and other workers who were essential to keeping the country fed and running, who were determined to guard the homeland with the numbers of other Home Guard groups around the country.

"There's the odd enemy plane comin' over at sea – lost their way I s'pose. But when they see us, that don't stop 'em from shootin' off at us, even though they c'n see we're fishing an' not armed. We got to throw everything aside and duck down when we see 'em comin'!"

Hannah drew in a sharp breath, "That's bad."

"Zach c'n tell what type of planes they are, an' when he shouts 'Duck!' we flatten ourselves pretty darn quick!"

He was off for the evening's training session even though he was tired from the day's fishing, but he'd got an easy day the next day, not having an early start.

"Because I've got the motorbike, they're goin' to use me as message boy between headquarters at Land's End an' Penzance an' Newlyn groups," he stated importantly, "I'll get free petrol too, which is handy."

"I'll 'ave the kettle on, but I'll leave yer supper out if yer late," she could hear him kicking over the engine as she closed the door.

Seth rode up the hill and over the moors, guided by the hazy moonlight and the shaded dimmed lights of the motorbike.

"Good job I d'know the lay of the land," he muttered to himself.

They were guarding the small Land's End airport that night, which was used for light aircraft training and also to fly over to the Scilly Isles, some twenty miles distant.

When he came up to the gates, he was challenged by Casely and Davy Pender who were on duty and whose shift he and Ben Pender were to take over.

"Ben can't get 'ere," Davy told him. "He's got a cow calving, so Eddy'll join Viddicomb in guardin' the perimeter an' area around it."

Eddy groaned, "M'legs'll be worn out by the end of m'stint."

"No help fer it," said Davy, "Seth an' Jacob'll be on the gates instead."

Eddy picked up one of the rifles put out for him, and with Viddicomb set off round the airfield, the miller going eastwards and himself westwards.

Seth and Jacob stood at the entrance to the airfield, where the others gathered inside the hut they used when the shift changed over.

The moon had disappeared behind cloud and the night had become cold and dark. They walked up and down along the road to keep warm, meeting up every now and again, Jacob muttering his grievances against the night, the cold in his aging bones, and the enemy for keeping him from his warm fire at home.

It was while he was at the gatepost, with Seth patrolling the far corner, that a dark vehicle appeared showing no light, and a figure came towards him.

"Password!" growled Jacob, brandishing his weapon.

"You know me, my man, let me through!" came the terse answer.

"Password!" Jacob repeated, "You'm testin' me, I d'know."

"Let me pass!"

Old Jacob Pendrea knew his training and thrust his barrel at the man's throat and held him fast against the gatepost.

"Password!" he hissed and stood his ground.

Seth was making his way forward when he saw the vehicle and approached it with his weapon raised.

"Password!" he challenged the driver who was standing stiffly at the side.

"I dunno!" he gasped. "But yer mate's got the sergeant pinned up against the post!"

Seth shaded his torch and shone it briefly on his face, then at the two figures by the entrance and recognised the sergeant from the Penzance group.

"Dear Lord!" he groaned, "Jacob! You've got the sergeant there – let 'im go!"

" 'e 'aven't given the password," Jacob demanded, not moving.

"Sir, it's Lighthouse," prompted Seth.

"Lighthouse," gasped the officer.

"Ah – yer took yer time!" Jacob lowered his weapon and saluted him.

"Pass!" he grinned.

Seth raised his eyes skyward, "Come wi' me, sir, an' I'll take yer to Davy Pender, he's in charge tonight," leading him into the guard hut.

" 'Ello Sir, you didn't warn us you was comin' tonight!" said Davy.

"Surprise visit – thought I'd catch you unawares. That crazy old man you got out there had me almost strung up against the post!" the sergeant spluttered.

"Ah, well - he didn't know it was you, an' you should've known the password," said Seth.

"I'll have to mention this incident in the log book you know."

"As an example of us all being alert an' of Jacob doin' his duty of course," suggested Davy, looking him straight in the eye, determined that the sergeant was going to make a good report of his group.

"Ah – of course," the sergeant was already on his way out, grumbling at his driver as they pulled away.

Which was fortunate timing in that he was out of hearing of the guffawing that came from the hut, when the fresh shift arrived to take over and were given an account of events.

31

It was late afternoon that the revenue man came to the cottage. Tamsin was up in the top lands with Ben moving the flock of sheep into fresh pasture, Zach and Seth were out at sea, so it was Hannah Jane who answered his knock.

He wanted to know the whereabouts of several neighbours around, including amongst them Zach and Casley. He was also inquiring about boats, who owned what and where they were moored.

Hannah answered to the effect that she was too busy to keep her eyes on her neighbours every five minutes, but as far as she knew she'd seen a few of them about now and again. As to boats, she didn't know anything about them, being a landlubber.

Just as she came to a break in her tirade and took breath to carry on, Tamsin came through the gate and the officer thankfully crossed over to her and repeated his inquiries.

She agreed with some names of fishermen in the cove and some who also fished from Newlyn harbour, knowing that he knew these anyway.

"And Casley?" he asked.

"Yes," she said in a level voice, "he's moored in the cove, I b'lieve."

When he'd gone, she felt panic. If the revenue were still not going to let the matter drop of what might have been hidden away after all this time, her grandfather, Casley and others would have to be careful shifting it.

She ran up to Zach's cottage, but he wasn't back from fishing and there was no sign of her grandmother. When she returned home it was to find that Jem and Pete had come home on a short leave.

"You're back!" she joyfully shrieked, but they were sombre-faced and her mother was holding Pete against her in a sorrowful embrace. Tamsin looked from one to the other.

"What is it?"

"Rob's gone!" Jem's voice was hoarse with his sadness as he held her gently.

"Oh, no! Oh, Pete!" Tammy flung herself at him, the tears welling from her eyes.

"Shot – in an attack," he mumbled, lost now without his brother. They'd always done things together, played, worked, and went to sea together.

Hannah opened a cupboard, bringing out the bottle of brandy she always kept handy, and poured out a generous measure, pressing it into his hand.

"Sit down and get this down yer," she said, "it'll ease yer heartache."

She held a glass out for Jem, "You'll need some too, to help 'im get through this."

"Oh, this war – it's terrible!" cried Tamsin, wringing her hands.

"I'm goin' down with Pete to his mum," Hannah picked up a basket with the brandy and bread from the table, shrugging on her coat and took Pete out with her.

Jem held Tamsin briefly, "See yer later," and left with them. She ran out, her eyes blurred by tears, and on up the stony track to the cliff top, where she stood gazing out over the sea to the horizon.

"Why, why?" she cried out in anguish. How would Pete cope without Rob beside him? She wandered for miles along the cliffs before she sank down exhausted in the heather.

The day was pulling in when she began to feel the chill in the air, and suddenly remembered the revenue man.

Hastily, she cut across the moor to Zach's cottage, which

was still empty, but his small car was there. She knew he wouldn't mind her borrowing it to drive over to find Casley, providing there was enough petrol in the tank, so she looked behind the back door where a variety of keys hung and found those belonging to the car.

She set off up the hill and over the moor until she pulled up in front of Casley's cottage, but there was no sign of anyone around.

"Casley!" she called out, jumping over the crumbling back wall into the overgrown garden, but the windows stared morosely out onto the heath.

On the way back she stopped at Jem's yard, but the green van that his father had recently bought from Eli's cousin wasn't parked at the side of the gate nor in any of the outhouses.

Then she heard the sound of an engine going up the steep shortcut, which wound up behind the cottages and came out onto the lane. Between the gaps in the willows at the far end of the field, she could see glimpses of the van being driven, she was sure by Jem, bouncing along the rough track.

She scrambled back into the car. If she hurried perhaps she could catch up with him, and she sped down the lane, following it where it went out across the moors. Here it twisted and turned between the cairns and crags and granite boundary walls, and going up the slow rise of Bound-an-a-Haf, she saw the van's roof sliding away in the distance ahead.

But when she came hurtling round the bends and down to where the lane met the Penzance road at Crows-an-Wra, it had disappeared again.

She swerved round the granite cross that stood by the way, and turned towards Penzance, hoping that Jem was heading for the quay. The light was gradually going as the evening drew in, and the hills of Bartinney and Carn Brea stood out darkly against the fading sky.

Past Catch-all, swooping down again into the coomb and over the narrow hump-backed Buryas Bridge, she caught up with two cars and saw the van in front of them. She drew out to overtake but the road was too narrow and turned almost back upon itself, so she pulled in intending to wait until it straightened out, about a mile ahead.

But when she reached that stretch of road the car in front of her began to overtake the other, so that she was still two vehicles behind the van.

In desperation she accelerated and scraped past the last car's bumper, its driver mouthing furiously at her as they rounded a sharp corner. Luckily the way was clear on the other side and she surged forward upon the next car, which only aggravated the driver in front of her, so that he went the all the faster, preventing her from moving up on him.

Jem seemed not to see her, and as she glared through the windscreen, she could see a vehicle with uniformed officers drawn up on the side of the road past the wooded grounds of Trereife. With a quick turn Jem had swerved off the road onto the side lane leading down to Newlyn.

The driver in front slowed when he saw the officers' vehicle, and there was a screech of brakes as Tamsin pulled at the wheel and shot across the road behind Jem.

She didn't catch up with him however, as he'd pushed ahead and rounded the turns of the lane into the village. Here he didn't cross over towards the quay as she expected him to, where the masts of boats and trawlers filled the harbour, but went over the bridge to take the road along the promenade. The sea in the bay was choppy and the rock of St. Michael's Mount rose up from the restless tide.

As she stamped her foot on the accelerator to catch up with him, she saw his tail lights flicker as he disappeared round the dock turning. A truck pulled out behind him as he carried on past the railway station and Tamsin craned her neck to see round the tailboard of the truck, just catching sight of him as he took the turning by the horse trough at Chyandour which led to the small village of Gulval.

This was not his intention, as he pulled away to the left, climbing upward towards the moors. As Tamsin followed, leaving the truck to carry on along the main road, she glimpsed dimmed lights behind her which must surely belong to the official vehicle.

Urging her car along for greater speed she drew away from the lights. The crossroads of Heamoor and Madron came up and she turned right sharply towards the moor road, then pulled in under the dark spread of trees that hung over the roadside.

She switched off the engine and lights and watched as the following car turned towards the village of Heamoor. Then she started off again towards Madron and saw the van's lights speeding over the heights of the moors.

The road wound itself in and out of the stark and solitary village then climbed higher still as the moon rose and shone on the vast expanse of field, plain and heathland in an eerie light. As she drove, she hoped that there was enough petrol in the tank, or she would have a long way to walk.

Then behind her came the lights of another vehicle again. She couldn't tell whether it was the same as those before, but she pressed her foot harder onto the accelerator. As she sped over the moors, catching sight of the van's red tail-lights every so often, the car behind gained ground, coming closer. Decisions chased each other in her mind as she realised that she could be leading them to where Jem was going.

She saw the van's lights disappear from a turn in the moor, so she veered off onto a rutted track to a farm and pulled up behind a high wall. As she stopped the engine she saw the other car going down where the lane dipped sharply away into the coomb. She slumped against the wheel, resting her head on her arms and closed her eyes, and could have gone to sleep. But then she heard the engine of the car coming back up the lane again. It sounded the same as the other, and she hunched down in the seat as it swept by and roared over the rise onto the other road.

Long minutes went by and still she waited. She would have lost Jem now, though there were only two ways he could have taken when the moorland road came to a junction with the coast road near the village of Morvah, bleak and windswept where the moor met the cliffs. He could go through Morvah and Pendeen or the other way to St. Ives.

She turned towards Pendeen, the tin mine village, the stone waste heaps rising above the roofs. The headgear, with its wheel whirring round stood out starkly against the darkening sky. The top of the van showed up momentarily on one of the corners, so she carried on past the mine, then saw it turn off at Botallack for the old Crowns Mine track.

She bounced over the rutted lane that went to the Count House and got out and shouted his name, her voice ringing around the towering crags of the cliffs. She picked her way across the lengths of iron and broken slabs and crumbling walls that were scattered about, abandoned by the owners now long gone.

There was a steep rab pathway, dropping away down the side of the cliff to the two mine engine houses below. They stood like sentinels against the restless surge of the sea, breaking upon the rocks at the foot of the cliffs. There was no-one around and the van was nowhere to be seen.

She ran and stumbled down the precipice of a path to the foot of the black cliffs, and called and searched the ruins. Then she climbed up and up, slipping and sliding on the loose rab and scree until she stood on the edge of the rough moor and trudged round the ore tips that were piled here and there around the heath. At last, she flung herself wearily down in the heather and decided that she would go home.

It had begun to rain, and when she looked out over the sea, she could see heavy night clouds gathering on the horizon. She made her way down to the car and set off quickly, turning onto where the road to Priest's Cove led off. The headland of Cape Cornwall thrust bleakly out into the sea, its mine stack pointing to the dark sky.

She got out, slamming the door behind her and scrambled down the wet heather and gorse, but all she found was the usual collection of crab pots, lines and boxes piled up. She stumbled back up to the car and set off for the crossroads where the road wound down to Porthgwyna, to see if Jem had been there.

By the time she had reached the cove, the wind had risen and was now beating the rain on the roof above her. She looked down the slipway and suddenly noticed that Casley's boat had gone. She searched the other berths and spaces where it might have been pulled up, but it was nowhere to be seen.

In a panic she ran, her breath coming in gasps, reaching the car and wrenching open the door to fall in, her jacket sodden by now with the water running down her legs into her boots. The engine spluttered before coughing into a roar and as she pushed it into gear, it lurched forward with a rush.

Where would he go? Not far, for the boat had only a small fuel tank, so the only cove where he could refuel would be Sennen, before he rounded the Land's End peninsular. Or on the other hand, he could take a chance in the dusk to try slipping into one of the inlets half-hidden amongst the rugged granite cliffs.

She swung off the lane onto a rough boulder-strewn track. The wheel threatened to wrench itself out of her hands as the vehicle jolted and jarred over the ruts and ridges, rattling its way up the cliff road that the wreckers used with pony and cart.

The wheels bounced and jolted and the engine roared and screamed as she stabbed her foot on the pedals and pulled round the sharp corners. The stones skittered beneath the tyres and threatened to throw her over the edge of the cliff that fell in craggy ledges down to the sea.

At last she reached the top and sped over the heather and gorse that spread onto the track. She roared across the top of the cliff as the dark cloud burst and a torrent of rain and hail beat against the windscreen, so that her visibility merged into a wash of mirages. The car swerved off the track, hit a boulder and lurched from side to side as she struggled to right it.

The turning to the next small cove came up sharply and she swung into it, bouncing over the corner stone, straining her eyes to see through the vapour and mist of the torrential rain. The wheels lurched wildly down the steep hill, roaring away to the valley winding down to the sea.

She stamped on the brakes, turning into a screeching slide, then leapt out, head bent against the sudden downpour that leashed itself upon her. The grey waves reared up in surging mountains, throwing themselves down upon the beach in white fury.

She ran across to the number of boats that were drawn up under the cliff and searched for Casley's boat, but there was no sign of it. Her vision blurred with the rain stinging her eyes and with the fear that the boat had come to grief in the rough sea.

Then shaking herself, she stumbled over the loose boulders back to the car and flung herself into the damp seat. The engine spluttered and coughed and she shrieked at it, turning the key again and again until it caught, then revved it up to screaming point, until she sent it lurching forward up the track that was awash with mud and debris.

She slewed across small broken branches and clumps of gorse and bracken that had been whipped and lashed by the wind. The wheels slipped and slid the higher she struggled up the narrow way. The track went up over the rise of the cliff and turned inward across the bleak moors.

It crossed the expanse of wet area which she chanced, hoping it wouldn't be a marshy bog by now. The ruts grew deeper and banked high with soft liquid mud that moved under the car's weight, pushing it aside into the bramble and gorse which rattled noisily against the doors and whipped against the windscreen, so that she had to pull hard at the steering wheel to keep it on the harder surface.

As the full force of the gale lashed the roof, the front wheel slithered into a deep rut and the engine roared as the back slid round and spun in the marshy ground. Somehow the wheel caught on something solid and lurched sideways dragging at her hands. She stabbed at the pedals and slewed to the opposite side mounting the water-logged bank, then rolled back.

Before the car sank into the rut again she swung the wheel and surged forward, urging it onward. She topped the rise that wound over the granite crag and bounced over rock and turf until she reached the summit where she could see the giddy drop of the serried cliff that fell into the raging sea.

The visibility was bad and she strained to see any sight of a boat or wreckage as she hurried the vehicle along, not daring to stop. She slid and slithered down the river of peat and mud running out from the cliff side. The rain beat against the roof with deafening fury, blurring the windscreen so that it was difficult to see the edges of the track going over the moor.

At the bottom she came to a ford and she prayed that it was still passable. Suddenly a faint glimmer flashed across her inside mirror, then disappeared in the darkness. She waited for the thunder but couldn't hear it, so she pressed on towards the bottom of the valley.

The sweep of light came again in the mirror, then disappeared into the mist. It wasn't lightning as she'd thought, it was another vehicle. Who else was out here in such weather?

There was only one answer of course. Those who were also anxious to find the boat. She urged the car on feverishly to go faster. The river loomed up dark and menacing with white flecks showing up in her dimmed lights. The ford was running high, sweeping the banks and flooding a great stretch of road.

Without hesitating she stamped her foot down hard on the accelerator, and with the engine screaming she surged forward, hitting the water so that it sprayed up into a wall each side of her.

The engine spluttered and coughed, but she kept her foot down and it picked up again as she neared the far bank and the car climbed up out of the ford. Then over the muddy rise it leapt, roaring up the track to the next summit of the cliff. The faint glimmer of a light showed for an instance in her mirror, then disappeared as she plunged downward into the cutting between high banks.

Then the ground rose up again onto a wide area of heath before running away into a valley that led down to a sandy bay. The car bumped and slithered over clumps of marram grass and sand dunes, and came to a lurching stop by a huddle of stunted willows. She leapt out and scanned the fore shore along the wide expanse of newly washed sand, to the black craggy rocks jutting out at the point.

The breakers thundered in white foam upon the beach, throwing up the surf high into the night, with the undertow rushing back seawards beneath the on-coming wave, meeting it head on with a riptide, scattering curtains of spray.

And there in the welter of foam, tossed the dark shape of a boat, trying to ride the breakers onto the beach.

Tamsin shouted vainly against the roar of the surf, and ran across the sands to the water's edge.

"Jem – Casley . . ." her voice rang out amidst the thunder of the waves, as she stumbled into the swirl to reach the boat.

As she grasped hold of the gunwale a wild breaker tossed the boat into the air, turning it over and throwing it onto the beach. Another wave lifted her upon its back and she could see that the upturned craft was empty. She watched as another wave rose towards the boat, smothering it and washing it out again. The wave lifted its splintered hull, and she caught hold of it again and hung on as she was taken out with it.

She heard a voice shouting, but the icy waters rushed over her, spinning her in a welter of foam. A hand grasped her jacket and with a wrench she let go of the boat as it swept past her.

The voice shouted again in her ear and she was dragged backwards in the surf until she felt the hard sand under her feet. She struggled against the dark figure that was pulling her towards the beach. Gasping with the salt water stinging her throat and blinking through the beating rain, she could see figures coming down to the shore.

She struggled, plucking at the hands that held her, wading through the surf and onto the sand. Then she staggered across the beach and into the dunes as she heard shouts following her.

She'd neared the safety of the bushes when she was seized by the shoulders, and as she turned she stumbled and fell with her captor into the soft marram grass.

She opened her eyes as a hoarse cry shouted her name and she saw the face and wild hair of Jem.

"Oh, oh, Lord !" she gasped, "I thought you'd drowned!"

"Keep down!" he pulled her further into the dune.

They kept low, hidden by the grasses, getting their breath back.

Men's voices wafted over on the wind as they examined the boat, which had been washed higher up the beach. Then as they moved away, Jem cautiously lifted his head.

"They've gone," he shouted in her ear.

"They've been going round asking questions," cried Tamsin leaning on her elbow, "I thought you and Dad might risk moving goods."

"We did – it's done!" laughed Jem, pulling her into the shelter of the grasses again. "Casley's gone off with them – though he won't be pleased about his boat – what we got to do now is wait till the coast's clear. . ."

32

Zach would help Frank Rowe and Tamsin now and then with the milking, and one afternoon as he sat in the farm kitchen and savoured the strong tea Frank had made, he said, "I shan't be in the weekend, you remember?"

"You off with the choir then?" Frank replaced the cosy over the teapot.

"We 'ave a last practise tonight."

"An' you're all off up to London town, then?"

"The Albert Hall it is – we should make a grand sound with the other choirs," Zach emptied his cup.

"You will too. I wish I was coming with you, but with Leah away . . ." Frank sighed.

"Well - see you when I get back," Zach scraped back his chair and set off for home.

He found Clarissa folding clothes to take with them, and she was still sorting them out that evening when the singing came drifting through the air to her from the chapel window – "Guide me, O thou Great Redeemer . . ." The harmonies were rich and smooth, from the bass to the tenor voices.

The men practised every week all through the year, and on this occasion for a concert of Cornish and Welsh Male Voice Choirs in London city. An enjoyable evening especially set up to entertain and boost the spirits of those who had suffered many nights of bombing, and the many British, Overseas and American service men and women stranded alone in the capital.

Jem, Pete and the few who'd had leave had long gone back to their ships, and with many more of the singers in the services the choir was short of members, and it was a task to round up enough men together. Many were away overseas and others were in the mines, fishing, on farms and essential work. Those who could, changed their days and shifts with their workmates to be able to go off with the choir, promising to make up the hours when they got back.

There had been a great business and bustle of arrangements of trains and hotels, and the washing of shirts and pressing of suits, by the women in the previous weeks.

Now the doctor, Andy Pengegon put down his baton and smiled at his group of men.

"Well boys, I think that'll do very nicely. We've worked hard and now we can enjoy ourselves this weekend with all the other choirs. It should be a great occasion, with a great sound of Cornish voices raising the roof," he closed his book. "I'll see you all on the station tomorrow. No gallivanting or drinking tonight, mind," he looked at the assortment of members, "save your voices for the day."

There was a noise of chairs and chatter as they went out, and there were those who headed into the Wink, but they didn't stay long.

Clarissa Rose fussed over her husband that evening as if he were going to visit royalty.

"Be still, woman," he said at last.

"I've got to see if everything's ready," she replied, "you'm be goin' off straight after helping Seth tomorrow, an' there won't be time for doin' anything then. After all, you'm be goin' up to the city an' you got to look right an' fitty."

"Aw, give over. Nobody's goin' to take notice of me among all they others."

"Well, I will . . ." almost all the wives of the village had saved meagre amounts of their money, and were going up on the train with the choir and had seats booked in the audience, "an' I'll be looking fer you on the stage."

"You won't see me amongst they lot."

"Yes, I shall. I'll not miss my husband singing up at the Albert Hall. What an evenin' it'll be."

Ezra had been having the same trouble and fuss that morning from his wife Ella, only he'd set off to the mine and left her to it. When he came home at the end of his shift she would still be at it. And she was – of course.

Tamsin was looking after the children for Seth and Hannah Jane and would look in on her grandparent's cottage.

"Mind you get boy Matt and Jessica off early enough for school," her mother reminded her.

"An' see that m'black out curtains are in place," Clarissa worried.

"Don't chaff the lass," laughed Zach, "she'll 'ave a nice pot of tea ready fer you when we get back."

"An' use that sparingly, it's on ration, don't forget."

"You all watch out fer they bombs. Get in the air raid shelters when the siren goes," Tammy said anxiously.

"They won't see us fer dust," grunted Seth.

Tamsin fingered the letter in her pocket that she'd had that day from Jem, and when everyone was busy she slipped away to sit by her window to open it . . .

' . . . the dusk here is as bright as day with firing of guns. What a difference Tammy, from our blacked out village at home. The big guns roar with shooting flames belching out black smoke in thick billowing clouds, soon blotting out sun and sky during the day. Dense fumes cling to our throats and dust and globules rain down, coating our hair and clothes.

I long for Porthgwyna and Newlyn, and I long to be with you by the singing surf and the clean wash of the tide. I long to see again the cottages huddled against the cliff and to feel the fresh salty air of the quayside.

When we near the shore, I watch the lithe-limbed, black-eyed children here, some running, some smiling, some alone, some

211

timid, hands grasping hands. I hear the shrill cries of women swathed in cool linen in the dusty shade. Then I read your letters and think of you, with your wind-blown hair, wide-eyed, carefree, walking the cliffs down to the slipway to watch the boats . . .'

The following day each member of the choir with wives and friends, were all milling around at the station waiting for the train. After spending the night at the hotel where they'd been booked in, they would attend the rehearsal the next morning to make ready for the evening concert.

While the men rehearsed, the women were looking forward to spending the day looking around the city and the big stores, even though they had little money to spend.

The train was late arriving and was soon crowded by personnel in various uniforms, Army, Navy, Air Force and a variety of other services, who all had priority on rail travel. It took quite a time to push a way into the packed corridors and carriages.

"We'll be lucky if they don't turn us out before we get to the city, to make room fer service men only," grumbled Zach.

Seth pushed Hannah Jane and Clarissa through into a carriage, "We'll stand in the corridor 'ere, you two make eyes at they sailors in there. They'll probably give you a seat," he winked at them.

The journey was long and tiring, with the train frequently coming to a standstill, making way for other trains which were held up by the threat of bombing.

When they eventually reached London, they found that the hotel booked for the choir was old and large, but the rooms were comfortable with high ceilings, although the bar and refreshments were closed by the time they arrived.

All the buildings were depressingly blacked out with not a

glimmer of light showing, with empty chasms and rubble in the streets where houses had been bombed and destroyed, and buildings that were shored up for safety.

Zach sat in his room and rummaged around in his suitcase, his hand groping underneath the pyjamas that Clarissa had neatly packed. He pulled out a bottle of whisky.

"Zacchaeus Trewin! D'you mean that's come all the way up with us?" she was speechless.

"Ah – well, I put'n in, in good stead in case of emergencies – an' a good job I did too, 'cause there ain't nothin' to be 'ad nor vitals around 'ere as I can see," he poured out a good measure in the flask cup, "you 'avin' one?"

"No, I'm not. I'll have what's left in the tea flask," she put his pyjamas out on the bed.

"Ergh! That'll taste 'orrible by now. Go on, a nightcap'll help you sleep."

"I'll sleep without that – well – I'll 'ave a dram in m'tea."

"I doubt I will, sleep that is, with the racket of this traffic going on all night. Cars, fire engines, ambulances an' all."

"Oh, come on into bed. It'll quieten down later on," Clarissa lay back against the pillow and closed her eyes.

Zach sat on the edge of the bed sipping at the cup in his hand.

"I shan't sleep a wink," he mumbled to himself.

But he did – and woke the following morning with a crescendo of the city's traffic still roaring in his ears.

They had breakfast in the hotel, then Clarissa left him to join her friends as they set off to browse around the city's shops.

"Us'll 'ave no money left," grumbled old Jacob.

"Ah, vicar'll be down on his takings for the next few weeks," Zach eased his toes in his new shoes, "they 'aven't got much to spend anyway with this war on. Come on, let's get over to the Hall and let's hear some good Cornish voices."

It was a longish walk, through alleyways and streets and sand-bagged buildings, and outside the Hall they met up with great numbers of other choirs.

Inside, the stairs and corridors were filled to overflowing with late-comers trying to join up with each other, and officials and stewards dashing to and fro. Each choir was being guided to places beneath and to each side of the huge organ, and there was a great hub-bub of voices as the chairs were filled, row upon row, as more and yet more filtered through the narrow entrances.

Richard Glyn-Porter was there, waving his hands excitedly in his dramatic manner to both singers and officials. For this was one of his flamboyantly publicised events, and he had pressed and cajoled upon almost every choir in the county to come. His enthusiasm in his own expertise swelled to capacity as he gloried in the newsmen and photographers, who interviewed him and who hovered from side to side, deciding on angles and light. The organist was running through introductory chords, and still the never-ending flow of singers slowly filed through the gangways.

The Porthgwyna lads had been waiting around in the outside corridors, moving forward gradually a few feet at a time.

"M'legs is killin' me," muttered Eli, "I could do with a sit down. How much further is it boy?" He prodded Ebeneezer in front of him.

"Not much, by the look of it. I c'n see the doorway comin' up," he craned his head over those in front of him.

Out in the main hall, a short pin-striped figure was also craning his neck above the numerous heads.

"Mr. Porter – Mr. Porter . . ." he urgently waved his arms as he pushed his way through to him.

Glyn-Porter looked up, "Glyn-Porter," he impatiently reminded the harried gentleman.

"Yes – Glyn-Porter – yes," he looked round, "a word with you please." His hand guided him to the side of the aisle, "We're almost full – we've not enough room for all the choirs!"

"Not enough . . .?"

"No – yes – that's right. We're full, and there's half-a-dozen more choirs to fit in," the small man was flustered.

"Nonsense! Get everyone to move along," Glyn-Porter flung out his arm.

"They're already packed like sardines, my dear sir. You'll not get any more in the front area."

Glyn-Porter glanced hurriedly around at the crowded hall, then turned back to him, "But we arranged all this with you. I've spent weeks writing umpteen letters with the most particular instructions," his voice rose to a high squeak.

"I know – I know," his shoulders slumped with resignation, "but you've oversubscribed your numbers."

Glyn-Porter opened his mouth to protest again – when he remembered that he'd rashly pressed additional choirs to his original figure, "Well – do something!" he panicked. "You've got to fit them in somewhere." He thought of all the numbers of singers still milling around in the corridors waiting to come in.

"We can have more rows spreading out each side," suggested Morgan Jones.

"There you are then. Get on with it! I'd better go and sort it out." He eased his way past those in the aisles, to the full passages behind the hall, and stood at the top of some steps and raised his arms, "Gentlemen, please – gentlemen!" The voices subsided as they turned to him, and he saw the face of Andrew Pengegon not far from him. He cleared his throat.

"Gentlemen – the front of the hall is now full, so we've decided to fill more rows on each side. So if you turn to your right, that'll bring you out into the appropriate aisle." The murmur of voices rose once more with the change of direction.

"It must be time to get rehearsin' soon," said Zach.

"Aye," Jacob blew into his handkerchief, "about time we got started."

"Alright men," Andy Pengegon let his breath out slowly, "let's get along an see where they're going to put us."

They moved towards the passage that went off at right-angles, and going along the length of that, turned right again down the next one. They came to steps and stairs and another couple of passage-ways going off each other.

"Goin' round an' round the mulberry bush," Davy Pender laughed.

"Hurry along, they'm waitin'," Ben nudged him. But when they came to a junction of three ways, they knew they had mistaken the directions.

"This place is a circular building," Zach scratched his head, "if we keep going we'll come back to where we started!"

"I thought I recognised that bit with the crack in the plaster, way back," Davy nodded.

"Then if we go up these steps 'ere, we'll go round again and come out in the same spot, only a flight higher," Zach went on.

"An' if you keeps goin' up an' round, an' round an' up, you'll end up in the roof," laughed Ben.

"This way, boys," Andrew indicated with his hand and they walked on, coming to a door at the end.

"At last," he pushed against it and it opened onto the pavement and the roar of traffic.

"Aw, hell – us goin' to give a concert on the street – haw, haw?" smirked old Gundry.

"Shut yer gob!" growled Seth, as he saw Andrew Pengegon coming to the end of his patience.

"Aw, I'm fed up," Eddy leaned wearily against the wall,

"There's a pub a little while back that we passed – let's go an' drown our sorrows."

"We might as well . . ." a few others around commiserated with him.

"Boys, boys – please," Andy turned to them, "let's find our way back."

Eventually they came to the right corridor and took their places with the huge numbers of Cornish and Welsh choirs, and rehearsed with each other in a great swelling of sound that filled the hall to its rafters.

When they'd finished they emerged from the building into sunlight, and wandered down a wide thoroughfare with a park on one side and buildings on the other which merged into a busy centre. It was nearing lunchtime when they found a dim dusty Ye Olde Red Lion establishment.

"No, no – boys – boys . . ." Andy protested as they drifted inside, where it was warm and comfortable. They ordered up snacks of pies and spam sandwiches, and with a tankard of beer each, sat and stood around eating and talking.

"I'm ready fer this," Seth bit into a pie with an assortment of filling.

"They're quite tasty ain't they, considering meat's on ration?" Zach examined his, "Ain't a patch on a pasty though."

"Ah – cor – I'm starving," Eli scratched his nose.

"I'll get another round," Zach picked up their glasses and moved towards the bar. It was crowded with a fair mixture of cockney and foreign accents and the landlord beamed upon them, pleased with the sudden influx of customers.

Jamie trod on Jacob's foot which was stretched out alongside the table. "Here lad, me feet are killing me as it is."

Jamie grinned, "Good exercise – walking."

"Not on these pavements it ain't – they're some hard on yer

217

soles."

"Beer's good though," nodded Zach.

Andrew Pengegon emptied his glass, "Come on now, boys, we best be getting back."

"What for?" Zach looked up at him, "There ain't nothin' to be goin' back fer 'till this evenin's concert."

"He's right there," nodded Jacob, " 'ere Davy, fetch us another beer an' save me feet," he pushed some coins into his hand.

"Give us a note, Andy," said Zach, "an' we'll 'ave a few of the old songs."

Pengegon sighed, and closing his eyes, hummed in the back of his throat and started up with - 'Twas down in Albert Square' - in his deep voice, and the others merged in with their harmonies until a swell of rich sound filled the old inn.

The landlord stood with pleasurable uncertainty as the tones floated round his ears. They went on to – 'Going up Camborne Hill' – and – 'The Old Grey Duck' – and the beer began to flow and the till began to ring. The rest of his customers joined in here and there, and stayed on longer than their accustomed dinner hour. Usually, he ordered out anyone starting up with their harsh ditties or wailing, and even had a sign up which stated in large letters, 'No Singing.' But this was an event not to be snubbed at, and as he passed the sign he quietly turned it to the wall and continued with a grin to pull the pints as long as the beer lasted. They were good drinkers as well as good singers it seemed.

"What're you all doin' around 'ere?" he asked.

"Well – we shouldn't be here at all . . ." Andy took another sip at his beer, "we're singing with all the choirs this evening at the Albert Hall."

"Oh, one of them wallahs are you?" Tom Peak polished the bar top with a chequered cloth.

"Yeh, our wives is up with us an' all – an' it's fer charity," added Ezra.

"A shame it is," said Tom, "that it's nearly time fer me to close."

"Time flies," Ezra put down his glass.

"What're you goin' to do fer the rest of the day?"

"We got to hang around 'till tonight, that's fer sure,"

" 'Ere, if you're collecting fer charity, we've got the Lifeboat collecting box 'ere on the end of the bar. After the concert tonight, why don't you all come back 'ere, when it'll be full an' give us yer company? You can make a collection fer the lifeboats at the same time."

"Well – what about it?" Andy turned to the others.

"It'll be doing something useful, as we'd be at a loose end," put in Davy as the bell was rung for closing.

"Now, I'll tell you what," suggested Tom, "if you'd all like to go round to the alley by the side door 'ere, you'll find yerselves in Papalinos's. I'll 'ave a word with 'im an' he'll set you all up with a good meal." He let himself out of the bar and opened the side door, and they followed after him.

The alleyway was dark and narrow and smelled of cats, but it turned at the end into a surprisingly attractive courtyard, with iron tables and chairs. There were miniature patios and terraces hung with hanging baskets of scarlet geranium, trailing yellow nasturtium and white alyssum, and flower filled tubs set in the crannies. They sat about in the warm sunlight that shone through the spaces between the buildings and chimney tops, while they could hear Tom shouting for the Greek owner, who appeared through the double French windows which opened onto the courtyard.

"Andros Papalinos. My friends have come to eat," beamed Tom, as Andros's eyes swept happily over them.

"Aah – certainly. For my good friend Tom, I promise you

something delicious," he waved his arms excitedly.

" 'Ere, I'm not 'aving any of that foreign stuff – turn me that will," old Jacca looked under his eyebrows at him.

"You may order English or French dishes besides," exuded Andros.

"I like a bit of spice m'self," grinned Ben.

"You are welcome to order now and look around, or if you go through the latch gate, it will take you into the park."

"I could do with a dish of tea, if it's goin'," Ezra sank into a chair, his bones complaining at the complications of the day.

"In a few moments," Andros smiled happily, and raising his voice shouted for Larisa his wife to bring tea, and for Rosina and Athene, his daughters to bring the menu.

Tom went back to clear up at the bar, while the older men sat and took their ease and the others went off into the park. The clattering and chattering of Paplinos and his cook in the kitchen came through the windows and later, he and his daughters served a fine repast to their hungry customers.

They lingered lazily over the meal and then drifted back to the hotel to get themselves ready in well-worn suits and jackets for the evening's concert.

Clarissa Rose and Hannah with their group of wives and friends were seated far up in the high gallery enjoying the concert, though they hadn't been able to actually pick out Zach or Seth amongst the huge number of choir members. The arena and balconies were filled with service men and city folk, all happily soaking up the rich sound of melodious voices in song that swelled to every corner of the Albert Hall.

When they walked back to the hotel amongst the dark blacked-out buildings, they didn't expect to meet up with the men until later, knowing that most of them would drop in for a drink somewhere before they returned.

It was the beginning of the weekend, and as the choir arrived at Ye Olde Red Lion it became busy with many out for a night's enjoyment. After a couple of tankards, Pengegon struck up a note and the rest of the choir joined in.

"Here's the Lifeboat box," said Zach, "why don't one of you go round with it while there's a good crowd in?" He lifted the collection box off the end of the bar.

"I'll take it," offered Eddy and he pushed his way around the crowded inn as 'The Little Old Church in the Vale' echoed under the old beams.

There were people standing in the doorways and outside in the dark on the pavements, as money was passed overhead to the bar and glasses went to and fro and back again, and the evening became hotter and closer. There was a hub-bub and mingling of voices that was rarely heard in that corner of the city for a long time.

When Tom rang the brass bell for 'time' the soft harmonies of 'The White Rose' drifted through the dark night, as people made their way out onto the street and wandered into the park. There was a hazy moon that shone a pale light down onto the blacked-out city, as 'Little Liza Jane' carried on through the evening, with Tom, who had come with them joining in the bass line.

Eddy had already filled the collection box and Tom had found another one for the Blind, and he went in and out of the listening groups who were sitting round on the grass. As the audience and choirs spilled out of the Albert Hall and were taking an evening stroll in the park, they heard the sound of the old Cornish songs upon the air, and in curiosity they wandered over and joined in, swelling the singers until a great sound soared into the night sky.

One of these was a newsman who'd been there to write an article on the evening's concert at the Hall, and he pushed his way up to Pengegon and pulled him aside as the soft harmonies of 'Amazing Grace' surrounded them as they talked.

Some of the women were drinking tea as they rested at the hotel and listened to the wireless.

"It went well, didn't it?" said Biddy.

"Lovely, dear, lovely," Hannah Jane sank back in a chair.

Ella suddenly sat up, "Here, listen to that - that's Andy Pengegon isn't it?"

A news programme had brought his voice on the air and the commentator continued . . .

" . . . just listen to this magnificent singing coming from this choir from the furthermost tip of Cornwall that we've invited into the studio . . ." and the glorious strains of 'Guide me, O Thou Great Redeemer' rose in full voice. "I should think when the London pubs called 'time' everyone ended up in the park and the charity collection there has already filled numerous boxes, and there are still crowds coming in – they're coming in across the streets and the park – I've never seen so many for a long time – what a terrific sound – it rivals even that of this evening's Albert Hall concert – just listen to this choir . . ." and the harmonies swelled and filled with 'Bread of heaven, Bread of heaven, Feed me till I want no more . . .'

" . . . and it's now coming up to midnight and the choir have now gone back to the park, and I'm told that the police are trying to move everyone on – but nobody's moving while the singing's still going. What an uplifting sound to raise the spirits of our servicemen to take with them into conflict, and for those who have suffered losses at home . . ."

"Oh – Oh!" shrieked Hannah Jane, "Seth Trewin! I'm goin' down there this very minute!" and off she scuttled, clutching her handbag, while some of the other women rushed to follow her. Outside they hailed a taxi and drove off amid breathless instructions to the driver. He dropped them off at the park amongst a great crowd and Clarissa Rose, with Hannah and the others behind her, pushed their way towards the men and there joined in the singing.

Eventually an officer had a word in Andrew's ear, who nodding his head, took the choir to a last rendering of 'Good Night Ladies' into the night, and motioned to the men to begin to move off.

They could hardly make headway through the crowd, with newsmen also following their footsteps, and had only gone a few paces when an upright grey-haired figure came up to Andrew.

"Marvellous – such splendid voices," he said, "Major Graham Sinclair – I wonder if all of you would join up with the band in the morning at the Band Stand – St. James's Park?"

"We certainly would," smiled Andrew, "the men'll be very pleased to."

When they arrived back at their hotel and the lounge and receptions rooms began to fill with the choir members, and their wives and newsmen who had followed them there, he told them of the invitation and they all looked forward to singing on the following day.

Suddenly, there came the raucous wailing of the air raid siren.

"Oh, dear life!" shrieked Clarissa.

But they'd all read the notices that had been put up by the hotel manager in each room, about going to the underground station nearby, so they made their way out and onto the street. Standing and sitting in the shelter, they could hear the drone of enemy planes and the explosions of bombs coming down a few streets away, but to their relief nothing came any closer.

Hannah Jane sent up a prayer that no-one had got caught by

the raid, and when the 'all clear' siren sounded some time later, she took in a deep breath, "Let's hope that's finished, Seth, and we can get to our beds."

That night Zach eased off his now street-dusty shoes and slept soundly, without reaching out for the whisky tucked away inside his case.

The morning was warm with the sun shining down from the clear blue sky into the park, where many people were strolling or sitting on the paths and grass.

News of the choir on the wireless had brought those from far and near to the Band Stand to hear them.

They weren't disappointed. The band played marches and airs and the choir sang happily, swelled by many belonging to the other choirs who'd come along to join them.

When they had played and sung their last, there was a commotion of well-wishes between players and singers, and for a good journey home, and when the men had collected their luggage from the hotel, the newsmen even followed them to the station as the train pulled away.

News from the wireless had travelled fast and when the train reached Plymouth, there to their surprise, they were greeted by the city band marching onto the platform, which played in their honour. News had already spread all over the west country, and at each station where the train halted, there were waiting groups of local bands who struck up their congratulations.

When they arrived in Penzance, there was the Mayor with the whole platform crowded with friends, relatives and townspeople. The town band tuned up and there was a great noise as the train emptied, and when the band came to 'Trelawny' the whole crowd stood and sang the last song of the day.

"An' you remember when you'm out there in that boat, who

bin singing their lungs out fer 'ee," Eddy nudged his brother, who was in the Lifeboat crew.

"Ah, an' who bin suppin' of liquid refreshment all the way down from London town?" his brother winked at him. "I reckon breweries 'ave 'ad a charity day too, by the look of things!"

"Well, it's all in a good cause, ain't it?"

"With you it is. I bet it was you homing in on the nearest pub that started the whole thing off!"

33

Lucille, Zach's widowed sister, hurried to open the side door of the old manor to the loud knocking, and Jarvis rushed in, slamming it shut and shooting the bolts hard home.

"Where've you been to, son?" Lucille gasped, for he was drenched to the skin. "Where've you been out in this wild night, fer it's gone midnight? The clock 'as long done chiming its hour and the dawn is creepin' in."

Jarvis sank down into a chair and wearily closed his eyes. Lucille rushed to get a blanket and dry clothing.

"I thought I heard the sound of feet hurrying down to the shore. I'm afraid fer you, of what you've been up to," she whispered.

Her son took in a deep breath and sighed, "Your ears are gettin' hard of hearing, mother. You've been dreaming, go back to bed. You know well that neighbour Tonkin passed away only yesterday an' I've been to his family's wake."

Lucille spread the blanket over him, "But what're you doin' there so late at night? I'm sure I heard the chink of bridle bit and muffled hoof going across the moor."

"Ah – you only heard the footsteps of those paying respect an' the chink of the sexton's thrust as he shapes the grave, an' strikes his blade against the stone."

She raked the warm ashes in the stove, putting on more wood to set it burning again, and filled the kettle to make a hot drink.

"But I thought I saw a flicker of light through the cracks in the window shutter, and when I looked, I saw moving shadows an' heard voices," she said.

Jarvis stretched his arm and groaned, "A-ah, yer eyes are fading mother, fer we laid old Tonkin in his coffin an' the light you saw came from the mourners throwing their rays on the grave, an' their shadows goin' by with their voices murmuring their mournful hymn."

She began to take off his jacket and he uttered another moan when she lifted his arm.

"Dear life, what's happened 'ere! I c'n smell cordite an' there's black grains on yer sleeve," she gasped, "an' there's a red stain spreading on the cloth an' dripping from yer fingers onto the hearth stone!"

"Let me rest fer a while mother," muttered Jarvis.

Lucille placed a cushion under his head and ran into the yard shouting for Will, who was sitting up with a weak calf in the barn. "Get over to Dr. Pengegon an' bring him 'ere, urgent – then go an' find Seth or Zach."

Will stared at her frightened face and hurried to the shed. He jumped on his motorbike, and roared off down the lane.

Lucille poured warm water into a bowl and snatched up clean towels, taking them into Jarvis and putting them on a nearby table. She picked up her scissors and began cutting the sleeve from his arm to ease off his jacket.

"I knew I heard what sounded like a crack of a firearm," she cut the shirt sleeve and pushed it back, revealing a wound above the elbow that was bleeding heavily. She bathed it and with a clean towel pressed above the wound and slowly the bleeding lessened.

Heaving a sigh of relief, she wiped his pale brow and straightened his trembling limbs, as she pulled off his wet clothing and helped him into dry ones.

"Don't ask where I've been an' don't let anyone know," Jarvis urged, "an' take this gun out of m'pocket an' hide it away."

"Well, you know Zach'll guess," Lucille pulled out the weapon and hid it in her own pockets in her skirt, as she heard Will's motorbike returning in the yard outside. The door opened and Andy Pengegon appeared, his hair wind-blown by riding on the rear saddle.

"My car wouldn't start," he said, following her into the kitchen. Will quickly turned round and went off to find Zach. The doctor lifted the towel from Jarvis and looked closely at his arm.

"You're in trouble my lad, the bullet's still in there. What've you been up to?" he opened his bag.

"Will's gone to fetch some help," Lucille told him.

"Clear the table here, and tear up a clean sheet or cloth."

As she was carrying clean water and towels, both Zach and Seth arrived in Zach's car.

"What's young Jarvis bin doin'?" Zach bent over him. "Good grief! You let one of they revenue men get too close!"

Jarvis groaned, "He didn't see me – it was a stray shot."

Seth snorted, "What did yer 'ave on you?"

"It's in the graveyard," his voice was fading.

"Never mind that," demanded Pengegon, "steady him while I give him an injection."

Between them they then lifted Jarvis onto the table, and with Zach holding his shoulders and Seth grasping his legs, they watched as Pengegon probed and searched inside the wound.

Lucille mopped the blood away with clean pieces of cloth, and eventually Andy found and held up the stained bullet for them to see.

"Fortunately it was lodged in the muscle so no harm is permanently done, it should heal nicely," he showed Lucille how to attend to the wound, "and tell him to keep away from these hair-brained schemes," he warned.

Lucille brought out brandy and made hot tea before Seth took the doctor home in the car, a more comfortable ride than on Will's vehicle.

"Give us a torch," said Zach, "tell Seth when he gets back

that I'll be in the churchyard."

He set off down the lane, going quietly in case the revenue men were still about. When he came to the church wall he climbed over, and shielding the torch, he began to search around the gravestones.

A rustle came from the other side of the bushes and he hid the light and froze.

"Zach!" a hiss.

"Here!" he saw Seth appear in the gloom of the early morning.

"Found anythin'?"

"Not yet. You look over that side, I'll finish 'ere."

They eventually found the cache hidden against the wall where it leant at an angle, with several fallen stones scattered on the ground.

"Let's see what we got 'ere," Zach uncovered barrels of claret and bolts of silk and lace.

"Jarvis 'as got some fancy goods 'ere right enough," chuckled Seth.

"Now I get it. He's gettin' married to preacher Zekel's lass, Amy May, in a few weeks time," Zach laughed, "he's got all this finery fer her, that's how 'e chanced his luck with the revenue."

"Daft beggar! Well, we'll 'ave to move it somewhere safer," Seth peered through the hazy light. "Ah, old Tonkin was buried yesterday, an' there's a new grave dug beside 'im fer Silas Noy, but 'is funeral's not till next week."

"Then we c'n put this lot in there. We'll get it out again before the ceremony," Zach began to move the nearest barrel over the grass and let it roll into the grave. They pushed the rest of the barrels into the ground and carried the bolts of cloth, placing them on top and covered everything with a couple of feet of soil that was piled up on the side.

When they arrived back at Seth's cottage, they related the plights of Jarvis and his lucky escape to Hannah Jane over breakfast.

"That Jarvis!" she exclaimed, "I suppose he wanted to impress Amy May."

"He'll survive," Seth laughed, "an' Pengegon won't say anythin'. I'm off now, to catch the tide."

And within a couple of days Jarvis was up and about, much to Lucille's relief, though very sore and stiff. Zach and Seth helped him to move his merchandise over to Amy May's cottage when her father, preacher Zekel was out of the way, and she was in 'seventh heaven' over the silk and lace, which had become very scarce.

Tamsin related the story of Jarvis and his coming wedding as she wrote to Jem. But being mindful that her letter would be read, mentioned his wound as having been 'winged' and 'gifts for Amy May', knowing that he would read between the lines as to the real meaning.

' . . . and the mackerel landings are high, Jem, though the market price this morning has dropped. But your Seamaid landed her catch yesterday and so caught a good price before it fell. We had a fierce gale blowing hard for two days, before it quietened down. Some of the roof slates went flying off and several trees were uprooted.

The lifeboat went out today to a large cargo boat whose engine had broken down, and she was drifting towards the rocks. Eventually her engineers managed to re-start the engine and she continued on her way.

There are oystercatchers on the shore, darting here and there searching for food, and also a grey seal in the harbour. The fishermen were throwing it some mackerel which it was cleverly catching and swallowing.

After a while it had enough and dived under the water and headed out to sea, but it has turned up again each morning this week, following the throbbing sound of the engines of the fishing boats.

From my window this evening I can see smoke curling up from the old fireplace of the inn, and hear voices rising in the air in a swelling sound of harmony from those inside, with their tankards of wine and ale . . .'

34

They ran Seth's small boat out, first pulling out the chocks, loosening the rope from the chain that held her, then turning her bows towards the surf and running her swiftly down the steep slipway.

Pushing her out into the coming wave, Zach held her steady for old Jacob to clamber in and help Seth to load the gear. Bait, dans and fishing floats, and stacking the coiled ropes and lobster pots.

Casley was giving Davy a hand at the farm, and the only other person they could find to go with them was Jacob.

"He ain't goin' to be much help," grumbled Seth.

Zach grinned at him, "He c'n bait pots an' coil rope, he'll be alright."

"You watch what yer sayin' – I bin fishing more times than you've 'ad hot dinners!" spluttered Jacob.

They both leapt into the bucking craft, riding on the breaking comb of the wash, with the engine coming to life with a spit and snarl and thrusting the boat out through the channel.

On each side the black cliffs rose behind them as they headed out towards the flags of the dans, which marked the position of the lobster and crab pots below amongst the rocks and sand of the seabed.

They circled and Seth reached down and pulled in the floats and the weed-covered rope from the sea.

"Ha – he's in!" he exclaimed, as up came the first pot with a lobster.

Then up came the others with crabs and starfish, and he passed them on to Jacob who took out the starfish, throwing them back into the sea and storing the shellfish in wet sacking and baited the pots again with fish-heads and mackerel.

"A good catch today," he shouted as Zach stacked the pots, then threw them overboard to catch again and they moved on to the next set.

They'd pulled a hundred or more pots by midday, but as they turned to land their catch for the market, the mists came down and all sight of the coast had disappeared. A fresh breeze freshened, whipping the wave in a frothy curl and chilling showers of spray swept over them.

Zach peered through the thickening mist and turned the boat.

"That's north," cried Seth.

"It's where we were, on the last string of pots," replied Zach.

"We'd circled round by then," Seth argued.

Jacob lifted his head, sniffed at the air and listened.

"I c'n hear breakers," he said, "that means the reef is to the left, and the shore to the right."

"Na – turn us round again," scoffed Seth.

But old Jacob had been at sea from a boy, and knew the coastline and its sheltered bays and rocks by the slightest echo and sound of the waves. He turned his weathered cheek to the wind and to the spray.

"You're gettin' nearer the reef! Pull back," he urged Zach impatiently.

"I hope you're right," Zach turned the boat and slowly steered her forward, "I can't see a darn'd thing!"

"But I c'n hear surf," cried Seth.

"That's the shore under the cliff," Jacob could feel the spray on the breeze, "the channel's to the left."

As Zach steered cautiously on, the mist near the shoreline began to lift and he saw the outline of the rugged cliffs, "I c'n see the channel!" he shouted.

"I c'n see the slipway!" cried Seth with relief, "You're a canny old seadog Jacob."

Jacob chuckled, "I d'know my sea. Take in the scent of her -

feel her touch on yer face – listen to her song – you got to treat her just like a mistress."

35

Jem was back on leave again, but before he'd reached his own door he met Seth going down to the quay, setting out for the day's fishing.

"Jem!" he shouted to him, "Come on! You c'n let us know what you bin up to, on the way out."

Jem flung his kitbag over the wall of his back yard, and went off with them to board the crab boat as the morning sun filtered pale and wan, flooding the waves with fingers of light.

The dawn lay heavy upon the grey sea, lifting the waves restlessly, and the small fishing fleet trailing hook and line, formed shadows against the breaking day.

The seagulls hovered above the masts, swooping and calling as Jem flung and waved his arms to send them soaring up to the sky.

As they made their way out to sea, one of the gulls flew into a stay and plummeted down onto the deck. Jem picked it up and held the limp stunned bird, stroking the fluttering wings. Seth reached out to toss it aside, when it moved and struggled to stand.

It toppled and staggered with a mewing cry, squawking and pecking at Jem's arm, so he covered its beak with his cap and then saw that its leg was injured.

He tore his handkerchief into strips and bound the leg with splinters of wood. When he let it go, it flapped about on the deck as he tried to tempt it with scraps of bait.

"That'll never fly again," snorted Seth.

Casley laughed at him, "Yer wastin' yer time, throw it overboard."

Jem put it to the side of the boat as he and Casley pulled in crab pots, emptying them of crabs and lobsters and baiting them again. By the end of the day the seagull was clumsily hopping behind Jem as he worked.

He spent the rest of the week fishing with Seth and the bird would perch on his shoulder and feed from his hand.

"I wouldn't 'ave believed it," said Casley, as it stretched and tried out its wings.

When Jem took off the splints its leg was scarred, but it gingerly took small hops about the deck, then took off and flew and circled around, to land again on Jem's shoulder.

"You got a friend fer life there," chortled Seth.

On the following days the seagull would follow the boat, calling again with the other seabirds and diving into the sea for any fish scraps they threw over the side.

Tamsin stood in the morning sunshine looking down at the figure which lay on the sand – motionless, dirty, snoring. He stank of fish and beer. His torn fishing smock was covered in stains and mackerel scales, and his hair stuck up unevenly in tufts. He had spoiled the early freshness of the shore that was new with sea-washed sand and empty, except for the cries of the gulls and the panting of her spaniel.

Jem had only once come to the cottage since he'd been home on leave. He'd spent his time with the fishermen out at sea, and drinking down at the inn.

She turned to look at the white surf of the waves as they broke, and watched as the incoming tide crept nearer. The first rivulets of the wash licked the sand around his feet leaving soft wet pools. She walked towards the higher rocks and dunes and sat amongst the grasses and sedge and waited.

The tide crept in, lapping around his knees, his thighs, then rippled over his waist. To her glee, the icy water jerked him from his sleep and he rolled sideways, slapping his arms in the waves, sending up spurts of spray. He roared into the morning and pushed himself onto his knees, swaying and blinking in the bright sunlight.

A rolling wave surged towards him, reared upwards and broke over his shoulders, pushing him over onto the sand again. He staggered up onto his feet and stood glaring at the ocean, then swung round and saw her watching him.

She sank back against the bank, but he was now striding over the beach waving his hands and shouting her name. She whistled to the dog and started walking quickly towards the cottages in the cove.

"Wait – Tammy – wait!" he called, stumbling over the rocks, but she ran through the narrow alley and slammed the door.

When he reached it he hammered the panels with his fist, but there was no answer. Only her mother pushed open the upstairs window and thrust her head out, shouting at him to stop his noise.

He asked her to fetch Tammy to speak to him, but, "Haven't seen 'er . . ." came the reply, with a bang of the window.

He sagged against the granite stone wall shaking his head, then pushed himself upright and went slowly down to the harbour.

There he leaned against his boat which had been drawn up onto the slipway, and breathed in the morning air. The two figures that joined him were in no better shape than himself. They guffawed and pushed at each other and leered at him in the sunlight.

"She doan't want a know 'ee now," grinned Casley, and Ben giggled. "You'm done fer."

"Get off . . ." snarled Jem.

"I told 'ee."

"An' I tell 'ee now – leave off!" He strode off down to the quay.

It was true that he was warned not to go on to Tammy's after coming out of the Black Knight, but he'd ignored it. His amorous instincts, roused by the liquor he'd consumed, craved for her warmth and love.

He fingered the small square box in his pocket and drew it out, flipping back the lid. The stone, as ice-cool as the surf, winked back at him.

The good Lord forgive him, but he'd had it in his hand when he'd barged in through the cottage door, seized hold of her around the waist and asked her to marry. Swaying with his drunken stupor and breathing beer fumes all over her.

She'd pushed him away against the dresser, making the crockery rattle, and shrieked her horrified refusal out to him, then slammed the kitchen door and ran up the stairs. Hannah Jane had thrust the broom at him and bundled him out onto the flagstones.

All was now in ruins. He should have waited until today. Or better still, he should have gone straight to her the first evening he was home on leave, instead of being waylaid by that rowdy group of his mates. They'd been collecting for the Lifeboat fund, and had started to egg and urge each other on to have chunks of their hair clipped off for a shilling a time. It was necessary of course to have a round of drinks between each bet, and soon they'd fetched up around fifty pounds in the kitty. Which was good, but his life was now wrecked. He thrust the box miserably into his pocket, then pulled it out and raised his arm to throw it into the sea.

A shout came from the right and he swung round, pushing the box hurriedly back into his pocket. Jacob was shuffling on his rheumatic feet towards him, and the old boy paused and slowly sank his weight down onto a crab pot. He pressed the tobacco into his pipe with a gnarled finger and struck a match, puffing away with the smoke rising into the air.

"I heard 'ee last night," he grunted. "Some racket goin' on."

"Well . . ."

"Ain't no peace around 'ere, now-a-days."

"Nope," Jem sighed.

"Yer Da is lookin' fer 'ee," Jacob warned.

"We're not goin' to sea t'day."

"He's still 'ollerin' fer 'ee," Jacob pushed himself up with his stick.

Jem groaned, "He wants to start paintin' the boat, I s'pose."

"Ah," the old boy moved off along the wall to the long wooden bench and joined the rest of the aged salts, basking in the sun.

Jem heard his father's voice coming down the lane, so he jumped up and went quickly into the boathouse. He rummaged amongst the tools on the bench and found a paint scraper and brush, and started work on the boat. When his father appeared, he was busy scraping the old flaky paint off the bow.

"Well – already at it?" he said.

Jem grunted in reply.

"I didn't think to see you – after last night."

Jem grunted again and brushed the side of the boat down. He went to fetch the paint tin and began slapping the paint on to the timbers.

"Hey!" yelled his father, "What colour's that s'posed to be?"

Jem looked down and saw that he'd opened up a tin of yellow.

"That's fer yer mother's kitchen – fer dear soul's sake, go and sleep off yer hangover," his father gave him a shove.

Jem flung the brush down and stalked off across the quay.

Tamsin sat miserably on the edge of her bed. She wouldn't ever go near him again. To have her love turned into a mockery, leering in a drunken sprawl over her. She swore she'd never go near him again.

She tightened the scarf over her head and went down to feed the dog. Her mother came in with a bag of groceries from the cove shop.

"Your Jem raised over fifty pounds las' night," she said.

"Ha . . ."

"Had 'is hair all chopped about – all of 'em 'ad their hair chopped about – daft varmints!" Hannah Jane laughed.

"What!" Tamsin swung round, "Was that what it's all about?"

"Raised over fifty pounds fer the lifeboats – it's all over the village," nodded her mother admiringly.

"Oh . . ." wailed Tamsin, as she ran out of the door and down to the harbour.

Jem was sitting on the sand, leaning against a crab pot and staring forlornly out at the waves.

She flung herself down by his side and he caught her hand and just held it.

"I 'ad to give m'self time to think – out 'ere on the boats – out 'ere on the shore – a time from the madness of the war goin' on back there," he told her.

"You gump – you should've said," she breathed against his neck.

He took out the small box from his pocket and opened it. The small diamond sparkled up at her in the sunlight, and tears came into her eyes as he pushed it awkwardly onto her finger.

"But Jem – you 'aven't seen," she swallowed, "us girls did the same as you – we got over forty pound the other night!" She pulled back her scarf, and amongst her long waving curls, her head gleamed with chopped spikes.

He was horrified, his mouth dropped open as he clutched at her shoulders and shouted "Tammy!"

Then, "Yow!" and he was laughing and shouting, and she was laughing and shouting, rubbing their hands over the stubble on

240

each other's head.

Then he kissed her – and she kissed him – and they fell onto the sands, laughing and kissing and holding each other, careless of the incoming waves.

36

Where Wheal Venton stood on the moorland, the headframe sheave-wheels went round as the cage descended underground with the rumbling sound of the turning drum.

In the ray of yellow lamplight stoper Simeon Trewin drilled into the stone, and the rock and caverns trembled as he bored the holes for firing. Water tickled down the walls in the hot clinging air. When he'd filled the holes with cartridges of gelignite, the miners swiftly withdrew from the face, the last setting the fuse alight.

In the dusty dark, the thunderous blast blew out stone and ore amidst acrid-choking fumes.

Swirling vapour clouded the warren of dripping tunnels in curling threads between dank walls, coiling about the weeping granite, red dust husking the mens' laboured breathing.

As soon as the smeech settled Ezra and Jory hammered and pounded, breaking the rock that filled the tunnel into smaller pieces, their half-naked figures dripping with perspiration.

Another breaker, Bevil Penhalligan joined them, splitting the stone. With the clang of pick and shovel and the fall of each hammer blow, the rock was worked through the 'grizzly' to roll down the chute. The swinging of tool and iron and the strenuous toil of shovelling broke up the ore as it rattled down into the buckets below.

Yellow rays danced on the dark walls from the piercing glow of their helmet lamps, flickering across the slime pools thick with the red of iron oxide lying between the rails running into the gloom.

Searching beams lit up the silhouettes of grimed features and dust-rimmed lining of the miners' gleaming eyes, and the broken lumps of tin ore that filled buckets for the trammers to move the mass of rock away from the working face.

Janner and Grenfell shunted the loaded iron trucks along the rails, ghost figures riding the laden trucks, rumbling through the black tunnels. A curving line of grey tin ore going back and forth with the trucks swaying and lurching, and stopping in turn to tip and fill the skips which then went up to the surface above.

With a signal given on the bell, the skips in the cage rose upwards, level by level and old man Mathias was there to work the winding gear.

There was the bell for fourteenth level, another for the tenth, another for the seventh. Tin ore and miners rose up and down with the power of the winding engine.

Deep down in the bottom level, beneath Venton ground worked the miner who was known as Big Bryok. More than seven feet he stood, with a fiery temper, his hard fists making any man stand back.

From pocket, from pack, he stole by sleight of hand any coin he could, and any woman he took from rival or friend. Any coat of cloth he took by stealth, fighting his way, putting any man down and with his hard-drinking gait and because of his stance, his height, his width and his girth, he was known far and wide as Bad Bryok - Bryok the thief, Bryok the liar, Bryok the hound.

"We keep well clear of the likes of 'im," Ezra told Zach.

Simeon was working his shift, when down in the bottom level came a rumbling tremor and a shuddering quake.

All the miners stood still, holding their breath, listening, with fear in their hearts.

Feeling the ground all around them shaking, they dropped their tools to make their escape. Stones and debris rained down on them in a deafening sound, striking and engulfing them in the dark tunnel. Simeon looked back, shouting to Bryok, but because of his immense height the large man was wedged by a huge slab of rock lodged against his broad shoulders, so that moving would cause the roof to collapse upon them all.

"Come on, Bryok!" shouted Simeon again. But Big Bryok stood there, unwilling to move, holding up the roof upon his wide shoulders in the choking dust, holding up the roof upon his broad back.

"Run, boys, run! – I'll hold up the prop!" he bellowed. "Run, while I c'n hold fast – get out boys!"

They ran, digging with their hands, their fingers, their nails, with pick or shovel, to move the fallen rock blocking the way. One by one they scrambled through, fearful in their haste to reach the surface, the warning hooter sounding throughout the mine. As each one passed, each touched him farewell, and soon he was the last to be left underground. Then as he tried to ease himself out, the rock moved and with a roar came tumbling down.

The rescue team searched through the levels and dug their way through the fallen debris for survivors, but failed to find any trace of Big Bryok.

It was a sombre Ezra who met Zach and Seth on the quay, as they returned from the fishing grounds at the end of the day. They sat in Clarissa's kitchen talking about Big Bryok as a boy and the way of life he'd chosen.

"He wasn't all bad," muttered Zach.

"He wasn't all good, either," grunted Ezra.

Clarissa sighed, "Well, I hope he's now at peace, poor soul."

The men went out and joined others down at the Black Knight, huddled around the old pew seats clutching their tankards of ale, commiserating on Big Bryok and his widowed mother.

Hannah Jane and Tamsin made up a basket of food, adding a well-hoarded small packet of tea as a little something to help Bryok's mother, for she'd be short of his wages in the days ahead.

"I'll take this up to 'er now an' see if there's anythin' we c'n do fer her," Hannah picked up her coat. She opened the door just as Clarissa Rose came to the gate and joined her on the same errand.

Tamsin sat sadly at her window and re-read Jem's letter that had arrived that morning . . .

' . . . everything's covered in dry sandy dust 'ere, Tammy, an' on the shore you'd never believe the insects 'ere, all swirling in the humid heat of the burning sun. Whenever we have a break, we huddle in any shade we can find on the ship.

The glaring white of the sun sears your eyes and the winds blow hot and thirsty, and there are days when everything lies still in a lifeless air. I see the rippling seas slip and slide in the shimmering haze, and I dream of the salt-laden westerlies, ice-cold, and the swooping gulls with their noisy cries, where the Celtic seas roar and fling up their showers of white surf.

I often think of my boat in the harbour and of going out to sea to fish for mackerel, or setting crabpots for lobster and crab an' watching the sunrise light the horizon.

The stars are brilliant in the dark sky tonight, star-spangled I think you'd call them, in very bright clusters.

How long will it be, I never stop thinking, before I hear our church bells chime again? How long will it be before I touch your hand - before I see once more your long hair blowing wild? To see your bright eyes brim with unshed tears of happiness and the curve of your quiet smile, that haunts the dreams that I left behind . . . ?

And down - way down - in the far deep down, lies a big, big man in a deep dark grave. No longer the bad, no longer the hound, but Bryok the brave.

Above that place, his fellow miners and men, and all those whose lives he had helped to save, raised up a stone with his name inscribed –

'Bryok the brave lies here'

37

The early evenings would find nearly every cottage door in the village and cove wide open to the last warm rays of the sun, the women and young girls sitting in their doorways busy with lengths of wool and knitting needles.

They knitted their way through numerous pairs of gloves, of socks, of scarves and woollen hats, to send in bulky parcels to the men at the warfront. Drawers and cupboards were searched for unused jumpers to unravel and wind up into re-usable skeins.

"I wish we could 'ave a bit more colour to work with," said Tamsin.

She and Kathy were trying to keep up with the clicking needles of Hannah and Clarissa Rose.

"It's got to be like that for camouflage," her mother reminded her.

"I know," giggled Kathy, "but you get a bit tired of khaki, browns and blacks."

"Oh, you young things're always after somethin' bright," sighed Hannah Jane.

Clarissa came to the end of her ball of wool, "You wouldn't want Jem or Pete to be shot at while waving rainbow gloves at the enemy."

"Hold out yer arms, Kathy," Hannah picked up another skein of wool, looping it over Kathy's wrists and began to wind it into the next ball for knitting.

Kathy moaned, trying to keep her arms steady, "This's the worst job – it's the very devil fer makin' yer arms ache."

As well as using the wool from unravelled knitted garments, the women would go out and help at the farms at sheep shearing time. In lieu of payment for rounding up the flocks and rolling the fleeces to be sent away to the mills, they could take away a certain amount of the fleeces that they wanted.

Hannah and Clarissa would bring a fleece down from Pencherrow, that Eli had saved for them, and take it into Gracie to spin. Of the many spinners who spun yarn in the cottages and farmhouses dotted around, Gracie Bussow was one of the finest.

She would sit in her doorway at her spinning wheel in the evening sunshine, and Tamsin would often help her to clean the fleece and card it into a rollag. Gracie would then spin it onto a bobbin, using the foot pedal on the spinning wheel.

"When you've spun two bobbins you c'n put these on the 'Lazy Kate' an' twist the yarn together. That makes a thicker and stronger thread," she told her as her fingers flew around the whirring wheel.

Clarissa would dye the skeins, mostly in dark colours for knitting woollen items to include in the parcels for the servicemen. But she also made lighter colours by using blackberries, onion skins or flowers for knitted clothes for some of the family.

When the cooler weather came, in autumn and winter, Gracie would sit in the corner of the room on a low stool, spinning with busy hands and singing to herself, her nimble fingers darting about the whirling wheel, twisting the threads onto the bobbin.

From her window looking out onto the bay she could see the boats at anchor and the fishermen working on the decks or coming ashore, while she entwined the yarn into sombre shades or into the colours of summer flowers.

Gideon Lidgey was a recluse, living in a solitary cottage on the side of Carn Kenidzhek, a hoary cairn of great slabs of rock rising up from the moor. He was one of the old style weavers who still worked a weaving loom, and was able to weave rich intricate patterns in contrasting shades of colour.

When a special piece of cloth or garment was wanted, the villagers would buy the skeins from the spinners and trudge their way along the stony track going up the cairn to his door.

Mary Anne would spin the wool from Eli's Pencherrow sheep, then take some of the dyed skeins to Gideon to weave into a shawl, a scarf or a length of cloth.

He would blend her fine spun wool, winding the greens of the fern and bracken, the emerald of the woodpecker and the rufous of the vixen of the valley into the cloth, the quivering loom with uncoiling skein threading a tawny of the buzzard, a blue-black of the chough into a pastoral fabric.

Biddy Penhale at her spinning wheel spun the fleeces from Job's Carn Gazick flock, and Gideon would weave patterns of the nut-browns and leaf-greens of the patchwork fields for her, with the milky cream of the seagull and barn owl.

From Trevarrick sheep he would wind Martha's spun skeins into sapphire blues of Botallack's wild seas, the pewter granite of Crown's tin mine, the subtle shades of the copper and tin ore, the filament of rose quartz and hazy amethyst crystal.

Tamsin sat watching Gracie at her spinning wheel and suddenly realised that it was her mother's birthday the next month.

"You've given me an idea for a present."

Gracie nodded at her bobbin, "You'd like some wool?"

"Some of your pretty shades, they'll make mother a lovely shawl."

"She'll like that," Gracie smiled, "I 'ave these 'ere, blue's, purple's, yellow – take yer pick."

"Oh, they're really fine - just right."

Gracie gave a chuckle, "Gideon'll come up with an 'andsome

pattern with these."

"Don't you say anythin' to her," warned Tamsin.

"Not a word," Gracie left her wheel to pick out the skeins for her.

The cairn was shrouded in mist as Tamsin climbed the track up to Gideon's cottage. She could hear the clatter of his loom as she drew nearer and lifted the latch of the door, which was half open.

He smiled at her, having already seen her coming past the window, and she saw that he was working at the loom on a design of rustic colours with the thrumming rhythm of the shuttle and frame.

She unwrapped Gracie's skeins of soft shades, "For mother's birthday, perhaps a shawl for her?"

Gideon nodded happily, "Always a lovely spinner is Gracie," he said, and was finishing off his present item as Tamsin made her way back down the steep path.

That evening he began to set up the frame to work on a shawl for Hannah Jane, with the golden strands of dusky thread interlacing the warp on the loom, and the waltzing dance of the flying shuttle turning the weft through the twisted yarn. He entwined the yellow of the gorse, the snowy flecks of the cascading surf, the blush of seapink and white bryony, the purples of the heather and viper's bugloss, his fingers weaving nature's tapestry.

A shawl in such colourful hues of the summer flowers that made Hannah Jane's eyes twinkle with delight when she opened her gift.

"Oh, Tammy!" she sighed. "How beautiful!"

38

Ferris, the son of Zekel the preacher, lodged with his cousin in Penzance, as they both now worked on one of the trawlers. Whenever he was ashore he would wake up to a vibrant call as the grey dawn broke upon the sky. The harbour would be bright with the glowing warmth of the rising sun, and his attic room rosy with it's light.

The shrill cry echoed along the quay, up and down with a clarion note, a clear voice ringing like a bell, "Who'll buy my fresh mack'rel?"

The fishermen knew her as Penzance Polly, trim and round, with her basket of harvest from the sea. She walked along the streets, with her father leading the donkey and cart loaded with fish, the early fleet having just come in and landed their catch upon the quay.

Ferris would leap out of his bed and run down the stairs into the cobbled street, shaking the sleep from his eyes, to catch a glimpse of her long fair hair, as her nimble feet tripped away to sell her wares.

He would meet up with her to follow and talk with her along the way, on the quay and on the street corner, and began to court her with a smile and a touch of her hand.

If he was at sea, he'd walk with her in the evenings after coming ashore, or as the setting sun sank slowly down the fading sky, he'd wait for her just to hear her voice.

One day he gathered up his courage and fervently asked her, "Polly dear, will you marry me?"

But she looked at him with laughing eyes, shaking her hair, and dancing out of reach, "Not to a poor fisherman!" she said. And so it was with heavy disappointment that he sailed the next morning on the ebbing tide.

He came over to Porthgwyna at the end of the week and was sitting on the bench by the sea wall with some of the cove men, when Zach asked him, "Why don't you fish 'ere with your own boat?"

"Well - " Ferris scratched the side of his head, "I got to put in a couple of new ribs an' do one or two other jobs on 'er."

"I'll give 'er a look over fer you when you're ready."

Ferris nodded his thanks, "I've got to get together some money fer that yet," and he started making a list of the items he'd need, as he made his way back to Penzance.

There was the usual group of Naval officers in the town from the recently anchored destroyer in the bay. They were seen everywhere, in the inns, in the pubs, eating and drinking, and he suddenly saw Polly sauntering past arm in arm with one of them.

He started towards her, but, "What's the use? She don't want the likes o' me," he thought and turned away.

Every now and again he would see them together in the street, the officer glancing at her with a roving eye as they wandered up and down the promenade on a fair evening, showing off like a pair of gay peacocks.

He had obviously given her the new silk dress she was wearing and the rings on her fingers.

All through the summer whenever the warship was in harbour, they were like two bright young butterflies, flitting here and there, living without thought or care.

No longer was Polly seen on the quay in the early mornings to meet the fishing fleet coming in. Her father with the donkey and cart would walk the streets alone selling his fish.

When Ferris woke with the sun's soft rays, her voice no longer smote his ear with its joyful note and trilling cry, "Who'll buy my fresh mack'rel?"

But then there came the time when, with officers and crew

the ship left the bay with orders to join the fleet again, and when the autumn winds came sweeping round the corners of the town, the nights began to draw in.

Many months went by, but there was no news of the ship and how she fared, and Ferris would see Polly standing on the quay searching the sea for any sign of the vessel.

He tried again and again to befriend her, but she bitterly wept and cried. She threw off all her fine silks and jewellery and walked the shore, forever seeking the horizon.

Eventually she rose once more at dawn with the donkey and cart to meet the fishing boats as they came in, but all the pertness of her voice became a hoarse and husky cry that croaked out in the morning air.

She didn't feel or care that the cold winter's fierce gales whipped her hair in tangled strands, the salt spray from the sea and all the dank and swirling mists drenched and chilled her to the bone, until at last she pined away.

Ferris grieved for Polly, his heart seemingly to be frozen in an icy grip. He would wake and imagine he still heard her voice in the early dawn, a faint voice calling up and down along the quay.

He would run out into the street and search until his eyes grew dim, but couldn't glimpse the like of her who called on the morning tide.

Her voice seemed to echo round and round, calling from the quay, drifting through the morning air. His sweet Polly, trim and fair, her clear voice ringing like a bell, "Who'll buy my fresh mack'rel?"

At last he went to the recruiting office and enlisted, leaving the town and all he knew behind.

Sadly, Zach and Seth pulled his boat high up the slipway away from the water's edge and tide.

253

"We'll keep an eye on it fer 'im," Seth carried the oars to the boathouse.

Zach nodded, "He'll be alright once he gets in with the other lads."

39

Ephraim tramped from barn to barn on the many outlying farms, taking his ease and spending nights amongst the straw put out for the sheep. He kept away from those that housed cattle because being larger animals, they took up all the space and also ate the bedding, leaving him with scant covering.

He would do some work for the farmers for his food and meet up with some of the farmhands on his travels, and venture into the villages every now and again for 'vitals' and his whisky.

He came to know many of those working in the fields and with the farm animals, and he met up with Walt now and then for he also liked his whisky.

Both of them were sitting against the granite wall by the field gate leading on to a large area of plain, the Gump, where Carn Kenidzhek rose from the stunted windswept heath, rearing darkly crag on crag against the sky. The winds up here would whistle round the cairn, crying with an eerie wailing.

The plain was once dotted with circular crellas and round huts of granite walls with roofs of dried bracken where the Cornu-Britons once lived. They kept herds of beef and flocks of sheep with the curling horn on the hill slopes. Beyond were the moors where they hunted the boar and the savage segh, the moose deer, their segh dogs racing to hurl themselves upon their prey. And beyond the moors, the forest, where they ran with their dogs after bear and bull, hunting, fowling and hurling.

Scores of small barrows and cairns of stones still lie where many were slain and their ashes interned, after a great battle with Athelstan's Saxon army.

Ephraim lifted his rheumy eyes to the plain, saluting it with

255

the whisky bottle and took a long swallow, "They ancients made their liquor with berries."

Walt chuckled, "I bet it was potent."

"Don't know what it tasted like."

"I bet not as good as whisky," grunted Walt.

Ephraim turned his head, "Aah – who's this comin'?" He looked towards the end of the track where they could hear the engine of a motorbike coming over the rise.

"Looks like Zach," Walt hid his whisky inside his jacket. He'd just finished work at Lizzie's place and didn't want Zach saying anything to her. "Who's on the back of 'im?"

"It's young Matt," grinned Ephraim.

Zach came to a halt beside them, switching off the engine and straddling the machine, "Ephraim?"

"Zach – nice evenin' ain't it?" the old tramp waved his hand to him.

"Time you went on to Lizzie's, or wherever you're staying tonight."

"Goin' to Trevarrick."

"Over the moor?"

"Aah . . ." grunted Ephraim.

"Well, get there before it gets late," replied Zach.

Matt leant over from the back seat, "The Spriggans of the Gump come out at midnight – they'll 'ave you!"

"Haw!" spluttered Walt, " 'tis old wives' tale."

"You'll get 'mazed'," laughed Matt.

"Naw – we'll be gone by then," Walt sank back against the wall.

"You best be off now then," Zach kicked the engine into life, roaring off up the lane.

Walt slyly took out his whisky and drank. It was good after a day's work. He nudged Ephraim, "Come's on, we'll make tracks."

256

Ephraim struggled to his feet and they made their way slowly, gazing around at the moor with the sea in the distance.

"Tha's a nice sunset."

"Bootiful," Walt followed the path over the heath until Ephraim sat down against a boulder.

"Let's 'ave a rest 'ere."

They talked about the sheep they could see grazing on the plain, the farmhands, the fishermen, then they set off again, wandering about and sipping their whisky.

"I should think we're nearly there," Walt guessed.

"Look out fer the Little People," chuckled Ephraim.

The evening dusk was quietly falling, when faint whispers of sound came on the breeze.

"Hark!" Walt stood still.

"What?"

"That . . ."

" 'Tis Trevarrick's wireless."

"Hark!" Walt turned to face the breeze.

" 'Tis nothin'." Strange echoes of haunting music came over the plain.

Walt felt a compelling tingling in his feet and found them tapping and stepping to the rhythm. Soon Ephraim, his stiff joints complaining, joined in a swaying gait.

"Hey – look at you!" he cried.

" 'Way we go!" shouted Walt merrily, waving his whisky bottle to the tune.

Quicker and faster went the beat of the rhythm, rippling and trilling, that had their feet soon dancing away. They pranced and turned in abandon, and soon they thought they saw a frolicking throng joining in, of sprightly Spriggans in nimble frenzy, whirling around them and singing in lively song.

Hour on hour they danced over the moor, unable to stop, up to the cairn and across the heather, their weary limbs dancing

257

all through the night.

The hill was glowing with tiny lights that lit up the midnight sky. The Spriggans gave them morsels of fruit and wine, as they held their mystic revels with feasting and dancing.

As Walt and Ephraim gaily skipped and twirled, slowly the mists of morning light brought the dawn creeping across the horizon, and with the rising sun Spriggans and music soon melted away.

Walt wearily sank to the ground as the music softly faded, slowing the compulsive rhythm in their feet, and Ephraim gave a great sigh and lay outstretched in the bracken to rest.

When Zach found that the pair hadn't arrived at Trevarrick, he rounded up a group of farmhands to search for them. They went the rounds of the barns on the nearby farms, then spread out on the moor to look.

They found the two lying in the dew, not knowing where they'd been, where they were, or how they'd got there.

"Some party last night," grinned Walt. Zach pulled at his arm and with Grenfell on the other, hauled him to his feet. Janner and Casley lifted Ephraim and held him steady as he cackled, "You should 'ave bin 'ere."

"Where's everyone?" Walt waved his empty whisky bottle and gazed around the moor, his eyes blinking in the sunlight.

"You're on the Gump," Zach yelled in his ear. "You bin 'ere all night!"

"Aah – that so?"

"Time you got home, lean on me," Zach moved forward. But Walt's legs wobbled and wouldn't hold him after leaping about on them all through the night, and he collapsed into the bracken again. Grenfell and Seth had to carry him back over the plain to where Zach had left his car.

Casley and Janner didn't fair much better with Ephraim, who

waved his arms to a vague tune that he hummed.

Walt lay back in the rear seat of the car and when they reached Lizzie's farm, looked around in confusion.

"What's up with 'im?" she peered through the car window at him.

Zach smirked, "He's bin 'mazed' by the Spriggans magic. He an' Ephraim bin up on the Gump all night."

"Well, you better leave both of them to sleep it off in m'barn," she said.

"He'll never be the same again," laughed Zach, "an' as fer Ephraim – we all know he was already 'mazed' to start with!"

40

The women of the village were busy unwrapping white dresses from their tissue paper and searching in their needlework boxes for new ribbons, which were worn by the young girls and women for the midsummer celebrations.

Hannah Jane held Jessica's dress against her shoulders and looked at the short length.

"Oh, dear – you've grown too quickly this year," she sighed, "we'll 'ave to make you another."

Jessica giggled, "I'll really show a lot of leg in this."

Tamsin shook the creases out of her dress and checked it over.

"I've got a grass stain on one side. That's come from sitting on the bank last year, it must 'ave been damp."

Clarissa came through the kitchen door, "You can give Jessica's dress to a smaller child, an' maybe get a bigger size from some-one else. I don't know about yours Tamsin, I expect we'll 'ave to find some material somewhere an' make a new one."

"It'll be a bit expensive to buy," Hannah replied, "I'll ask around."

"We could sew a new panel in the side," suggested Tamsin.

"It won't match, you can be sure about that," Hannah sighed.

"We might be able to get the same material," Tamsin draped the dress over the chair, and took in a deep breath as she'd felt slightly queasy since early morning.

Clarissa folded the dresses into their tissue, "I'll take these round the village an' find out who's got what. We c'n make a list of exchanges for anyone needing a different size."

She met Zach in the lane who put his hand on her arm. "Go up to Zekel's house, he's just had word that Ferris has bin killed in an explosion."

Clarissa gasped, "Oh, Zach!"

"He's all on 'is own, just sittin' there in the yard, though his daughter'll be there soon," he went into the cottage.

Hannah Jane's eyes filled with tears when he told her, for the preacher, a widower, was a kindly soul and always had a good word for everyone.

Tamsin felt a cold fear sweeping over her as she thought of Jem. She had written a good many times but hadn't heard from him for months. Pete was on the same ship and his mother hadn't had any news from him either.

"I'll put the kettle on," but as she turned towards the range, the queasiness took a hold and she hurried out of the door. Her mother glanced up at her, with a slight frown.

Zach looked at the pieces of tissue left about, "You're getting' ready early."

"We'll need to. Jessica's grown out of hers an' Tamsin needs a new dress altogether," she said.

"Seth'll 'ave to dip into his savings then," Zach chuckled.

"An' I'll be off up to Zekel's an' see what I c'n do fer 'im."

The beginning of May became sunny and warm, with the fields and cliffs looking brighter in the sunshine. The blackthorn was out with snow-white blossom and the gorse in full yellow flower.

Suddenly, news broke out all over the country, with the announcement that hostilities had ended and the war was over. Windows and doors were flung open as the excitement from the wireless echoed up and down the lanes.

Villagers poured into the streets from their cottages and work places, laughing and shouting the glad news. Housewives banged their pans, lads rang their bicycle bells, drivers sounded horns, the baker and his daughters waved aprons and gave away trays of buns, the Reverend Glyn Owen rang the church bells. The fishermen and boats let off their hooters from the harbour, Crantok the blacksmith beat his huge gong with his hammer, the Black Knight poured out free ale and cider, farmers and farmhands waved their hoes at anyone passing by, and the mine sounded off its hooter, bringing all the miners underground to the surface, to hear the great news and join in the excitement and joy of relief that the war at last was over.

The black-out curtains were pulled down and that night the villages, coves and every farmhouse scattered around the countryside was lit up with lights shining from the windows again. Tamsin was jubilant, for it meant that soon Jem would be home, though at the same time she still felt anxious.

Everybody began to prepare for a celebration to be held in the village square if the weather was good. Each family gave what they could and every kitchen was filled with various aromas of cooking. Cakes minus currants, but with homemade jam in the middle, biscuits, jellies, butter and cream given by the farms for spreading on splits and buns, spam sandwiches and apple juice and cider.

Eli had brought a large ham from his own pig allowance to slice up to make real ham sandwiches.

The children cut out and strung up triangle shapes from coloured paper and pieces of cloth for flags, and joined up paper chains which were stuck together with glue made from boiling fish scraps.

Ezra, Simeon, Casley and Grenfell with their farmhand friends, hung them from windows, launders and drainpipes until the square was festooned with colourful bunting fluttering in the breeze.

The women made paper hats of witches, pirates, army and Robin Hood shapes from newspaper and coloured paper, while the girls plaited ribbons with wild flowers for their hair. Zach and Seth put together long trestle tables to set up in the square with a various mixture of chairs and school benches.

A great sound of laughter filled the air, with chatter and excited gossip echoing from cottage to cottage as the women set out large plates of food and the feasting began. Tamsin and Hannah Jane walked up and down filling a varied assortment of cups and mugs with apple juice and cider.

"Have one of these," her mother was passing around a plate of Eli's ham sandwiches, "I 'aven't had ham for ages."

"They're nice," Tamsin bit into one as she poured the last of the juice from her jug. She was taking a sip of cider when her face suddenly paled and she rushed round the corner of the nearest cottage.

"You're not looking too good," Hannah said when she came back.

"It must be something I ate. I expect it's the cider," Tamsin busied herself with taking round a plate of cakes.

The merriment went on till the late hours of the night, with many toasts raised to their lads in the services who'd fought for their country's freedom.

Zach appeared a few days later with a large package under his arm.

" 'Ere you are," he lifted it onto the table, "just what you've bin lookin' fer."

Hannah Jane unwrapped it, "Oh, Zach!"

"Parachute silk," he grinned, "one of Seth's mates in the Home Guard got it fer me."

"I c'n make two dresses out of this for Tamsin and Kathy. They'll be really pleased."

That evening the two girls were busy taking measurements and drawing patterns on newspaper, while Clarissa and Hannah pinned and cut the cloth and started sewing.

Tamsin had written to Jem again, for there hadn't been any news of his ship. Now the war in Europe had ended, her hopes had risen of seeing him again soon, but the war with Japan was still going on and she realised that he must still be out there.

Seth came home the following morning from landing his catch at the market. He had some mackerel which he slapped onto the draining board.

"I'll 'ave a couple of these fried fer m'breakfast. How about you Zach?"

Zach grinned, " 'andsome."

"They look good, I'll put the pan on," Tamsin washed and rolled them in breadcrumbs to make them crispy, then put the pan on the range.

Clarissa was helping Hannah to make bread. They found that it was quicker to do a big batch together. Tamsin turned the mackerel over, then caught her breath at the strong fish odour.

"Watch these mum," she groaned, "I got to go out a minute."

"She's lookin' peaky," Zach looked over at Hannah, "somethin' she ate?"

"She's bin upset a bit lately, I ought to – ah – oh – um . . ." Hannah glanced at Clarissa who gave her a knowing look, then raised her eyes heavenwards.

"I'll go out to her," Hannah murmured.

"What is it?" asked Seth.

"I'll make 'er a cup of tea, that'll settle 'er," Clarissa put the kettle on to boil, "an' I think a couple of plain biscuits."

Hannah walked with her daughter round the small garden, then left her sitting on the bench.

"She all right?" asked Seth again.

"Well – it's er . . ."

"Well man," Clarissa added, "You know . . ."

"Know what?"

"Now, say you won't go off the deep end!" Hannah sat down

264

beside him.

"Deep end?"

"Well - you've got family – you know all about it."

"What! You mean . . ?" Seth spluttered. "Who is it? I'll wring his neck to starboard!"

"Jem, of course," Clarissa said calmly.

"They're engaged after all." Hannah sat back as Seth leapt to his feet shouting, "That's no matter!"

" 'Tis natural," she said, "no more than you once were." Seth opened his mouth to protest then shut it as he met the twinkle in her eyes.

"I'll still get m'hands on him!" he muttered.

"You can't – he's missing – he might be dead." Tamsin appeared in the doorway, tears in her eyes.

Seth strode over to her and enfolded her in his arms, "Oh, Tammy, m'little bird. He'll turn up."

"I've written an' written, an' I've heard nothing," cried his daughter.

"His father hasn't heard either, an' he'd be the first to 'ave a letter from the Admiralty," Hannah Jane poured out cups of tea.

Seth remarked, "We c'n do somethin' about that. I'll go an' see our Home Guard captain. He c'n pull strings to find out about the ship."

"He'll get an answer a lot quicker than we will," added Zach.

"Oh, Grandfer," Tamsin hugged him. He patted her shoulder and watched her climb the stairs. She sat sadly at her window and looked out across the bay at the waves surging onto the beach. "Jem," she thought, "I know you'll come back, I know." She picked up her pen and began another letter . . .

" . . . when will you soon be on your way home? I'll wait for you Jem. I'm writing again in case my other letters have been lost. I'm writing with hope and longing for you. Remember

Casley's boat and when we lay low on Nanven dunes, and giving me your ring on Porthgwyna sands? I can feel our love-child stirring – your first unborn son trembling within me. I'll never stop believing that you're still alive. Will you soon be here for your first child's coming? Will you be here with me for your child's first crying? Jem, I wait for you . . ."

Midsummer dawned bright and sunny and the children and young lads and lassies gathered by the gate, then made a long winding procession across the field to the Dons Meyn stone circle. The pillars of granite stone, long stones, whispering stones standing in a mystic circle, each to ancestors gone, where the Cornu-Britons once stood in the first rays of light to pay homage to the dawn, to vow to the rising sun, to celebrate the spring and summer.

The girls in white dresses with head garlands of leaves and flowers, clutching posies of daisies and buttercups, the lads in white shirts, waving coloured scarfs, danced in and out between the granite standing stones.

Flower children weaving garlands, in tunics of leaf green, flower buds in their hair, skipped with light footsteps, hands touching, lips smiling, dancing and turning between the stones.

Gracie sat on a low stool, playing rippling notes on her celtic harp, as Tamsin, dressed in white with a circle of flowers in her hair, as Lady of Flowers, passed between the dancers with a bouquet of wild flowers as sweet offering.

As she danced with the children, she had sorrow in her heart, but in the celtic circle she also felt rays of hope for Jem.

Merry music filled the air with Jan and Ben on their fiddles, Dan with the mouth organ, Eddy with his accordian and old Gundry tapping away on his tambourine and drum.

Zach had brought Gracie in his car, leaning her harp against the back seat and then carrying it over the field for her.

"Now I'll know the touch of the harp when I get to the pearly gates," he told her.

"Well, I'll most probably be there afore 'ee, so I'll put in a good word fer 'ee," she cackled.

Straw bales were set outside the stone circle for the children to sit on and enjoy a 'tea treat' which were saffron buns, this year without saffron and currants, and apple juice.

As the evening drew in, Simeon and Jory with a group of miners had cleared a large granite rock near one of the old mines. It had a number of holes drilled in it by miners in the past, midsummer holes, which had been filled with explosives at their midsummer celebrations and fired, making a great noise. Simeon did likewise and set off a succession of explosions, delighting the children.

When darkness fell, the bonfires that had been built on the cairns around, which everyone had added to during the past week, were set ablaze, lighting up the night sky.

The Land Girls were still at Frank's farm as Leah hadn't yet come back. Tamsin had helped them with the hay making, then cleared out the milking shed as Frank let the herd out into the field, before heading for home. She was setting the table while Hannah was busy at the range, when there came a timid knocking at the door. It opened and Beth Pollard looked in at both of them.

"We've had a telegram," she told them, "Pete's safe – his ship went down, but he was picked up by another."

Tamsin gasped, "An' Jem?"

Beth shook her head sadly, "I don't know. His dad's had a telegram that says Jem's missing. He's coming down now to let you know."

"Sit down, Tammy," Hannah Jane pushed her into a chair.

"Pete'll be here in a couple of days. He'll come an' tell you about it."

"Thanks Beth," Hannah took her hand, "I'm so glad fer you. We'll see Pete when he gets home."

Tamsin gave a sad smile, then went out into the garden, "I know you're out there somewhere, Jem," she breathed.

All that week she was up at the farm early for the milking, and then worked hard with the crops and the haymaking. It was while she was on the hay cart, that she looked up and saw Pete striding across the field.

She climbed down and ran towards him throwing her arms about him. He drew her close. He had lost a lot of weight, his face drawn and lined.

"Oh, Tammy, I'm sorry, so sorry about Jem."

"But I'm happy to see you safely back, Pete. I'm glad that you're home again."

"But Jem – I didn't see what happened to him."

"I just know he'll be back - sit down here an' tell me," she pulled him down onto a hay bale.

Pete gazed into the distance, "We were torpedoed. The ship was hit an' fire broke out. It was pandemonium. We swung the lifeboats out an' rafts, but a lot of them were damaged, so we were leaping into the sea. I found a raft an' clung on to it fer hours. Then one of the boats picked me up, but I couldn't see Jem. We pulled in all the men we could find, some in a bad way, an' we were drifting along with the current when we saw another destroyer headin' towards us.

That was a great moment I c'n tell you. They brought us home, picking up other survivors on the way. I looked all over the deck where we were crowded into any spare space available, an' I asked any new survivors they brought in fer news of Jem, but I didn't find 'im. I'm sorry, Tammy – I'm so sorry."

Tamsin stood up, "I can't thank you enough for looking out fer him. I know you did everything you could."

She felt a hard lump of sadness gripping her, as she walked across the field and over the moors to the cliff. Here, she sat looking out to sea, watching the waves tipped with white flecks of surf, rising and falling.

41

At Penhale farm, Job had rounded up some of the sheep into a pen, and had one ewe gripped between his legs as he clipped the nail on her front foot, when he looked up and saw three figures coming towards him. They were in army fatigues and each carried a bag over their shoulder.

"We're lookin' fer work, sir. Would you 'ave anything for us?" asked the taller one.

Job let the ewe go to scuttle over to join the rest of the sheep, as he straightened his back.

"Out of the army are 'ee?"

"Demobbed sir. We 'ave our demob savings an' c'n pay fer our lodgings."

"I c'n certainly do with a hand. Our Land Girls are goin' back today an' there's hay to be got in while the weather's good, an' one of you c'n help trim these ewes' feet," Job explained, "I'm short of workmen this week."

"Ellery sir, and this is my brother Logan. When we got back to Plymouth, our house'd been bombed an' we lost our parents with it."

Logan added, "We've been movin' around working 'ere an' there, but haven't found anythin' permament yet."

Job shook them by the hand.

"This here's Sawle," said Ellery, "his home's gone too, an' he hasn't got over the bomblast when he was hit by a shell. We found 'im wandering about down at the docks, so he's come with us. He's a bit quiet but a good worker."

"Well, you an' yer brother go across the field there an' you c'n help Ben an' Jan get in the rest of the hay. I'll show Sawle 'ere how to handle the ewes." Job watched the brothers stride over the field and begin tossing up the bales onto the cart. He turned to Sawle, " 'Ere you are," he said, getting hold of a ewe. "Catch her by the scruff round the neck and turn 'em, an' they'll sit fairly quietly against yer knees."

He watched as Sawle copied him, "That's it, now I'll clip the nail. They grow long y'see, an' if you don't trim 'em they'll grow under the hoof an' split an' be painful to walk on, an' yer sheep'll go lame."

They worked until Biddy came out at midday with a basket of pasties and cake.

"Here's m'wife, she'll fix us up with some crowst." Job pulled out mugs and a large cider flagon from under the shelter of the cart, keeping cool from the sun, as Ellery and Logan joined them.

" 'Ave you got anywhere to stay tonight?" Biddy asked. Sawle smiled up at her, "Not yet Missus."

"Well, the Land Girls are going so you c'n 'ave their rooms. We made up the little cottage fer them when they came, an' they c'n show you round before they go," said Biddy.

"We can't thank you enough," Ellery shook her hand, "we'll pay you a fair rent."

"You c'n eat with us," decided Job, "Biddy'll see you're alright."

They worked until late evening to finish the field, and then sat down around the large table in the farmhouse kitchen, and Biddy did indeed see they were alright with a well-cooked plentiful roast.

Ben and Jan were eating with them as well, before going back to their own farm.

"What made you come down this far in Cornwall?" asked Ben.

Ellery helped himself to more roast potatoes, "We were looking fer work all along the way, but one of our mates, Ferris, lived around 'ere. We came to find his father, Zekel, a

271

preacher I b'lieve. Do you happen to know 'im?"

"Zekel!" Biddy exclaimed, "Poor man, he ain't got over losing his son."

"Well," said Job, "you'll be able to go an' see him an' ease his mind."

"We bin asking fer 'im all over the place," Logan told them, "I'm glad we've found 'im at last."

Job had passed the news on to Zekel about the mates of Ferris now working at the farm, and the following Sunday they went over to see him.

He shook hands with them, "I'm very pleased you've come. It'll be nice to hear about Ferris, especially as you were the last ones to be with him."

"He was a good lad. Full of everything, an' would give a hand to help anybody," said Logan.

"He'd bring out a faded 'photo of him an' his sisters, leaning by the cottage door 'ere. An' he'd talk of his boat the Girl Rachel in the cove, an' settin' crab pots fer lobsters an' crab," remembered Ellery.

Zekel sighed, "Rachel was his mother. He named the boat after her."

"He'd tell us about fishing fer mackerel, when we were in the trenches with the shells screaming over our heads, shaking the ground," Logan shuddered with the memory.

Ellery shut his eyes, "When we went over the top through that thick mud, he was just behind me when the world around us exploded, slamming us into the opening crater, spewing earth and stone that came raining down on us."

"We heard the enemy comin', treading us into the ground, running over us, their boots pounding the stone," whispered Logan.

"I lay there stunned, gaspin' fer each breath, my ribcage

cracking with a knife-edged pain. I couldn't move," Ellery felt along his ribs. "I heard Ferris groaning, then felt his hand dragging me out of the pit."

"We rolled them both behind a crumbling wall an' lay there," added Logan.

"It all went silent. Ferris moaned again an' pushed somethin' into m'hand. Then another shell exploded over us an' everything went black – we didn't see 'im again," Ellery muttered.

Logan looked over at Zekel, "I hope we don't make it harder fer you, hearing about it."

"It does - but it also comforts me to know he had such good fellows as you with him at the end," Zekel replied.

Logan went on, "They carried us out fer miles in trucks that jolted us about all over that bomb-blasted terrain."

Ellery brought out a crumpled envelope, "When peace finally came, Logan an' I were adrift. No home, no job, friends an' faces gone. We wandered 'ere an' there, looking fer work, with little in our pockets because we didn't want to dip into our demob money. Then one day, what Ferris had pushed into my hand in his last moments, dropped out of my pocket," he passed it over to Zekel.

When he opened it, he found a photograph of Ferris with his sisters, Amy May and Alyssa, leaning against his boat on the slipway.

Sawle looked up, "I had a sister," he said quietly.

"I remember this. Ferris was going to give his sisters a trip round the island," Zekel had tears in his eyes as he gazed at the photograph.

"You keep it," Ellery said, "it helped us to find you."

Zekel turned to Sawle, "And you Sawle, were you there too?"

"I don't know," Sawle looked down confused.

273

Logan said, "We've asked 'im, and named all sorts of places, but he can't remember. He can't even remember comin' back, but he's got his demob pay, so he's down on an official list somewhere."

"I can't remember," Sawle mumbled sadly.

A voice called from outside, "Dad – where are you?" A young girl came into the room, and Ellery came face to face with the girl in the photograph, that he had looked at so often in the trenches. She smiled at him.

"This is Alyssa," said Zekel.

When the hay had all been brought in and Job decided he would keep the three men on for a while, they would go down to the shore on their day off from work, and watch the fishermen going out to sea or bringing in their catch.

They liked to walk over the cliffs and moors and hear the seagulls as they called and squabbled over fish scraps. As they were sitting outside one of the boat houses Ellery caught sight of the Girl Rachel.

There she was – in bad need of repair – but still beautiful in his eyes.

"Girl Rachel," he pointed her out to the others. They walked across the slipway and looked her over.

Zach was stacking empty fish boxes, "She wants a bit of work done on her."

"You've said it," replied Logan.

"Seth!" called Zach. "Come over 'ere an' tell us what Ferris had in mind."

Seth joined them, "Ferris had quite a few jobs to do on her, but he never got round to them. Zekel says you were with 'im."

"We were – it's sad that he's not with us today," Ellery ran his hand over the gunwale. "I used to go out fishin' with m'Dad when I was a youngster."

Zach laughed, "Well, you're not much more than that now. Why don't you ask Zekel if you c'n buy the boat from 'im? Better than lettin' her rot away 'ere."

Ellery's eyes lit up with interest. He looked sideways at Logan, who looked sideways at Sawle.

"I'll go," said Ellery, "you two stay 'ere," and he was off up the cliff path.

"You liking it over at Job's?" asked Zach.

Sawle nodded, "Biddy's good to us."

"She bakes a real 'andsome harvest supper," Seth chuckled, "an' here comes Ellery back with Zekel."

The two walked over to the Girl Rachel. Zekel put his hand on the bow.

"She's yours," he said, "when Ferris gave you the photo of the boat, I think he meant you to have her."

"We'll help you with some of the tools you'll need," Zach examined the stern, " saw, drill, hammer, nails . . ."

They pooled their demob savings to refit her, and in the evenings and on their days off from work, they slaved away at her ribs and gunwale, happy as sandboys, sawing, drilling, sanding and painting.

When she was ready, Alyssa came with a bottle of wine and sprinkled some of it over the stern, as they pushed the boat into the water, and they drank the rest with a toast to the Girl Rachel and to Ferris.

With her bows thrusting through the green wave, riding the ocean sway, her mizzen sail blowing high and free in the wind, they knew Ferris was out there with them.

42

Zach looked at his chickens. They'd had feathers pulled out of them which were floating around in the air, and there were two of the birds missing. Reynard Fox had got in the chicken house.

"I'll 'ave that varmint," he roared and stormed into the kitchen.

"Didn't you shut them up last night?" asked Clarissa.

"Matt's supposed to be doing it. I'll go down an' 'ave a word with that lad."

"The fox is only catching 'is dinner. If you leave them out he thinks they're his, though that's put them off laying now an' we'll 'ave no eggs," Clarissa stated.

"He don't need to 'ave my fowls, he's got plenty of rabbits around." Zach hurried off down the lane.

"Matt!" he shouted when he reached Seth's cottage. Matt appeared at the gate, and as soon as he saw Zach he knew he was in trouble. It was his job to go up to his grandfather's and shut the chickens in at night, then let them out in the morning and feed them, for some pocket money.

"I'm sorry, Granfer, I forgot."

"I don't pay you to forget. I've lost two birds an' now I'll 'ave to get more from somewhere," Zach strode down the path to the door.

"I had a football match at school an' it went on late. I just forgot about the chickens," Matt admitted.

Seth came to the door. He wasn't going to sea that day, the groundswell had got up with a blustery wind.

"What's the shouting?" he asked.

"I forgot to shut the chickens up last night," said his son.

"The fox 'as had two of them" added Zach.

"Well, you know what to do about that. We'll get a few of the lads and a couple of dogs an' find where 'e hangs out," Seth grinned.

"Leave old Reynard alone," said Hannah Jane. "If you shut the chickens in at night, he can't 'ave them."

"Huh – I'll 'ave that varmint!" Zach growled.

The men met up at Eli's farm. He was on his grey mare, followed by his collie who was racing around. Job was on the big farm horse and had his two terriers with him, his gun under his arm. Davy Pender came on his cob, with his sons Ben and Jan on borrowed mounts. Zach and Seth had a couple of Eddy's horses. Old Gundry turned up on an ancient donkey.

"What've you got there?" snorted Zach, "You ain't going to catch anything on that animal."

"Ha! He c'n put speed on when 'e gets going," Gundry gave it a pat, startling the donkey and it took off across the field.

"Not yet – we ain't started yet – pull 'im back."

"Woa, woa," Gundry juggled with the reins until the donkey came to the wall and halted. "There – see? 'E's eager to get goin'."

Ezra and James with Matt and Harry and a group of farmhands were on foot. Eli pointed towards the moorland bordering the field, "I've seen that fox crossing the far corner a couple of times this week. That's where 'e's coming from."

So they set off, the dogs excitedly running here and there, noses to the ground and the horses fresh and lively.

Seth perched awkwardly in the saddle, "I'd choose a tossing boat any day."

"This is your idea," muttered Zach. "This horse's too fat, m'legs aren't long enough fer its stomach."

"Towzer – come 'ere!" shouted Job, "It's no good, he's off." His terriers tore off across the field and onto the moor, shooting off into the heather, going all ways. The horses followed, the donkey lagging behind, showing no interest in hurrying after the others, no matter how Gundry urged him on.

Job followed Towzer over the bracken, while Ben and Jan took off on the trail of the other terrier.

Davy yelled, "The devils are hunting rabbits!" as the terriers and the collie yelped after rabbits scurrying in all directions.

"Call 'em off!" shouted Ben.

"Well, they know the smell of rabbit more than fox," said Job.

Then, "There he is!" pointed Eli and they saw Raynard jumping over the field wall into the bracken. One by one the horses soared over the wall, except for the donkey who suddenly came to a halt and Gundry shot over his neck into the heather.

Matt and Harry flung themselves breathlessly down beside him, while the collie licked Gundry's face.

"Gerroff you sloppy thing," he pushed him away.

"Some fun, this," Matt panted.

They leapt to their feet and tugged at the donkey's reins, but he'd begun grazing and wasn't going to move.

"I'll get on 'im an' you two push from behind, that'll shift 'im," Gundry pulled himself into the saddle.

"Giddy-up," he yelled in the donkey's ear as the boys pushed at its hindquarters, but the animal wouldn't go over the wall.

" 'Tis no good, he's too lazy to jump," cried Harry.

"I'll tell you what – we'll get on him an' get 'im to go round by the gate," Matt helped Gundry to slide off sideways, then he leapt onto its back with Harry behind him.

The donkey taken by surprise at the two on top with two pairs of heels digging in his side, turned, and pulling on the reins, Matt guided him towards the gate, with the collie yapping at its heels.

The lads jumped down and Gundry scrambled into the saddle and they picked their way across the moor.

"I see 'im!" came the call from Seth and they caught sight of Reynard's red coat moving swiftly through the heather towards the cliff.

"Head 'im off! Don't let 'im go over," Davy Pender galloped past them, the terriers racing ahead. One of the dogs disappeared while the other ran along the cliff. When Zach reached the edge there was no sign of the fox, but Towzer was teetering on a narrow ledge, ready to go over.

Zach leapt from the saddle and crouched down, putting his hand out to reach the dog. He grabbed its collar and hauled him back onto the turf.

"That's a near one fer you Towzer," said Job. He looked down the steep cliff to the rocks below and searched the shore.

"I can't see Reynard Fox anywhere."

There came a call from behind them, "There 'e is!"

"I'll be blowed – he's doubled back," Seth turned his mount and was off in pursuit.

Matt ran across the cliff, "He's gone in the gorse." He and Harry crawled into the bank of tall furze, between the thick trunks of the thorny bushes.

"It's like a tunnel in 'ere," they scuttled through the furze stogs.

"Come out of there," called Seth, "you'll get scratched to hell."

When they backed out, the horses had moved on, and the fox was seen running beneath the cairn.

"Run, fox, run," chanted Matt, hoping they wouldn't catch up with him, as Ezra, James and some of the farmhands raced by to head him off.

Eli on his grey mare rode past at full pelt and Jan went along at a cracking pace, with the mud and turf flying fast, as they saw the red brush of Reynard disappearing over the hill.

Ben urged forward his mount, following through beck and heather only to see the sly old fox slipping past.

Engine houses of run-down and derelict tin mines stood scattered over the area, so they had to pick their way carefully, keeping the horses away from hidden holes and pits that threatened to lame them.

They galloped past small granite cottages with tiny gardens and washing lines, where the widow Ada shouted and shook her fist to them after they'd ridden through her washing. The moors were a purple and gold of heather and gorse flower, as they swept past a chapel and empty tumbledown abodes whose owners had abandoned.

The runners with Ezra and James spread out, as they came to a wild area of tussock grasses and boulders beneath the cairn. They stood on the high slabs of rock searching for any sign of the fox.

"There 'e is!" James jumped down and set off on his long legs, going down the valley which led to a stream, and waded through the rushes and brambles that grew over the water.

Zach saw a movement up near the cairn, "He's 'ere!" he shouted. The fox was sitting on a rock above looking down at them, his red coat shining in the sun.

"That's not the one we saw before," said Seth. "The first one had a split in 'is ear."

"There's two of 'em then," Zach turned his horse towards the cairn.

As they drew nearer the fox jumped into the bracken and loped off down the side of the cairn, towards the stream. They came to a stretch of marshland, where the horses floundered and kicked up peaty ooze over the riders.

"You're covered in black splodges," laughed Seth.

"No more than you, an' my backside is black an' blue with

bouncing about on this pesky saddle," Zach wiped the mud from his forehead.

They came to an inn tucked away on the moor, The Grape Vine, and decided to wait for the others to catch up with them, but as most of them were still scattered over the heathland, only one or two appeared.

Abbie came out with ale for them which they drank thirstily and took their ease on the bench.

"Lad, I'm goin' to be stiff as a board tomorrow," Zach sighed as he leant back against an old vine on the wall.

"Don't you touch that vine," cried Abbie, and Zach hastily sat upright from the branches.

"That holds the secret of m'red wine. That's known far an' wide fer its fine taste."

"Well, you take care of it an' we'll be back sometime for a sample of that," said Seth.

"That rascally woodcutter tried to trim the branches and I shouted at him, 'Don't you touch a twig of that old grape vine'," Abbie told them. "There's some like drinking the ale, an' some like the beer, but I like a sip of the red wine which comes from that old grape vine growing there."

"Well Missus, we'll be off again," Zach looked round for his mount. "Where's m'horse gone?"

Seth gazed into the distance, "He's over there. You couldn't 'ave tethered 'im right."

"Hey – hey," Zach shouted as he began running across the moor to where the horse was grazing and gradually moving further away.

Reynard Fox slipped quietly through the rushes of the bog, loping from tussock to tussock. Job on his farmhorse followed with his terriers scampering at his heels, as they came across the Boscregan marsh.

"Go, Towzer!" he shouted to the dog, urging his horse into a lumbering gallop, digging his heels into its sides. Suddenly the horse stumbled into a boggy hole.

Job went soaring 'ass over tip', landing in an old foxhole. His gun was sucked down into the marsh while the horse galloped off.

Zach had caught up with his mount as the riderless horse went passed him.

"Seth!" he yelled, "Get hold of it!" Seth set off at a fast trot, leaning over to grab the dangling rein.

"It's Job's horse," he came up beside Zach, "where is 'e?"

They searched the bracken and marshland and caught sight of movement in the rushes some way ahead, and heard the yapping of the terriers. When they came to the spot they found Job, head down, trying to get out of the hole, his legs struggling in the air.

"Where's the fox?" asked Seth.

"A pox on 'im," Job's muffled voice spluttered, "get me out of 'ere."

Zach held the horses, while Seth pulled at Job's legs. He rolled over in the rushes.

"You look some mess!" Seth laughed. "I don't know what Biddy's goin' to say to you."

"She won't let 'im in the house," chuckled Zach.

"Where's m'gun?" Job probed about in the mud.

" 'Ere it is, that'll need a good cleaning, or it'll be shooting mud pellets."

Zach looked up and saw that they'd come round in a big loop, and there was Gundry leaning against the granite wall, while his donkey grazed nearby.

They rode up to him and he cackled, "I saw you Job, going 'ass over tip', an' so did that fox. You with yer head in the bog. Reynard Fox, 'e took off and was gone mighty quick."

"That marsh is full of holes," Job muttered. "What's that donkey doing?"

"Well, 'e likes a bit of carrot, 'e does, so I let 'im loose and give 'im his head," Gundry nodded.

Zach grinned, "You'll get one given round your head, when Eli sees that donkey in his carrot field."

43

They were adrift. The wet mists fell on the restless sea, swirling around in a veiled shroud, and they'd set up a mast with a broken spar with part of a shirt end for a sail.

The ship had foundered, lurching as thunderous waters roared, spitting fumes and spume, and cries rended through the air, with hulk, bulk and masts in sway.

Torpedoed amidships, down she wallowed to her doom, slipping into the cold waters as they watched her sink.

With eight of the crew Jem clung to the splintered lifeboat that tossed and twisted for many days and nights. The strong winds blew on the stormy sea that reared and roared, green waves soared to the sky, flinging the boat through the white-tipped crests.

When the gale subsided, hunger came and searing thirst as they drifted beneath the hazy sky. Jem lay in a feverish dream, with tired limbs and shallow breathing, his hands freezing in their frigid hold on the gunwale, and with his consciousness falling into a nightmare.

His body shivered and shook with cold as the relentless seas took their toll of the crew, one by one, until they were down to five.

He could feel himself floating and slipping away as he tired and loosened his hold, and at times he thought he could see Tamsin's face hovering above him. His hand would reach out to her, but she always faded away into the mist.

He could hear the harsh breathing of the lad lying next to him, propped up against the side of the boat.

A rogue wave would come in over the stern, swirling around in the bottom of the boat and drenching their feet. They had found a baler hooked to the side of the boat, but everything else including the oars had been swept away. Phil had stopped baling, resting his arms on his knees.

Jem inched forward and took the baler from him and continued the struggle to try to keep their feet dry. It began to rain again, falling heavily, and they upturned their faces to the sky, drinking in the clean raindrops and moistening their lips cracked by the salt spray.

Jem stopped baling, rinsing out any salt residue and held the baler steady to fill it with fresh rain water. They passed it round, refilled it, passed it round and refilled it, again and again, each drinking as much as they could. Bert pulled off his waterproof hood to cover the baler, "That'll stop the salt water gettin' in fer a while."

He looked over the vast expanse of sea around them, and on the grey horizon he was sure he could see a dim shape in the distance.

"A ship!" he cried, "A ship!" He struggled to stand, waving his arms.

"Get down!" yelled Phil, "Don't attract attention. Wait till it gets nearer."

"It'll pick us up!" cried Bert.

"Keep down – all of you. Keep low in the boat. How do you know it's not the enemy?"

Jem said, "If it is, they won't rescue us, they'll fire on us!"

They watched agonizingly as the ship came nearer, but then receded into the rain cloud.

"They didn't even see us," muttered Bert bitterly, "I don't know as being fired on wouldn't be a quicker end."

Phil sank back dejectedly, "How's Russ gettin' on?"

Jem leaned over the slight form of the lad, "He's not too good. He's got oil in 'is lungs, so has Roy."

Bert rummaged about in the large pockets of his jacket, "Ha! I remembered eating somethin' when we were hit. 'Ere 'tis."

He brought out a screw of paper containing some soggy biscuits.

"You can't eat them. They've been in salt water." Jem snatched at Bert's hand and they watched the particles of biscuit disappear in the wave.

"You'd go crazy with thirst if you 'ave anything salty. Worse than now," warned Phil.

They tied the baler firmly so that they wouldn't loose any of the precious water. A pale sun shone down on them, warming their chilled bones and the waves became calmer. But with the sun came the thirst. They would take one swallow in turn, but the water wouldn't last long and they sank back into a huddled stupor.

Jem muttered, "That desert patrol we picked up were telling us that if you stretch out a piece of waterproof at night, the night's moisture will condense an' run down the sides, an' you'll get a certain amount of liquid."

"Ha!" croaked Phil, "Have to try anything I s'ppose."

With Bert's knife they cut a square out of his oilskin. He was the only one wearing one when the ship went down. That evening they stretched it tight, holding it in place by a couple of odd shoes that slopped about in the bottom of the boat.

"You cut a hole in the middle," said Jem, "an' the moisture gathers at the sides and runs down through the hole into a container."

"Container?" asked Phil. "We can't throw away the water in the baler."

"We ain't got nuthin'," mumbled Bert. "Not even a mug."

"Well, that's that!" Phil lay back against the gunwale.

Jem's eyes looked from side to side of the boat and lingered on each one, but they had already made a search and realised there was nothing that hadn't been washed away. Russ made a movement with his hand, "Smoker!" his hoarse voice grated.

"Smoker?" Jem leant over him. "Ah – right - Russ 'ere's a smoker ain't he? He must 'ave a baccy tin somewhere."

The lad wheezed heavily, trying to lift his hand again to pat his top pocket.

"Don't move," said Jem, "I'll look fer it fer you, if yer still 'ave it." He opened the flap and came up with a tin in his hand, "Here we are. I'll tip yer baccy in a piece of cloth 'ere, if I c'n find a dry bit, an' put it back fer you."

He wiped out the tin and Bert wedged it under the hole of the piece of waterproof, "All we got to do is wait 'til morning then," he wasn't very hopeful.

When they woke the following day, trying to move their stiffened limbs, Phil carefully drew out the tobacco tin.

"It's got something in it," he tasted it cautiously, "there's not much, but its not salty - its fresh water. It's worked!"

"We'll get more if we use the baler, depending on the temperature at night, but it's better than nothing," Jem felt more cheerful.

Bert sipped from the tin, "There's a flavour of baccy leaf, but at least it's wet."

"You'll make a scientist yet, Jem," grinned Phil. "Can't you figure how to rustle up somethin' to eat?"

"A fisherman ain't I?" Jem looked at the waves around them, "There's plenty o' fish in the sea."

"I'll eat 'em raw, I'm so hungry," groaned Bert.

"We got to catch one yet. We want something to make up a hook and line." There was nothing Jem could see in the boat that would do. They turned out their pockets to no avail, then Phil took off his belt.

"There you are," he held out the buckle, "just right to make into a hook," which was easier said than done without tools, but they managed to bend it and Bert sharpened it with his knife. They tore the bottom strip off each of their shirts, tying them together for a line.

"I dunno if it's long enough," Jem lowered the line over the side, whiffing it up and down as they did for mackerel in the bay. When his arm grew tired he passed it on to Bert and then Phil had a turn.

"The fish are lower down, if they're 'ere," Jem pulled the line in, "we'll 'ave to tear another strip off yer shirt."

"We won't 'ave any shirt left soon," Phil began tying the extra lengths together, then dangled it over the side. Eventually he passed it on to Bert, who carried on jigging the line, until his arm began tiring.

"Hey!" he suddenly sat up, "I felt something." Jem put his hand on the line.

"Yes – yes. Don't loose 'im!"

They cautiously hauled the line in, and up came a good size fish. Jem pulled off his shirt, working it under the flipping body, and scooped it into the boat. They all stared at it in amazement, not believing that they'd actually caught one.

Jem tapped it on the head with his shoe, and Bert cut it into edible strips.

"I don't know what fish this is, but – well - seeing it's raw," Jem chewed at the flesh, trying to ignore the taste.

Phil grimaced, "The Japanese eat raw fish, s'posed to be full of vitamins." He cut small slivers and slowly fed them to Russ and Roy.

Then they each took turns at the line again, but only caught one more before the light fell.

The clouds had passed over and the night was clear, with some stars shining in the sky. Bert looked up, "If we get clear skies, we might be able to tell where we are by the stars."

Jem shrugged and Phil looked blank. None of them knew much about it. There was a harsh sound from Roy, who gazed up at the sky and pointed, "North Star," he croaked. They followed the line of his finger and found the star.

"That's great," Phil touched his shoulder, and they tried to tell which direction they should be going, but with a make-shift sail and without oars they weren't going to get very far.

The mists came down again and seeped into their bones. The few fish they caught wasn't enough to keep their strength going, and they lay exhausted in the boat as it drifted on the waves.

Jem sank into a fantasy where he thought of Tamsin and Porthgwyna bay, with the cry of the seagulls as they soared above. As he floated in and out of his delusion, through his dream there came again the cry of the wild gull.

He opened his eyes and saw through the mist the grey shape of a seagull perched on the gunwale. Bert lifted a trembling hand, his tongue moving hungrily in his throat. He made a desperate lunge at the bird, and it rose swiftly with a noisy cry. His hunger welled through his salt-dried lips while the seagull hovered and circled above them.

It flew down again and perched on Jem's arm, while Phil and Bert moved quietly nearer, their mutterings rising with their hunger. The gull picked and pecked at Jem's tattered sleeve, but as the two men surged forward, it winged upwards with a frantic squawk. It then came down again in a swooping glide, uttering harsh mewing sounds and hopped up and down on the gunwale by his side.

Jem hoarsely whispered to it, stroking the feathers of white and grey. He held the bird in his roughened hands and looked at it closely in the misty light. On its limb was a jagged scar, and it carried an impudent cocky air with a gleam in the brightness of its eye, as it blinked boldly at him.

"It's my bird!" cried Jem, "We must be near land! I believe

this's the same bird with the same zigzag scar on the leg that I mended last summer, when I was out fishing on Seth's boat."

Bert reached out hungrily for the gull, but Jem quickly flung it free and it flew up with a screeching call, as Bert seized his arm. Jem moved stiffly over to the sail and tried to pull it round to manoeuvre the boat to follow in the direction that the seagull had taken.

Then to their ears came the sound of surf and as the mists lifted they saw the gull soaring to join the boisterous throng of seagulls that circled above, swirling and swooping with their haunted cries.

"I don't believe it! I don't believe it!" muttered Phil and the others joined him with a great uplift of spirits.

"I know where we are. We're off Land's End!" cried Jem.

"There's a boat coming! Help at last lads. Keep yer pecker up Russ," Bert's voice trembled with excitement.

It was the fishing boat Isabella, out from Penzance.

"Give us strength! You've had it rough, lads!" the skipper hurriedly shouted for a ladder to be lowered, and the make-shift stretcher that they kept on board for emergencies.

One of his crew climbed down into the battered looking craft and they strapped first Russ, and then Roy, onto the stretcher and the rest of the crew hauled them up. He then helped the other three up the ladder, pushing them up rung by rung, their joints stiff from the wet and cold.

Jem croaked, "I tell you, we're some glad to see you."

Eithna and Caleb Morgan went to Plymouth to see Jem at the city hospital, and came back wreathed in happy smiles, so relieved to have their son safely back home.

Seth accompanied Tamsin to the ward where Jem and the other members of the crew were recuperating to re-gain their strength, and where Russ and Roy were now beginning to breathe easier.

Tamsin walked down the long corridor, her footsteps echoing in the hushed crowded ward, to where they were at the far end. She was unsure, after all this time, of finding Jem as the Jem she knew, but when she saw his unruly hair flopping over his forehead and his hazel eyes twinkling to greet her, she ran towards him, wrapping her arms gently around him.

"Oh, Jem, I always knew you'd come home," she whispered.

He smiled, "Tammy m'darlin', I knew you were waiting fer me."

Sitting on the side of his bed, Phil chuckled, "You're a lucky chap, Jem Morgan!"

44

Clarissa Rose sat in the middle of her kitchen, surrounded by pans and baking tins, and surveyed the vapour rising from the cake that she'd just taken out of the oven, and the trays of baps and buns, fancies and saffron cakes, but in her heart she knew much of it would be wasted on the one for whom it was all intended.

"Clarissa – how are you doing?" Hannah Jane came into the kitchen and drew in her breath as she saw the display.

"My, you must've been at it since early this morning."

Clarissa waved her hand towards the table, "Six o'clock," she stated, "as soon as Zach and Seth left for the fishing."

Hannah nodded, "You'll be nearly ready fer tomorrow then."

"Yes, but not half of it'll be eaten, you know. Sit you down and I'll make us both some tea," she reached for the kettle.

Hannah put her large basket onto the worktop and lowered herself slowly into a chair, "I've brought trifles an' flans." Clarissa lifted the cloth and peered underneath, "Beautiful – you certainly have a way with you," she sighed.

Hannah shrugged, "You are in the dumps."

"Well," Clarissa sighed again, "you know as well as I that Zach'll be 'ere fer the first half-hour fer a bite to eat, then he an' his mates'll be off down the Black Knight fer the rest of the evening."

"As if they hadn't been seeing each other on the boats all day," agreed Hannah.

"An' us women'll all be left 'ere," continued Clarissa, " 'til they appear again at midnight. The men are always the same with any celebration – you won't change 'em."

"Still," went on Hannah, "Fifty years you bin married - that's serious – it's not like any birthday – he'll stay . . ."

"He won't," interrupted Clarissa, "he won't change if a gale of wind blew that place down," she set her cup firmly onto its saucer.

Hannah laughed, "Have you got a present fer him yet?"

"Not yet," Clarissa shook her head, "I'm going into Penzance town this afternoon. I've seen what he'll like."

Hannah stood and buttoned up her coat, "An' has he got one fer you?"

Clarissa shrugged,"I haven't seen any knowing signs."

Hannah opened the door, "Yer 50th anniversary is yer Gold Anniversary, so it's got to be something of gold, you know."

Clarissa laughed, "Seth has told him. That'll make a big hole his pocket."

Hannah laughed with her, "Here, what're you wearing?" She hovered in the doorway.

"Oh," Clarissa hesitated, "I 'aven't decided. Come up an' have a look."

She led the way up the narrow stairs into the bedroom and opened the wardrobe and took out two dresses.

"There," she said, "I got these in town last week. There's this deep blue with the wide pleated skirt, an' there's this one in rose with the frill on the collar."

She held each up in turn, flouncing out the panels, "What d'you think?"

Hannah Jane swung them both around, holding one after the other up to Clarissa's shoulder, "The rose is pretty, but blue is romantic," she said, "blue to match yer eyes and the summer sea. Zach'll see that alright."

Clarissa chortled, "Ha – he'll not notice that!"

Hannah lay the dresses on the bed, "Ah, well I'll see you in the morning."

As she went down the stairs, Clarissa held up the blue dress against her face and looked into the mirror. Her reflection gazed back, still with its dark hair, and though her skin now showed a few lines, her eyes were still a clear blue. Hannah Jane was right, the dress did light them up, and a romantic twinge tugged at her heart for the gawky young lad with salt-blown hair who had waited on the corner of the lane for her.

She remembered the walks along the harbour, and the same small cottage near the quay. Then along had come their sons, Seth, Ezra and Josh, always up to mischief, Seth now owning part of the fishing boat, the Clarissa Rose, with his father. Ezra now working at the mine and Josh at the farm, and Zach, his features weathered by the winds, still lean and sprightly.

He had called the boat after her with great pride, and it still rode its moorings after a day's hard work, with that presence and spirit that all sea craft have. But the romance had somehow faded in the harsh realities and rigours of the seasons.

She shook the past from her mind and put the dresses back into the wardrobe, patted her hair and hurried down to the kitchen. She took the precious wad of savings from the back of the drawer in the dresser, and set off for the bus to town.

Beckerleg's were an old family firm and had bay windows, each displaying shelves of jewellery, watches, glass and silverware, and anything else you could think of in gifts.

There was a worn red carpet covering the wooden floorboards that creaked, as Clarissa entered and walked towards a young Beckerleg who was sorting out a tray of rings. He must be the grandson of the present owner she thought, recognising the family features of dark hair and heavy brows.

"I'd like to look at your tray of watches," she said as he looked up. "Gold watches," she added.

His hand stopped in mid air, "Oh, gold," he smiled. Then he

opened the glass door behind him and took out the tray that she'd seen in the window the week before. She looked at the whole range set before her, gleaming in the artificial shop light, but there was only one that she'd set her mind on, and that was the one at the end of the first row.

"I'm afraid they're becoming rather pricey now," the young man said, lifting one out for her to see.

Clarissa murmured and pointed, "I'll take this one."

"A good choice," he said, taking it out, "for a present is it?"

"A wedding anniversary, my husband's - and mine," she said.

"Congratulations to you both," he smiled, "we have a gift-wrapped box and ribbons for birthdays and anniversaries, as our speciality."

Clarissa watched as the silver and gold paper was folded precisely at the corners and bound up in ribbon. Her savings were counted between the slim fingers, and the receipt written out and pressed into her hand with the wrapped parcel.

And several times on the way home, she glanced into her shopping basket at the rich gleam of the paper.

The Clarissa Rose rounded the end of Porthgwyna quay, on her way in from the fishing grounds, and after they'd landed their catch, Zach walked through the fishmarket to the office.

Seth and Ezra leaned against the doorframe as he received his catch money, then when he came out and handed Seth his share, they each caught his arm and steered him towards their van.

" 'Ere, I can't go into town like this. I got to change into somethin' decent," he protested.

"Well, you can't," said Seth, "Mum'll know somethin's up."

"Get in," added Ezra and half pushed his father into the back of the van, where Josh and three of his fellow fishermen were already waiting.

"What's this?" he asked.

"Witnesses," grinned Josh, "they're coming to see that you get a good, expensive anniversary present."

Zach looked from one to the other, "Huh, more likely comin' fer a pint."

They nudged each other as Jem started the engine and they drove into town.

When young Beckerleg saw the group of booted fishermen coming through the door, he smiled a welcome, knowing that they must be flush with their catch earnings and were likely to be generous with their money – or each other's. He brought out display after display of jewellery for them to look over.

"I don't like that," said Seth.

"Nor that," from Ezra.

Josh added, "It's got to be gold."

"Costs a fortune!" groaned Zach. "I'll just get Clarissa a nice little ornament, she'd like that just as well."

"It's yer 50th anniversary. It's a good job we came in with you, to see you get somethin' special fer mum," insisted Josh.

A tray of bracelets appeared.

"Aw," whistled Seth, "I like they. That one – with the blue stones set in the gold. They're the colour of mum's eyes."

Zach remembered suddenly the clear blue of Clarissa's eyes, "They are," he said. But when he was told the price, he took a step back and hesitated.

"Ah – well . . ."

"We'll take it," jumped in Seth quickly before he could change his mind.

"Now – wait . . ." began Zach.

Ezra urged, "It's gotta be gold – an' fer that you gotta pay!"

So Zach slowly took out his brown envelope and counted out

a great deal of its contents, emptying his wallet as well.

"I think we'd better 'ave that drink," he said weakly, as the package was wrapped up in its gold and silver paper.

"Ah, I reckon you got a good bargain there," agreed Seth, grinning at the others.

When Clarissa saw them that evening there were sly glances flickering between them and she guessed the reason. After some disjointed conversation, Zach slipped on his jacket and his sons followed him with a "See you later, Mother."

Hannah Jane brought Eithna and Wendy round to see the pastries. Wendy said, "My Ron is bringing along the barrel of beer in the morning."

Clarissa sighed, "A crate of spirits and wines all came today. We'll be chock full of the stuff and after half-an-hour they'll all be off down that pub – your husbands included."

Eithna said, "The only place they stay fer any length of time is on their boats."

Wendy winked at Clarissa, "Well then - that's where you'll 'ave to 'ave yer party!"

Clarissa laughed, "What?"

"That'd be fun," cried Eithna, clapping her hands.

Clarissa chuckled, "It's not on. There's no electric."

Wendy leaned forward, "I've still got the old carnival lights and the long lead. Ron can open the workshop on the quay an' you can use the socket in there. The quay and the boat'll look real pretty hung up with all they bulbs."

Eithna said, "Get your lads to tidy up tomorrow. Then there'll be plenty of space on the quay and on the deck."

"It'll be nice havin' the party outside," added Wendy.

"Start it off here," said Eithna, "and when the men go off, we'll move all the eats and drinks down onto the quay. Then you'll 'ave to think of something to get the men down there."

Clarissa laughed, "Don't worry. Zach'll come running, afeared we'll be doin' his boat some mischief."

By the time the two women had departed and Zach came in with Seth and Ezra, Clarissa felt a little flicker of excitement beginning to grow.

She cornered her sons in the kitchen. "Aw – Dad'll throttle us," groaned Seth, but they agreed to stack away the ropes and boxes as the boat turned homewards, and to leave the deck more ship-shape than usual.

The next morning there was a succession of women scurrying to and fro from the cottages around.

And early that evening, while Zach was struggling into his waistcoat, Clarissa hovered over the two dresses.

"The rose really is a warm colour. What d'you think, Zach?" she murmured.

"I like the blue," he said, thinking of the sapphire bracelet.

"Really?" she asked, surprised.

"The blue," he said firmly, picking up the dress and holding it up against her. "It matches your eyes," he kissed her cheek.

"Zach, away with you," she giggled, "the blue it is then."

Zach straightened his tie in the mirror and grinned slyly back at his reflection.

"Come on," he said, "I c'n hear half the village 'ave arrived downstairs already, by the sound of it."

For the next couple of hours there was a commotion of voices, clinking of glasses, drinking and eating. Zach brought out behind his back his ribboned parcel and watched with satisfaction as Clarissa's eyes lit up with delight as she lifted out the heavy bracelet, studded with the blue sapphire stones.

"My, that goes with your dress perfectly," exclaimed Wendy.

Clarissa Rose laughed, "What a coincidence that I chose to

298

wear this one tonight," she said, as she caught Zach's eye. He winked, and in turn she gave him her gift and he took out the watch from its box.

"Now, that's what I call a 'andsome piece of mechanism," he declared, examining it with awe.

Then they toasted each other and everybody else toasted them, and then one by one the men slipped off down to the inn.

"Seth!" called Clarissa as her sons were following their father out of the door.

"Aw, Mum," he groaned, pulling Ezra and Josh back.

"Quick, now," urged Wendy, "it's dark enough for nobody to notice anything going on."

So they hurried across the harbour and hung the quay and the boat with carnival lights on the masts and rigging. Tables and chairs, food, bottles and barrel were set out on the quay with the record player and a stack of records, then Josh was sent off to get his father. When he reached the inn, he flung open the door and pushed his way into the crowded room until he found Zach at the dartboard.

"Dad - Dad – er – there's people on the boat!" he blurted out, the only idea he could find in his head.

"What!" exclaimed Zach, and he dropped the dart he was holding and rushed out, with a curious crowd following behind him, eager to see what was happening. They hurried along the quay, and just as they reached the Clarissa Rose, Seth threw the switch and she was lit up like a galleon in a story book.

Zach stood rooted to the spot, and his mouth dropped open, astounded, as music filled the evening air and her decks were dotted with people dancing. And there stood his Clarissa Rose in her blue dress, smiling, her hand reaching out for him.

He laughed, and taking her arm, away they went, swaying to the waltz that played on into the summer night.

Esme Francis

The author has spent almost a lifetime living on the shore. Experiencing baiting crab and lobster pots in cove boats, setting long-lines for turbot, whiffing for mackerel and Pollack.

Crofting in granite hedged fields for potatoes, salad crops, strawberry, raspberry and summer fruits, and breeding sheep.

Descending into the levels of Levant tin mine under the sealed cap where the sea broke in, and living the way of the Celtic Cornish life, that is still going on.

Front & Back Covers
Surf at Gwenver